THE SEVEN YEAR ITCH

LYNDSEY GALLAGHER

ISBN: 978-1527241756

PROLOGUE

I never imagined I'd be the type of woman to fall in love with someone else. I was far too sensible for that. In my mind, that kind of woman is a certain stereotype; flighty, impulsive or unbalanced. I wasn't any of those things. I was average, normal and, if brutally honest, a bit boring.

I sought a simple life, without stress or drama, preferring a bucket full of fermented grape juice and my own company most evenings. My girlfriends called me a wino, but the wildest I got was three glasses on a school night.

On the odd occasion, I'd committed to an irregular fad of exercising I would update the WhatsApp with a daily progress report. 'My name's Lucy O'Connor and I haven't had a drink for three days.' As far as vices go, it could have been a lot worse than a couple of quiet snifters on my couch.

I wasn't looking for Him. The thought never even occurred to me as a possibility. It was inconceivable I would ever meet anybody else, me that's so sensible and predictable. I'm a neat freak, control freak and serial planner. I'm the person who knows exactly what I'm doing for the entire year ahead and have it clearly marked out on a wall calendar. Change terrifies me. Fun, I could be, spontaneous, I could not.

This was back in the days before Tinder and Grinder, or whatever else the singletons (or marrieds) do these days. Nobody admits they went out looking for trouble, but genuinely I was not looking for another man. He found me anyway. By God, did he find me.

It was like a bolt of lightning exiting the sky, and striking the very core of me, waking me from my meaningless, although not entirely unpleasant existence. I never believed a love like it could exist, let alone that it would happen to me. Nothing would ever be the same, regardless of whether I pursued it or denied it. Something had awakened in me. I'd seen the light at the end of a very long and lonely tunnel and could no longer pretend that things would ever be right.

Nobody had it all, and I had a lot. I had a magnificent job, a roof over my head and the best of friends. Fun loving Rachel, whose alter ego 'Raquelle' got the blame for everything that occurred post wine. Sensible and sensitive Katie, mother of two, and fellow dental hygienist. Clara, my work practice manager who had formed the Wednesday Wine Club, to which I was a regular attender.

Before the night that changed everything, I holidayed three times a year with my mum, who was young and full of fun. Sometimes I felt like I was the parent, I was so sensible and predictable.

I went out for dinner with my girlfriends, drank cocktails at the end of a long day with my colleagues. I worked hard, six days a week, primarily to escape the building I called home.

I suppose I should mention I had a husband of seven years. I was only twenty-seven myself. A child bride, and it's not like I was pregnant when we got married. I'm sure our extended families waited with bated breath for 'The Joyful Announcement' for months afterwards, but the chance would be a fine thing. I'd been dating an American guy on and off for a year. When his visa expired, he faced deportation, unless of course we got married.

I knew I wasn't in love when we got married. Foolish maybe, but this is the crazy bit. I thought I was being clever you see. So many times, I'd seen people close to me fall head over heels, crazy in love. I even envied them, wondering when this magical thing would happen to me. The 'can't eat or sleep for thinking about him' kind of love. The 'I need to see him right now or I might die' kind of love. I wanted it for myself, until I saw first-hand the damage it was capable of.

It was all-consuming, overwhelming, and I witnessed it suck the life out of those involved from the inside out. It seemed to me love was like a tornado; it powered in hard and fast and destroyed everything in its path, before fading and disappearing as quickly as it arrived.

More often than not, it wasn't actually love, of course. It was infatuation. A person couldn't think straight amidst its throes. Rational people became irrational, alienating their friends and family, making countless grave decisions, sacrificing everything they'd ever known before. All for this higher power 'love' which took priority over everything and everyone else. The things people did in the name of love baffled me. I didn't want that for myself, didn't want to feel helplessly controlled by an emotion generated by chemicals which caused only chaos in the real world.

My twenty-year-old cynical young self assumed if I wasn't crazy head over heels in love to begin with, then I couldn't really fall out of love. It seemed fool proof at the time. I knew what I was going to be left with in the end, because I already had it. Not the most exciting relationship, but a life partner. What I needed was a steady, secure relationship, not something that would wither and die as the chemical reactions lessened on my brain and body over time, similar to a heroin addict continuously searching for the unobtainable soaring high of the initial hit. I wanted a life partner to work with. Someone with the same goals. I was playing the long game.

On reflection, with hindsight only age and experience bring, at that at that point in my life I was vulnerable. I wanted someone of my own, as tragic and as desperate as that sounds now, years later. After much instability in my youth, I wanted someone solid to stand by me, someone that wouldn't uproot everything and leave. I craved normality, emotional security, a family of my own. A partner who I could lean on and who could lean on me, the safety of our own home, and eventually one day, maybe children.

I knew within three months of marrying Rob I had made a

mistake. A big one. He certainly wouldn't up and leave, but solid he was not.

The cracks appeared almost immediately, but I was too pig-headed and stubborn to even admit to my own mother I'd made a mistake. Shame prevented me from confiding in my friends. Instead, I attempted to wallpaper over the enormous gaping cracks that emerged throughout the core of us as if they were nothing. I was too proud to admit I was wrong.

I adopted the role of his mother instead of his wife. Instead of having someone to lean on, I stood on my own two feet at all times, carrying the full weight of a grown man-child on my back.

Rob worked on a building site. He was studying a construction management degree at night. I cooked, cleaned and dealt with the other dull aspects of adulthood, to give him more time to study. But the more I did for him, the more he let me do. Which would have been fine, if he actually passed the exams. But he didn't. It frustrated the life out of me watching him with the text books open, staring blankly ahead into space.

Trying to engage him in conversation was like pulling teeth, and I should know. Ultimately, I knew my work colleagues better than I knew my husband. There was no depth there. During the frequent silences between us, I'd ask him what he was thinking. He would always reply that he wasn't thinking anything. And I honestly think he meant it.

How could a person not be thinking anything? There's always something on my mind, even if it's something as trivial as wondering, why aren't blueberries actually blue? I was the human version of the computer with seven million tabs open. Was it any wonder I struggled to fall asleep each night? We were very different. So much for opposites attracting.

The void between us became increasingly obvious. I tried to talk to him, but he failed to understand what I wanted and what the problem was. I wanted to light a fire under his arse and kick-start some sort of drive in him. I wanted conversation, I wanted to communicate on a deeper level with the bond that I thought marriage would bring. I don't think that deeper level existed in him. The lights were on, but there was nobody home. Over time, I stopped trying. I accepted it.

We slipped into a rut of resentment. Well, I did. He was happy being pandered to. We no longer wanted the same things, or if we did, he wasn't willing to work towards them with me. The drive had left him since we got married; he lacked ambition and desire.

We were supposed to be a team. He was supposed to be my equal. I felt enormously let down, deflated even and deprived, without the initial high of ever actually being properly in love. But having made my bed, I lay in it.

Rob and I lived separate lives under the same roof, under the pretence that the situation was normal, though we both knew deep down it was far from it. I'd accepted that it was just going to be that way. Now and then, somebody would ask that really awkward question: 'When are you guys going to have a baby?' It wasn't entirely unreasonable I suppose, given we were married for seven years, but there was zero chance of that happening. We all know how babies are made and there was none of that going on. There hadn't been for years. Plus, I already had the man-child to look after and I could barely manage that, let alone anything else.

I had a good life in many ways, bar the complete lack of any form of romance or intimacy. Intimacy seemed overrated to me, anyway. I completely and utterly lacked desire. Until that night in June.

I didn't bank on really falling in love. With somebody else.

I met him one unsuspecting night I June. Bang, The Universe dealt me a brand-new hand of cards, the Royal Flush. The prize was phenomenal, more than I could comprehend, but so were the stakes. I'd never played cards or gambled with anything before.

Cupid's bow struck me hard and fast when I

I fell head over heels, crazy in love. The 'uncontrollable, over- thinking about him kind of love'. The irrational anything for. Chemi- whelming, all-consuming love I would active than the purest drug cals, though they might be, were mon ought? The only teeny tiny in the entire universe. Who would to somebody else. little problem was, I was alread

Chapter One

FRIDAY 29TH JUNE 2012

It was the weekend of my future sister-in-law's hen party. The day was seasonably humid; the surgery lacked air despite the open sash window, and my blue scrubs stuck to my clammy skin. It was four o'clock in the afternoon. I pretended to be listening to what the patient in the dental chair was telling me, an art I had perfected over the years. Sympathetic, yet professional. I nodded my head and leaned forward as if to hear better, but in reality, I was repositioning my backside which was numb from the day spent sitting on the saddle stool peering into people's mouths.

'And when I pushed on my gum pus just oozed out. It was loose anyway,' the patient rattled on. 'So, I gave it a little twist, saved myself eighty pounds for the extraction fee,' he bellowed in a brash, northern accent. I could smell his gum disease from across the room.

Most days, I absolutely loved my job as a dental hygienist. It's not a career you could afford to be squeamish in. But I loved the patients, loved my colleagues, loved being able to help people and to make a difference. I saw fifteen patients a day and getting to know them was the highlight of my profession.

Some of them could be a little challenging. Take Lord and Lady Mountjoy-Row, for example. I used to shudder when their names appeared on my day list. They would waltz into the surgery, drop their coats on the floor, before proceeding to insult me in various ways.

'Are you even qualified?'

'Couldn't you be bothered to do the extra years to train to be a dentist, or were you just not clever enough?'

And my absolute favourite of all time: 'That was quick' when I'd spent way over the allocated appointment slot, sweating, my fingers crippled with a cramp from removing several years-worth of persistent tobacco staining in half an hour. The next two patients would be tapping their feet impatiently in the waiting area because I was running late.

But most of them were absolute diamonds. My favourites were the old ladies who brought us biscuits at Christmas, despite the fact we spent our lives telling people to avoid sugar. I lived for the patients I could talk to, the ones I could actually relate to, and connect with on a human level.

At four-thirty, I finished up with Mr Missing Premolar, and booked him in for a check-up the following week. A commotion downstairs in the patient waiting area sounding largely like a heard of elephants in stilettoes, alerted me to the arrival of my girlfriends. I removed my scrubs, washed my hands and raced down to join them. We were heading to Bristol, and Friday afternoon traffic was a bitch in any city. I figured it would be worth it when I was sipping a Cosmo in the Harvey Nichols bar the following day.

My future sister-in-law asked me to be her bridesmaid, despite the fact we weren't close. English wasn't her first language and she had a tendency to translate exactly what she was thinking. Her delivery was often offensively blunt. My brother met Heidi while touring Europe with his band eighteen months earlier. Her mousy hair was cropped short in a boyish style and she had a sturdy frame to go with her five-foot eleven height. Her hobbies included body building and calorie counting, neither of which I was very good at. She wasn't what I'd have imagined him going for, but to be honest, I was in no position to judge.

I tried to welcome her into our family, for the sake of my brother, but she didn't make it easy. She seemed to take pleasure in insulting people, enjoying their discomfort. I hoped marriage might soften her.

Optimistically, I hoped we might forge some sort of bond over the weekend. I was wrong.

'All set ladies?' My spirit soared at the prospect of a weekend in a city full of unexplored bars and shops with eleven other women for company. I was a woman's woman; I lived to connect with other like-minded creatures and longed to be accepted by my peers.

'Raring to go, Lucy,' Clara, shrieked four octaves higher than necessary.

Clara was the practice manager in the other dental surgery I worked in. I split my regular work between Dental Connections and Appollo Dental Practice, both of which were in Winchester.

Over the last four years, Clara had become a great friend. We had the same messed up sense of humour and loved the same sports; shopping, sunbathing and of course, our Wednesday Wine Club.

Heidi lurked awkwardly in the doorway with a Bride-to-Be luminous pink sash on and flashing willy earrings. Clara clutched a bottle of prosecco under her arm and four plastic flutes. Our friend, Ruth, stood between them, looking fabulously understated in jeans and a white bardot top. She was engaged to one of my childhood best friends, Oliver. We clicked the first time we met. When Oliver left the room, she asked if I'd ever been with him. Her earnest question caused me to dissolve into a hysterical fit of laughter. The answer was a resounding no, but I loved that she just came out and asked. The visible relief that swept over her features was endearing, and something every woman could probably relate to. We've been firm friends ever since.

The rest of the hens were travelling by train, so it was just the four of us travelling in my little BMW one series, nicknamed Betsy. Betsy was well accustomed to long trips, I spent hours driving around the coast sight-seeing, merely to escape the nothingness at home.

We bundled into the car and set off with Heart Radio pumping out Carly Rae Jepson, "Call Me Maybe". The girls sang along raucously fuelled by the prosecco. It was a long drive.

It was six-thirty before we pulled into the Hilton Hotel car park, where we were due to spend two nights. I couldn't wait for the shopping, cocktails, and more shopping. I wondered if perhaps my friends were right, maybe I was a wino. Either way, it wasn't going to change this weekend. I'd go to the bar with the rest of them and stop worrying about it.

We checked in and found our rooms. I was sharing with Heidi, but thankfully, the room had two double beds. I couldn't imagine spooning Bridezilla after a few too many Cosmo's.

After a quick shower, I changed into a little black dress. My tan and nails were fresh from the night before. It never ceased to amaze me the lengths we women would go to when we knew we were going to be surrounded by other women. I certainly hadn't put the tan on for the sake of any man. With one last squirt of Chanel Chance, I skipped out the door.

Clara and Ruth beat us to the bar and were already ordering from the cocktail menu. The lucky bitches were rooming together. How I ended up with Bridezilla was beyond me. I wanted to bond though, and maybe this would give us a chance.

The hotel bar was impressively understated with huge red leather couches and gleaming glass coffee tables. The bar itself was long; expensive marble, with high leather stools. Windows spanned from floor to ceiling and the streaming sun illuminated everything it touched. The evening was still warm and bright. Couples were scattered around the room, groups of friends called back and forth across the tables. I ordered two Cosmopolitans, one for me and one for Heidi, we joined the rest of the hens who were arriving in dribs and drabs.

'To Heidi,' I toasted, and we clinked glasses. I really was going to try hard to get close to her this weekend, after all she'd be part of our family in a few short weeks.

She didn't make it easy.

'Hope you're going to get a boob job before the wedding, Lucy,' Heidi sneered. 'If I go along when you get the facelift, they might give us a discount.' And just like that, I realised my hopes of bonding were futile. She had no desire to be my friend.

The girls roared with laughter, not detecting the underlying animosity. Clara and Ruth pulled a face behind Heidi's back, and I thanked God for my loyal friends.

The hen party consisted of me, Clara, Ruth, and five of Heidi's coworkers from Costa Coffee. There was a traffic warden called Emma, a nurse called Catherine, who was Emma's best friend and the daughter of a local politician. Her accent was heavily affected, very Ab Fab Darling, and ultimately hilarious. Lastly, there was Ann, a small blonde girl, who was dating another member of my brother's band.

When everyone had arrived, we strolled the ten-minute walk to Brown's for dinner; a listed building with high ceilings, fancy chandeliers and mirrored walls. The modern décor was a complete contrast to the traditional architecture of the building, yet they complimented each other beautifully.

At the table, the girls integrated seamlessly. I positioned myself between Clara and Ruth and enjoyed the easy company of my closest friends. Even Heidi was smiling, which was an unexpected bonus. I pulled my phone out of my cream Mulberry clutch to take some pictures, relieved to see I had no messages or missed calls. Not that I expected any. Rob barely ever texted, unless it was to remind me to put out the bins.

After dinner we bar-hopped around Bristol. The city was buzzing with life, projecting that epic Friday feeling. We found ourselves in a nightclub called Melandras. The bass resonated through the club. Cheap drinks ensured many limbs were loose enough to congregate on the dance floor. Clara shouted in my ear, but with bodies everywhere, pushing, jostling, I couldn't hear a thing. The air was stifling. Ruth lost a shoe. Heidi propped up the bar drinking tequila with her work colleagues. Emma lap danced on a table with Catherine egging her on. It was two in the morning and my feet were killing me. I signalled Clara towards the exit and she grabbed Ruth and her one shoe and dragged her reluctantly out with us. I typed a message on the WhatsApp group to the others, telling them we were heading back to the hotel, assuming they'd follow us back in their own time.

Back at the Hilton, we were surprised to see the barman still serving drinks. A group of twenty lads congregated, their contagious laughter rippled through to the reception area.

'One for the road?' Ruth suggested.

Clara and I were more than happy to oblige.

We ordered a bottle of Chardonnay and the three of us spread out on two of the red couches. The hens trekked into the bar in twos and threes. There was no sign of Bridezilla. I was simultaneously guilty and relieved. The awkwardness was gruelling.

The lads began to mingle with some of our hens, an unavoidable eventuality at this hour of the night, given the combination of high spirits, low inhibitions and copious amounts of alcohol. I kicked off my six-inch black lace peep toes, the cold tiles a welcome relief to my burning soles. As I quietly admired my burgundy toe nails, engrossed in my own thoughts, tiny hairs pricked on the nape of my neck. The sensation of being watched overwhelmed me. My head snapped to the left. A man now occupied the previously vacant space next to me. I hadn't seen him coming. Literally.

And there it happened, as innocently and unintentionally as that. My life changed in that moment forever. There *he* was.

'He's had a bit too much to drink,' his mate explained, nodding at him. 'I'm just going to leave him sitting there for a while, if that's ok?'

At first glance, he appeared like just an ordinary guy, which lulled me into a false sense of security. There was something disarming about the gentle manner in which he acknowledged me. With no explanation or reasoning, I was instantaneously drawn to him. He simply looked like a nice man. 'No problem.'

He didn't look drunk to me. In fact, he looked extremely sober, holding a pint steadily in his right hand.

Even as he sat, his height was obvious. His build was slim and athletically toned. Fair skin and red hair set him apart from a crowd. High cheekbones and a chiselled jaw line boasted exceptional bone structure. When his lips curled into a grin, I noticed his upper right central incisor slightly overlapped his left. A perfect imperfection, but what really shook my world was his eyes. They were the colour of the Caribbean ocean. A person could evaporate in those eyes, they exuded an intelligent, knowing depth, as though he could straight into my soul, and glimpse my every secret.

Ordinary became extraordinary on closer inspection. The attraction was not only instant, but from the way his eyes bore into mine, it was apparently mutual. It pulled at the strings of my hammering heart.

It was so much more than the way he looked. He radiated an over-whelming sense of familiarity. Déjà vu devoured me.

'You look nice, you must be married,' were the first words that fell from my mouth.

I was attracted to him; it was blazingly obvious. But I needed him to know I wasn't available. A tiny fragment of my previously untouched heart willed him to be married, so I could enjoy his conver-sation for what it was, without the risk of it leading anywhere.

'I am, surely.' His low Irish lull lit up my insides, but I was simulta-neously relieved and disappointed with his reply.

'I'm in safe hands then.' I held up my left hand, showing him the wedding band I wore like a coat of armour.

'You couldn't be in better hands.' His deliberate innuendo set my pulse racing.

'Fabulous accent.' I changed the subject.

'You're one with the accent,' he said, with another brief flash of his white grin.

His eyes were trained intently on mine. They burned through my pupils, setting my sleepy insides alight. I was under no illusion. He could clearly see way past the platinum armour I wore, the shield on my finger. I couldn't bring myself to look away. It was then the thought first occurred to me that I could be getting myself into trouble. How much trouble I had no idea. I'd never met anyone who sparked this type of reaction before.

'What part of Ireland are you from?' I attempted to negotiate a safe topic of conversation.

'County Mayo.'

'I've never heard of it.' I was embarrassed at my ignorance. I don't know why I cared what he thought of me, but I did.

'It's between Galway and Sligo. It's the best county in Ireland.' He winked and took another sip of his pint.

'I have a friend in Galway. Great city, I loved it. Like a mini-Edin-burgh with the cobbled streets and little pubs.'

'You live in Edinburgh?' His eyebrows burrowed together ques-tioningly.

'Not anymore. The weather got me in the end.' I looked down at my tanned arms and legs and shrugged my shoulders. I was just back from ten days holiday in San Francisco with my mother. Escapism was a means of survival at this stage. 'I'm John, by the way.' He extended his hand out to mine and I shook it without breaking his stare. His hand was warm and firm, and I found myself holding onto it slightly longer than necessary. The physical contact sparked an erratic pounding in my chest. Like an electric shock, he jolted; his darkening eyes piqued with interest.

'Lucy.' I introduced myself, before standing to leave. 'I'm going to the bar. I better get the girls another drink.'

I had to put some distance between us before I got carried away with myself. The chemistry was immediate and practically painful. The scale of the attraction was nothing I'd experienced before. It shocked me, leaving me vulnerable, newly aware of every tingling cell in my body.

'I'll give you a hand.' He didn't miss a beat, stood up and walked with me towards the bar.

Now I was in an even bigger predicament. For a fleeting second as we crossed the room together, I fantasised about how it might feel like to have come out with him tonight, as a couple on a date. A feeling of longing scorched my insides as I allowed myself to pretend it was the case. I shouldn't do it to myself. I looked at him and swore he could read my mind as he sized me up. His twinkling eyes roamed the entire length of me; a boyish smirk hinted he liked what he saw. A redness crept into my warm cheeks. I didn't recognise this version of myself. I wasn't sure I liked her.

We perched on two high stools while we waited for the barman's attention. I rested my bare feet casually on the bottom of his chair in an intimate gesture, as if I'd known him my whole life. I ordered a bottle of white for the girls and a gin and tonic for myself. He ordered the same as me. I dropped the bottle down to the girls while the barman mixed our drinks. Before I could finish ordering the round, John paid for it, and gestured to the barstool next to him for me to sit again. It seemed he was enjoying my company as much as I was enjoying his. A shiver of excitement coursed through me, but a niggle of worry warned I was treading dangerous ground.

'Sit down, Lucy, I promise I won't bite.'

It wasn't him I was worried about. I took a sip of my drink, unsure what to say.

'Tell me about yourself.'

I wracked my brains for something other than, 'I'm a fucking hot mess in your company and I can't be trusted not to throw myself at you'.

He rubbed a thumb thoughtfully over his chin, his eyes sizing me up in a way that probably wasn't appropriate for a married man. I glanced at his left hand. It was without a ring, or even the tell-tale mark of one. His gaze followed mine and he shrugged, a small smile curling at his lip. I was entirely unsure what he was smiling at, because to me, there was nothing remotely funny about the intense, crackling attraction between us.

What could I possibly say to him? He didn't know me or my situation. I'd already told him I was married, so I had no appearances to uphold. I decide to tell him the truth and see if that sent him running for the hills, or to the nearest airport to catch the first flight back to Ireland.

'When I was nineteen, my father died. He was sick but it was quite sudden. Shortly afterwards, I finished from college. Although my graduation was something I had been striving for, I felt like I'd lost something; the routine, the familiarity of it, and the daily banter with my best friends. Everyone started making plans for the rest of their lives. One by one, they began to leave the city we'd all settled in.'

I paused to swallow, his eyes watched intently as my lips revealed truths that I had never spoken to anyone, not even my best friends. 'Something about everyone leaving terrified me. Then Rob, my boyfriend at the time, was going to have to leave too. His visa was on the point of expiry. I couldn't face another loss – of any sort. So, I married him.' I took another large gulp of my drink, allowing the gin to work its magic and take the edge off my new found nerves. Never before, had I admitted my reasoning for doing what I did, out loud – not even to myself.

'And is that a decision you've since regretted?' His head tilted closer towards me, and something like sympathy mirrored in his eyes.

'It's a decision I've deliberately never analysed or spoken about with anyone before.' There was something about John's familiarity and his earnest interest that led me to reveal my deepest truths . I assumed I'd never see him again, and it was liberating knowing he was from a completely different country, that we would more than likely never cross paths again.

'Do you want to talk about it now?' His warm hand reached out to clasp mine, and the same crackling charge of energy surged through me, its intensity triggering the tiny fine hairs to rise on my arms, along with tell tale goosebumps. I pulled myself back, before it could pull me further towards him, and carried on talking. It was safer than the alternative.

'My parents' divorce when I was a child. I craved stability, strength and support. It's funny because now, I'm well able to support myself, I have a great job and great friends. As a married woman, I'm strangely more independent than I ever was when I was single.'

So used to pretending that my life was a perfect fairy tale, it was liberating to be honest for once. I figured he must have some empathy being married himself, no marriage was absolutely perfect, even the great ones supposedly needed two people working at it. So they tell me anyway. As the words escaped my chest, the weight I'd been subconsciously carrying shifted. It was a shocking revelation, even to myself, and it set inevitable wheels in motion. I could no longer deny the situation needed addressing. Change loomed ahead, regardless of how much it terrified me.

John listened more intently than any therapist might, sensing the relief of admitting my truth. Never before had I been so honest about my situation. Even to myself. It was cathartic, but unnerving.

The only thing I didn't tell him was that I still longed for an equal partner, someone I could respect rather than resent. Someone strong enough to challenge me, to carry me the odd time I needed it. I'd doubted what I had in mind existed – until this very night. But from the way his eyes bore into mine, I could only assume his unnervingly sharp senses saw it all.

'Tell me about yourself, John.' I fired his own question back at him, seeing as he hadn't run a mile at my deepest, darkest revelations.

'I'm a farmer.' His enthusiasm for his job echoed in the words that he spoke.

'Seriously?' It wasn't what I expected.

'I have a dairy farm.'

'I've never met a farmer before.'

Out of all my confessions this evening, this was the one that caused him to laugh outrageously.

It seemed our lives were worlds apart, not just in location. He described his family, and his parents' pub in Ireland. Bizarrely, I found myself longing to meet them. A picture of them formed in my mind and I liked them already. As he spoke, I attempted to conjure an image of where he lived, imagine the kind of life he led amongst the country-side and cattle.

'Do you live near the sea?' I grew up on the Isle of Wight. Once you live by the sea you get spoilt, you always want to be by the sea. There's something so reassuringly familiar in the swell of the waves and the sound of the sea lapping the shore.

'You could say that.' His smile hinted he could say a lot more on the topic, but he chose not to elaborate.

He was so different to anyone I had ever encountered before. I couldn't get enough of him. Maybe it was his rural upbringing, so alien to mine. His accent definitely helped; I could have listened to him talk forever. He was self-assured, but completely grounded. His manner was wholesome, understated, and with more than a hint of sexy. The attraction heightened with every exchange.

Hours passed unbeknown to us. The bar emptied; the night drew dangerously close to an inevitable end. I did something I'd never done in the course of my married life.

'Shall we swap numbers?' I was undeniably infatuated with him. The alcohol had made me brave or stupid. I wasn't sure which.

'I thought you'd never ask.' A chuckle escaped his full, smirking lips. He took my number and rang my phone, so I'd have his.

Guilt ate at my stomach lining, but I told myself I hadn't techni-cally crossed any lines yet. My situation might change one day, and if it did, the thought of never being able to speak to him again was unbear-able. I'd always wonder.

'Visit me in Ireland, anytime. No strings attached...' He seemed genuinely to mean it. Something about his open manner made me trust him completely. Call it instinct. I felt safe in his company. His quiet confidence allowed me to imagine for once I might be able to let someone else take the reins, and hand over some carefully collected control that I normally relinquished.

'I might just do that.' The words fell loosely from my tongue, but I meant them.

It was embarrassingly late, or early, whichever way you wanted to look at it. Eventually, we were the last two in the bar, even the barman had gone home. The impending goodbye loomed, and the thought physically nauseated me. The sun had risen without us noticing, soon breakfast would be served in this very room, as if everything was normal, as if my world hadn't been turned upside down in the space of a few short hours.

There was no excuse for me to still be here, yet I couldn't tear myself away.

'I wish I wasn't married,' I blurted out truthfully before I could overthink it.

'*I* wish you weren't married.' John glanced wistfully at me.

'It was never my plan.' Apparently, I hadn't quite finished unburdening *all* of my secrets. 'We have nothing in common. We're a habit. Like an old jumper with bobbles on. There's a familiar sort of comfort in it but you know you should throw it away, it would never be good enough again. Except it isn't a jumper, it's a person. A person I made a promise to in front of all my friends and family, at a point where I thought it was what I wanted. Needed, even. I got married knowing I wasn't in love. But I was looking for a partner, not that mad head over heels, crazy in love. I don't believe in that.' I paused and swallowed the lump forming in my throat. 'I didn't believe in that.' I corrected myself, fleetingly wondering if it were possible to be falling in love with this stranger already. The attraction pulled so deep, a fizzling slow burn of sheer longing tugging at the strings of the heart I'd forgotten I owned.

Was this what it felt like?

'I don't want to be the person that failed, that gave up. But there is nothing there. And to be honest, there never was. I'll never have a family with him. I don't want to be forever tied to him, so I've accepted I'll never have a family.' The cold hard facts stung as I uttered the words out loud. I blinked back a tear threatening the corner of my eye, praying it was just the gin making me so unrecognisable to myself.

Oceanic eyes gazed thoughtfully back at me.

'It never bothered me before. I often find myself thinking if I got hit by a bus in the morning, I've had a good life. I'm twenty-seven. It's no way to live. It's not easy being married, is it?' Silently, I pleaded with him to acknowledge my truth, tell me that none of it was simple, and everyone felt this way to some extent.

I wondered about the woman he'd married. If they were happy. How I envied her right now. How I would love him to be mine, to put my arms around him and feel his skin against mine. Even imagining it ignited every nerve ending in my neglected body.

He hesitated for several seconds before quietly revealing, 'The thing is, Lucy, I'm not actually married.'

'What?' I'd spilled my soul to this man, opened up my heart, only to be told he'd lied to me from the beginning. Maybe that was what happened when you let your guard down.

I wanted to be mad, I really did. But instead, it provided the faintest glimmer of hope when I was in no position to be hoping for anything. Anxiety bubbled in my stomach. Things were spiralling out of control. An unfamiliar, dangerous stirring of butterflies, rippled through my insides.

'I knew if I said I was single you wouldn't have talked to me. You are the best-looking woman in the bar.' He looked at me from under indecently long eyelashes.

'I'm the only woman in the bar.' I waved my arm at the empty silence surrounding us. 'You are a wolf in sheep's clothing!' I cringed, remembering all I'd shared with him, unsure if I was mad or delighted. Our entire encounter was morally wrong, but something about it felt very right.

We stood together in unison. The shift in the atmosphere was clear. Now the cards were on the table. The ball was in my court. I gathered my handbag and my heels and walked barefoot with him to the lift. My room was on the first floor. His was the fourth. A heavy silence lingered between us for the first time that night. The atmosphere was charged with illicit possibility. I could barely meet his eye, the was attraction so intense.

As the lift doors opened on the first floor, my empty bed awaited me. I stood motionlessly staring at his questioning features, my feet cemented to the floor, unable to leave. The doors closed again, and the lift progressed upwards to the fourth floor. Our eyes locked on each other in an unspoken agreement.

My clammy hand felt small in his as he guided me along the narrow corridor to his room. In his bedroom, we stood a foot apart, our hands still entwined. It was dark, despite the fact it was broad daylight outside; the heavy curtains had been long since drawn. My breath caught in my throat as he attempted to close the distance between us. The masculine scent of his aftershave lingered in the air around us, enveloping me. I desperately wanted to feel his arms around me. The temptation was like nothing I'd experienced before. The devil on my shoulder whispered in my ear and begged me to take a big juicy bite from the forbidden apple.

Guilt ripped through me. My heart hammered in my chest. I couldn't do it, this wasn't me. It went against everything I claimed to believe in. I'd never wanted anybody more before in my entire twenty-seven years, but I wasn't allowed. I signed a contract to prove it.

I bolted before I could change my mind, running out the door as fast as my swollen feet would carry me, tackling the stairs two at a time until I reached the safety of the first floor.

From my cold crisp bed, I sent him a text. Bridezilla lay snoring four feet away from me.

Lucy:

I'm sorry.

And I truly was. For myself, as much as him. A deep sense of loss penetrated my core, though it had no right doing so. My heavy heart was crushed by my own stupidity. I should never have put myself in that situation, or let it get that far. Though I couldn't bring myself to regret it fully. My eyes had been opened. Change was imminent.

Chapter Two

SATURDAY 30TH JUNE 2012

I had less than two hours sleep. My mouth was like the bottom of a birdcage and my head pounded. Nausea hovered in my gut. It wasn't the alcohol. Raw, acidic guilt stripped the lining of my stomach. I had sailed dangerously close to the wind, and the worse thing about it was, it had felt so right. I'd felt at one with John right away. I knew in my heart if I crossed the line physically, I'd go home to my husband and confess. And it would be really ugly. One thing I did not do well with was guilt and secrets. No one could punish me more than I would punish myself.

Entwined with the guilt was a shattering sadness. For the first time in my life, I had glimpsed a different path. I met a younger, carefree version of myself. A version that didn't have to maintain a façade or uphold a life where everything was planned, clogging the emptiness inside.

I found something I didn't realise I was missing; a part of me I didn't know existed. I'd felt alive. I'd felt young. I'd finally seen the light, there was a world of opportunity out there that I had cut myself off from. I'd imprisoned myself in a box. It had felt like security at the time, but in reality, it was an obstacle course of limitations constructed of fear and insecurity. An odd moment to accidently stumble upon such clarity.

Heidi pulled back the curtains and the sun shone in brightly in the window. I squinted looking up at her and she handed me one of her stolen supplies of Costa Coffee orange juices. She wasn't all bad, I suppose.

'You look like you need this more than me.' Her crisp tone heavily articulated each syllable.

'Thank you.' I gratefully accepted and drank quietly, trying to gather my thoughts.

John was still in the same building as me. I wondered if he was awake. I pictured him entangled in his crisp-white sheets, only wishing things could have been different. That I could have woken up in his arms. Even in the light of day, the need for him was strong, unreasonable but undeniable.

They were also staying for two nights, the same as us. There was a chance I might run into him again. Oh, how desperately I wanted to. I couldn't decide if it was one of my best ideas, or one of my worst. My brain was foggy from the gin and sleep deprivation, yet I couldn't sleep another wink now if I tried. 'Good night?' Heidi asked.

'Too good,' I replied genuinely.

'And there was me thinking it was my hen, yet you're the one sneaking in in the early hours of the morning.'

Bollocks. I thought I'd gotten away with it. 'One of us had to have some fun.' I tried to sound breezy about it.

'What time are we going to the West Coast Park?' she asked.

Shit. I'd forgotten about that. The West Coast Park was a fifty-minute drive from Bristol and involved us women donning sumo wrestler suits and fighting with giant foam poles. I mean seriously, whatever happened to a nice relaxing spa day? Or a bubbly afternoon tea? Or even just a bit of shopping and a few glasses of wine? Still, it was what she wanted, and it was her hen. I scrambled out of bed.

'Ah, I think we need to be there at ten.'

'Where do you think you're going, Lucy?' Heidi said as I searched the sideboard looking for my car keys. I was still drunk, there was no point denying it.

'Looking for these?' She waved the keys in front of me. 'If you think I'm getting into a car with you like that, you can think again. I'd actually like to make my wedding day. I'll drive.' Her tone was stern, even by her standards.

Thank God. Bad enough having to go, let alone drive as well. And she had a point, I would have been way over the legal limit to drive. I headed into the shower and tried to brace myself for the day ahead, wondering how to go about 'accidently' bumping into Mr-So-Wrong-He's-Right.

————

We met the girls in the hotel lobby an hour later, kitted out in wellies, shorts and vests all ready for the mud fest that was ahead of us. I was never as happy to see Clara as I was that morning. My thoughts were consumed with John, it was all I could do not to shout his name from the rooftops.

'Hello, Mrs, how are you this morning?' Clara said.

'I've often felt better.' It was the truth.

'You were up late with that ginger guy last night.' She gave me a playful nudge in the ribs.

'We were only talking. He's married.' I repeated his cover story, crossing my fingers behind my back as if it made any difference.

As we headed out the door into the sunshine, I scanned the lobby twice, but there was no sign of him. He was probably still in bed. That was the right place to be. I squeezed my eyes shut and tried to force the image from my mind.

Heidi drove my car to the venue, concentrating on the road while Clara and Ruth dissected the events of the night before. I was there in body but my mind was elsewhere. In the light of day, I couldn't under-stand how I could have felt so drawn to a man I'd just met. Which only fuelled my curiosity. I needed to see him again, to see if what I'd felt was real. It was overwhelming and irrational. I couldn't get him out of my mind. He was everything I deliberately avoided.

We arrived at the games in good time and were promptly issued animal fancy dress outfits to put on. I thought it was bad before I had to wear a sheep costume. Now it was fucking ridiculous. Once the photos were taken, I discarded the costume and lay in the field with the sun shining down on my face. Then, I closed my eyes and allowed myself to think solidly, without interruption. The girls duelled in their costumes, laughing, fighting and falling over each other. My good self and the devil on my shoulder were also duelling; the devil egging me on to find out more while I had the chance.

I tuned everyone out, replaying our conversations over and over again, thinking about how close he got to kissing me, imagining what it might have felt like, trying not to smile at his humour, and not to cry at the complete unfairness of the situation. Longing dragged at the pit of my stomach, and as unwise as it probably was, I knew I had to see him again.

After what seemed like an eternity, we headed back to the car and returned to the hotel. At least at the hotel there was a minute chance of seeing him. We had no hope dressed up as farm animals in a field fifty miles away. Probably a saving grace.

I agreed to meet Clara and Ruth in the lobby twenty minutes later to get some shopping in while we had a free couple of hours. Retail therapy was the best therapy, so we hit Cabot Circus. If I'd hoped to take my mind from John, it didn't work. I wondered would he prefer a scarlet or a nude lipstick. I bought both, but decided on the scarlet for that night. Hung for a sheep as a lamb...

———

That evening, I was the first of the girls to reach the hotel bar. I couldn't deny it to myself; I knew exactly why I was there first, who I was hoping to bump into. There was no sign of him or of his friends. I checked my phone on the off chance he might have texted me, but it showed no new messages. When the girls appeared, I fell into mindless chatter before being pulled into a taxi.

The Comedy Club was good fun, the food was crap, as you'd expect, but the comedians were brilliant and the stage turned into a disco afterward. Clara wasn't feeling well. She suffered with her tummy and mixing cocktails and wine last night hadn't agreed with her.

'I might go back to the hotel.' Her tone was apologetic.

'I'll come with you.' I grabbed my bag.

'Don't be daft. Stay here and enjoy the night. No need for you to leave as well.'

I welcomed an excuse to leave, desperate to bump into John again. One thing was for sure, he wasn't in The Comedy Club. But there was a chance he may end up in the residents' bar at the hotel, and I was going to make sure I was already there.

Disappointingly, I hadn't heard from him all day. I'd been so sure he'd felt what I'd felt. I'd checked my phone a hundred times and there had been nothing. I considered confiding in Clara, but I couldn't find the words. Even she didn't know how bad things were at home. Never before could I admit out loud that anything was less than perfect. She had a fair idea, everyone did. But nobody said it out loud. The topic of my marriage was off limits, even to my mother.

'Are you sure? I honestly don't mind going back myself.'

I did not need any encouragement. I apologised to Bridezilla that Clara wasn't well. She didn't seem to mind us going back to the hotel. Ruth came with us.

We sat in the hotel bar in the relative quiet, Clara sipping on a brandy that was apparently medicinal. I was more than happy to sit with her, unwittingly turning my head each time the door opened. I ordered a gin and tonic again and looked longingly at the two empty stools at the bar we'd been sitting on only a few short hours ago.

'Anyone would think you were waiting for someone,' Ruth said, digging me in the ribs with her elbow playfully.

'Ha! As if! Just keeping my eye on the door in case Bridezilla decides to come in and pee on my bonfire!' I joked to mask the truth, trying not to choke on my drink, willing the threatening blush to stay away. The girls laughed as I checked my phone underneath the table for the hundredth time.

They were my best friends, but I could barely process what had happened myself, let alone try to explain it to them. I wouldn't get away with it for long though, that was for sure. My facial expressions gave me away every time. It was impossible to be fake with them even if I tried. That's probably why none of them openly asked about my marriage, it would be uncomfortable for all of us, me openly lying and them pretending to believe it. It was an unspoken rule in our friendship. No one ever asked how Rob was. Only now did it occur to me how fucked up the whole situation was.

Two G & Ts later, I excused myself to go to the toilet and took my phone with me. It had bad idea written all over it, but I decided to call John. It was now or never. Tomorrow he'd be back in Ireland and I would never see him again. The gin made me brazen. I pulled the phone out of my bag, shaky hands reapplied the deep red lipstick while I rang his number. The dial tone rang as if he was abroad, but then I suppose technically he was. After two rings he answered.

'Lucy,' he said in a bright tone; his familiar voice soothed my soul. The lads shouted in the background and loud music echoed over the line.

But that voice… it sounded like home to me.

'Where are you?' he shouted over the noise.

'I'm in the hotel bar. I wondered if you'd like to have a drink with me?' I had nothing left to lose at this point. Oh yeah, except absolutely everything… but it was a chance I felt compelled to take.

'When you didn't reply to my text earlier, I assumed you didn't want to see me,' he said.

'What text?' I'd checked enough, let's be honest. I couldn't have missed it.

'I text you earlier, to see how you were after everything. When you didn't reply I thought you had seen sense and remembered I was ginger,' he said with a snigger.

'I didn't receive any text, and I'm fully aware that you're ginger.' I exhaled a girlish giggle. The sound of his voice sailed through my soul, lifting my spirit.

'Give me half an hour and I'll be home,' he promised.

Home. If only. But the hotel bar would do for now. I headed back to the girls and tried to hide the fact that my mood had shifted a full one-eighty while I'd supposedly only been going for a wee.

Seventeen people came into the bar, including four of his stag friends. Seventeen times my head snapped round, only to be disappointed. The eighteenth person was him. My heart swelled with joy and I raised my hand to him unashamedly.

He wore a simple navy slim-fitting shirt and jeans, his hands tucked effortlessly into his pockets. He nodded at me, and I caught the secret smile curling at the corners of his mouth. He headed over to where we were sitting on the same couches as the night previously.

'What's the craic ladies?' His casual demeanour was one of the things I'd been most attracted to last night.

'Zero craic,' I said. 'How was your night?' I tried to act normal in front of the girls but my hands became increasingly clammy and the blush threatened my face again, revealing my obsessive attraction to him.

'Can I get you ladies a drink?' he asked.

'No thanks.' Clara yawned, looking ready to hit the hay. She rested her head on her hand and her eyes started to close. I smiled at John and he fake coughed, his daze darting to Clara. She had opened her eyes and was looking between the two of us. Why was she so reluctant to leave us? Please, could she just go?

The message must have delivered. Clara got to her feet and arched her eyebrow. 'Sorry, I can't keep my eyes open any longer. See you in the morning.'

'I should go too.' Ruth said, standing with a smile. She followed Clara out the bar.

'And then there were two...' I said.

'Sadly, not for long.' John gestured to his friends heading our way and soon the bar was packed again.

A tall man with dark hair and tanned skin approached us shortly after. He clapped John firmly on the back in a familiar manner and smiled warmly at him.

'Well, this must be Lucy.' He extended his hand to shake mine firmly. His smile was bright, but I wasn't sure it fully reached his eyes.

'Nice to meet you.' I shook his hand firmly.

'I'm the best friend. Owen.' His accent was almost identical to John's.

'I'm the random married woman, but if you know my name, I'm sure you know that already.' I tried to make light of the situation but I wasn't sure Owen was convinced of my honourable intentions. Darting glances inferred he was still making up his mind about me, but he sauntered back to the rest of the stag party, leaving us alone again.

We sat side by side on the couch. John's thigh leaned against mine, electricity pulsing rapidly between us. I hadn't imagined a thing from the previous night. The attraction was acute. Again, I found myself imagining what it would be like to be his. To hold him, to be held. To feel him physically against me. I felt so powerlessly drawn to him.

He took out his phone and showed me the message he had sent me this morning. I spotted the mistake immediately, only because I had received the foreign dial tone not half an hour before or else I probably wouldn't have noticed. He hadn't put the UK area code in, so the message wasn't delivered. The knowledge that he'd tried to contact me warmed my heart.

'So, Lucy,' he said knowingly. 'What are we going to do with you?'

I knew what I'd like him to do, but it was never going to happen in a million years. I wasn't that kind of girl, married or not. I'd learnt the hard way. If you wanted a man to respect you, you made him wait. Regardless of what every fibre in my being was telling me.

'I don't know, John. What would you suggest?' I batted the ball straight back into his court.

He looked at his watch for a second thoughtfully and said, 'I could have my car over here in about thirty-six hours to collect you and your belongings and bring you back to my house. No one would even think to look for you there. And then I'd have you all to myself, to do exactly as I pleased with you.'

'Ha. If only it were that easy.'

'Well, there's not much more I can suggest. But the offer stands.' He shrugged.

We changed the subject, knowing nothing would be resolved tonight. But it was reassuring that we were on the same page. We moved up to the bar stools again to steal some privacy away from the others. The more time I spent with him, the more time I wanted to spend with him. Conversation was effortless, and I lowered my armour once again. He was easy company, in addition to being unnervingly attractive.

The hours flew by all too quickly. The barman loaded the glasses into a dishwasher, clearly pissed off with the lot of us. It was five in the morning and there was no sign of anyone going to bed yet. But I knew at some point I'd have to say goodbye. This time it could be forever. Who knew? The thought sickened me.

'I can honestly say meeting you has been an eye-opener.' I meant every word.

'Lucy, you are an absolute lady. I'd love if you'd come to Ireland sometime...'

'I'd love to, but I have to face into a truck load of shit before that can happen, unfortunately. But never say never.' I took his hand and held it for a minute and allowed myself to look at him properly for a few seconds, hoping it wouldn't be for the last time. He met my eye, and with one look we exchanged more than words could ever say. A sense of sadness, longing, hope, possibility, understanding.

There was nothing left to say. I gave him a lingering cuddle and slunk away up the stairs to the first floor, feeling like I'd just let the best thing that could have happened to me slip through my fingers. One thing was clear, though. I couldn't go on like this.

Chapter Three

SUNDAY 1ST JULY 2012

Another night with less than two hours' sleep. I was physically wrecked but there was a drive charging me that wasn't there before. I showered and put on a black cotton maxi dress and diamanté flip flops for the drive home. Bridezilla had already gone for breakfast so I had the room to myself. I toyed with my phone and contemplated ringing John, but what more could I say?

I headed down to the breakfast room although I could barely stomach a thing. Joining Heidi at her table, I scanned the room for any sign of him. Nothing. I managed to drink a cup of tea and shovel enough food around my plate to make it look like I'd eaten something.

Heidi was looking forward to getting home. I was not. Still, it was time to crack on with it. I hadn't heard from Rob all weekend and I didn't know if he would be home when I got in or if he had plans. Who was I kidding? He'd be sat on the sofa watching the cricket with a can of Stella, waiting for me to come home and make dinner.

At the reception desk, we handed back our key cards and checked out. I couldn't help noticing the stag party John was with was congregated in the lobby, ready to go. I glimpsed a fleeting view of him, our eyes locked and a sad smile curled on my lips. He nodded and raised his hand. There was nothing we could say to ease the goodbye, especially not surrounded by thirty of our alcohol poisoned friends.

I threw my weekend bag into the boot of the car and rounded the girls up. There was no point delaying the inevitable. The drive home was quiet, the girls tired after the weekend's debauchery. I drove on autopilot, wondering if John had boarded the flight back to Ireland yet. Such a weekend it was. I'd never felt so high and so low in such a short space of time.

One thing was for sure, though. Something had to change. I'd seen another way, that there may just be someone out there for me who could make me smile and ignite some life back into me. Even if it wasn't John, even if I never laid eyes on him again, he had awakened something in me. I wanted more. I couldn't carry on pretending everything was ok when it was far from it. It wasn't fair on any of us. I had a sinking feeling that, given the chance, I could actually fall head over heels, crazy in love. And for once, the thought actually excited me.

I dropped the girls back at each of their houses, waved at my brother, Simon, from the car. I couldn't face talking to him. My body was raw, aching with confused emotion. I drove the last few miles back to my own rented house slowly, deliberating what to do for the rest of the day. It was only lunchtime.

Heading through the back door, straight into the kitchen, I heard cricket commentary blaring out from the television in the lounge. I rolled my eyes and followed the sound. There he was, predictably sprawled on the couch, can in hand and another discarded at his feet.

'How's things?' Rob didn't turn his head; his eyes never left the screen.

'Fine, thanks. How are you?' I picked up the can from the floor.

'All well here. Had a lazy weekend.'

What's new? I refrained from saying it out loud. Upstairs, I unpacked my weekend bag. It took all of ten minutes. The house felt claustrophobic. I needed to get out. Pulling on my gym clothes, I headed out the back door again, only shouting I was going out as an afterthought.

I thought I heard, 'What time's dinner?' but I chose to ignore it, banging the door defiantly.

The gym was a five-minute drive away. I was surprised to see the carpark almost full. Great. Just when I was hoping for a bit of solitude. I remained in my vehicle, staring searchingly at my phone. Would I ever hear from him again? Was it just a bit of craic for him? Or did it feel as real to him as it did to me?

After a brief internal contemplation, I decided then, shit or bust, to ring him. If he answered, I'd see where it took me. If he didn't, I would never ring him again, just simply draw a line under the weekend. I'd let fate decide. For all I knew, he could have been exceptionally charming over the weekend, and then not give our meeting a second thought. It was complicated, to say the least. It wouldn't be any wonder if a person didn't want to get caught up in what was about to be the car crash of my life.

I found John's name in my recent calls log, chewed my lower lip and pressed the phone tightly to my ear.

'Welcome to the Vodafone messaging service, your call cannot be connected right now, please try again later.'

Well, that was that. Fate had decided. It was a great weekend. Nothing more. Sort your life out Lucy O'Connor, you are in no position to be hoping for anything. It had served its purpose as a complete eye-opener, regardless of what happened from that point.

In the gym, I found a free treadmill overlooking the car park and started the machine. Pure alcohol streamed out of every pore. I increased the pace, the physical burn distracting me from my self-inflicted heartache. My feet pounded the rubber, thumping thunderously with each step. Old school dance music blasted from my eardrums as I attempted to drown everything else out; how I'd felt for those few hours with John, how impossible the situation was, regardless of the fact that I was actually married. The odds were massively stacked against us. We lived in different countries.

He didn't answer. Write it off, I repeatedly reminded myself.

I was two kilometres in when the music cut out, and I looked down at my phone in surprise to see John's name flashing up on the caller ID.

I hit the emergency stop button and swiftly positioned a foot either side of the running belt.

'Hello?' I panted.

'How are you now?' That fabulous accent melted my heart instantly.

'Good thanks,' I replied out of breath. 'Just in the gym. Needed to burn off some steam.'

'You're some woman,' he said. 'I'm in the pub with the lads, we stopped off in the local on the way home but the network's not great. I only saw your missed call now.'

Missed call? I didn't leave a message, and it went straight to answer phone so I thought I'd gotten away with my borderline stalkerish behaviour.

'What missed call?' I denied feebly.

'Vodafone sent me a text to say you tried to ring me,' he explained slowly, like I was simple.

'Oh, right. I must have hit it in my pocket by mistake.'

'Oh. Well, I just wanted to say thanks for a lovely weekend. It was great to meet you. If things change, or if you need anything, even to talk, you know where I am.'

'Thank you. I'll be in touch. For sure.'

I didn't know how or when, but I knew this wouldn't be the end of us. 'Enjoy your day.'

'You too, Lucy.'

Then he was gone.

Chapter Four

MONDAY 2ND JULY 2012

Monday morning came too soon. I was starting a locum position in a small NHS dental practice on the outskirts of Bournemouth. It was for a three-month period on a Monday only, and it was an hour's drive from my house in Winchester. I didn't mind the commute, driving gave me the solitude I desired to think.

Resentment had built at home in the mere twenty-four hours since realisation struck. Tiny things I used to tolerate quietly were becoming massive issues I was ready to explode over. I'd had to pick up more Stella cans from the living room floor this morning and the room had smelt like a brewery.

I didn't want to watch our marriage shatter, crumbling both of us into pieces of our former selves. I'd far rather, if it was going to happen, that we had a fast, clean break so there was no time for things to get really ugly. But I still didn't know what to do. There was no doubt in my mind I had to leave, though.

What would I say? What would I tell my family? Where would I go? What would he do? It wasn't my responsibility to look after him, he was a grown man after all. But I couldn't help feeling some sense of responsibility. His family were in the States. Could he go back? Would he even want to? I felt like I barely knew him at all.

I pulled into the driveway of the dental surgery to begin my day. It was a relief to do something practical after all the pondering I'd been doing all night.

At lunch time I sat in the staff room with my new short-term colleagues and dabbled in polite conversation while slyly checking my phone. No messages, but I had a friend request on Facebook. It was a certain John Kelly. My stomach did a little lurch. I clicked on his profile picture but couldn't see much as he was up a mountain togged out in skiing gear.

It was nice he'd bothered to search for me. I'd accept it tonight. I didn't want him to think I sat desperately waiting by the phone, even if it was ridiculously close to the truth.

The day passed quickly. It wasn't long before I was in my car again, mentally and physically exhausted. I dreaded going home to that house, to Rob. Now I had it in my mind I needed to leave I wanted to do it ASAP. But I couldn't just up and leave. My brother was getting married in four weeks and it would cause a complete uproar before the wedding.

I thought about it throughout the night. It would be completely selfish of me not to just wait a few weeks. Plus, it would give me time to decide what I was going to do with my life, to come up with some sort of plan.

In the night's darkness, I toyed with the idea of moving back to Edinburgh. I'd been so happy there, bar the weather. I still had a lot of contacts. I'd have no problem finding work. Some of my best friends were still there. Edinburgh is a really short daily flight from Dublin; I'd be lying if I said that thought didn't cross my mind. But whatever I did, it would have to be for me. Not on the off-chance John was the man of my dreams, even if he seemed absolutely perfect.

I needed to sort myself out and get my shit together. For me, not for anybody else. Whether things ever worked out with John, he had shown me a fresh perspective. I had to make the change, as unnerving as it was. I had just needed the kick up the arse to motivate me to do it.

It wouldn't be pleasant for any of us. Nobody gets married thinking it will end in divorce. But I couldn't waste any more of my life like this, in a stale, loveless marriage. At the prospect of leaving, a tiny glimmer of relief flickered on the horizon. Until now, I hadn't realised it had been there in the background the whole time. I hadn't realised how weighted I'd been, hadn't wanted to see the massive elephant in the room. So, I'd closed my eyes.

I pulled up at the house, poured myself a generous glass of Rioja and ran a bath. Rob was home already, sitting in front of the television.

'What's for dinner?' he said.

'I don't know. What are you making?'

He looked blankly at me, frown lines creasing his forehead. The lights were on but, as usual, nobody was home.

'Look, there's pasta in the cupboard. It will only take fifteen minutes. There's a sauce in there too. Just do enough for yourself, I'm not hungry.' I was subtly trying to prepare him for the real world, the one where everything wasn't done for you.

Twenty minutes later, I heard him banging around in the kitchen below, so I gathered he'd taken my advice.

I got into bed early. Rob fell asleep on the couch watching television. He always slept in the spare room, it started because he snored, but that was just an excuse. We just preferred to be apart. I accepted my new Facebook friend, did some cyber stalking, wondering if he was sitting in Ireland, doing the same.

I slipped into a deep dreamless slumber, with the lamp on dimly next to my bed. Exhaustion from the weekend finally caught up with me.

Chapter Five

TUESDAY 3RD JULY 2012

On Tuesday I often locumed, but I hadn't looked for work, and nobody had phoned from the agency. Too much time on my hands was proving to be dangerous. With the house to myself, I cleared out anything I hadn't worn or used in six months and bagged it for the charity shop. I was ruthless. It enabled me to feel productive, even in my new uncertain state of mind. I cleaned the windows, hoovered the entire house, cleaned the bathroom and mopped the floor.

I also googled 'how to get divorced' with shaky hands and a guilty sense of nausea. It wasn't something I'd ever seriously considered before. Other than witnessing my parents' divorce, I knew nothing about the process. Apparently, there were several options. After the weekend I knew without a shadow of a doubt that it was my *only* option, if I was ever to be happy in myself again.

It sounded heartless; I know. But my eyes had been prised open to the fact that I felt completely and utterly nothing for Rob. Nothing bad, nothing good, just completely and utterly indifferent. A while ago, my friend Fiona asked how I'd feel if Rob met somebody else. I actually laughed. I'd genuinely be delighted. It would be a relief. That alone should have been enough to make me realise I had to change something, but I was always too scared to open that can of writhing worms.

We'd been coexisting. That crack of light at the end of the tunnel was getting closer. I imagined what it would be like to get my life back, to go wherever I wanted, to do whatever I wanted. I never realised how weighed down I felt until the prospect of not being weighed down occurred to me.

By lunchtime I had all the household chores done. The idea of phoning John consumed me. I convinced myself it could do no harm, as he was in a different country. How much trouble could I really get into at this stage? Besides, the damage was already done.

I lay on my bed and stared out the window, willing him to answer.

'Hello?' he said slowly. The grin spread across my cheeks, right up to my ears.

'It's Lucy.' Talk about stating the obvious, I was fairly sure in this day and age even Ireland had Caller ID.

'Give me a second.' I heard him excusing himself, then the rustle of him moving away from whoever he was with.

'Sorry, I can talk now. I'm just having lunch with a friend.'

'Sorry for interrupting you,' I said. 'I was thinking about you. I wanted to say hi.' I had no right to wonder who the friend was, or feel envious of them, but I couldn't help it. An unreasonable jealousy attacked my stomach. This was exactly why I never wanted to fall in love – or into infatuation. The craziness was creeping up on me already. I couldn't fully control the emotions he stirred in me, but I was in too deep already to care.

'I wanted to call you last night,' he said. 'But I didn't want to put you in an awkward situation. How did your first day go in the new job?' He placated me without even realising. Lovely of him to remember in spite of all the gin and tonics.

'It was fine. Thanks for asking. Are you working today?'

'Yeah. Well, right now I'm standing here in the pissing rain talking you. My shirt's soaked through. I must be mad in the head.' I could hear the smile in his voice, as I tried to envision him in my mind.

'Sorry! Go back to your lunch. I only called to say hi.'

'Listen, I'll send you a text later, ok?' he checked.

'Perfect.' I looked forward to it.

I tried not to spend the afternoon and early evening checking my phone, but it was practically impossible. I was infatuated with John Kelly and I couldn't understand it. Never had a man had such an effect on me before. I'd always been so cool; I was practically cold. I was supposed to be the sensible one in my group. I'm not sure if it was good to be proved wrong, or bad. The jury was out. One thing was for sure though, someone was going to get hurt with the stakes this high, I silently prayed to God it wouldn't be me.

At seven-thirty, my phone vibrated with a text message.

John:

Good to hear from you earlier. If this text doesn't deliver, we'll have to try smoke signals next.

I beamed from ear to ear, but waited half an hour before replying.

Lucy:

Don't light any fires on my behalf. I'm in enough trouble as it is.

John:

Nowhere near enough trouble yet.

Lucy:

I can see you are going to be a bad influence on me.

He had influenced me profoundly already, whether he realised it yet or not was another thing.

John:

I'd like to be.

Before I could reply, he sent another message. He cut straight to the point, like only a man could.

John:

What do you want out of this?

. . .

Lucy:

I really like you. I didn't expect to meet someone like you. I need to sort my life out. Maybe we can be friends and if anything comes of it, it will be a bonus.

There it was, heart straight out on the sleeve. No point beating around the bush. Let's face it, it wasn't like I was going to bump into him in my local Sainsbury's anytime soon.

John:

I'll settle for friends. For now.

Chapter Six

THURSDAY 12TH JULY 2012

Clara and I were out for dinner at our local Prezzo. It was busy for a weeknight, but we managed to get a table for two in the window overlooking the city. I watched a hundred strangers coming and going; imagining them returning home to their families, imagining what kind of life they might lead. The evening was bright; the weather had been kind to us this year. People were out making the most of being able to wear their shorts and T-shirts after a long day at work. I pushed a pile of untouched rigatoni around my plate.

'I've never seen you so distracted, Lucy, what's going on?' Clara asked.

'Nothing really.' Nothing in reality, and everything in my head.

'The last couple of weeks it's like you're here, but not really here.' She probed a little further as I twiddled my napkin between my fingers.

I took a massive gulp of wine before I could say, 'I think it's over. With me and Rob.'

Her eyebrows shot up at my acknowledgement of it rather than the truth of it.

'What happened?' she whispered. We were in proximity to several other tables, and Winchester was a small place.

'I suppose it's been on the cards for a long time. I've just been avoiding accepting it. We're like chalk and cheese. It's just not enough anymore. I thought I could just get on with it...' I glanced up from my tattered napkin.

'Go on,' she murmured, without a hint of judgement, probably still in shock that I was prepared to discuss it.

'Then I met John.' There, I said it. It was out there.

Silence at first, until the penny dropped, along with her lower jaw.

'That ginger guy from the hen?' She couldn't mask her shock. 'Lucy, apart from the fact that he lives in a different country, he's married,' she reminded me.

'Ah.' I forgot I hadn't fully disclosed the truth about that one.

'He's actually not. He just said that so I would spend the night talking to him.'

'So, what exactly are you telling me?' She still wasn't getting it.

'There's nothing to tell, really. Apart from that night changed everything. Don't get me wrong, I'm not going to run away to the west of Ireland with some complete stranger, but I suppose it awakened something in me. The short time I spent with him I felt more like myself than I had done in years.' I swept my hair back from my face, tucking in securely behind one ear before continuing. 'Not to mention the fact I was massively attracted to John. I can't stop thinking about him. I can't actually sleep for thinking about him. There was just something about him. It's hard to put it into words. I'm turning into one of those crazy women that I used to feel sorry for.'

'You certainly are.' She covered her mouth to suppress a laugh and hide her surprise. 'I actually can't believe I'm hearing this from you, of all people! So, have you spoken to him?'

At that exact second, my phone vibrated with a text on the table in front of us.

'Oh no, it's worse than I thought.' Clara's head fell into her hands. 'That's him, isn't it?'

'How did you know?' I grabbed the phone from the table quickly, before she could snatch it and pry.

'Your face says it all, Lucy. You're like an open book. Your smile could light up Blackpool for a year.'

'I can't help it,' I said honestly. 'He's intriguing, funny, and he seems to really care. I'm borderline obsessed already.'

'I honestly didn't think you had it in you. You're normally so sensible, practical. Sometimes I think you're old before your time.' She took a sip from her wine glass before leaning conspicuously across the table. 'Well, what's he saying?' She squinted, attempting to read the text upside down.

'Just asking how my day was. Saying he's watching the football.'

'So, what are you grinning about then?' She still didn't seem to get it.

'I'm just glad to hear from him. He texts every day. But this was the first one today. I thought he might have gotten bored sitting around waiting for me.'

'Oh no.' Clara's face was crestfallen. 'This is so much worse than I thought.'

'Don't say that, Clara! I promise you, nothing happened. We've only been talking.' I so badly didn't want her to judge me. Technically, nothing had happened... yet.

'That's even worse,' she exclaimed. 'You're like a lovesick puppy over a man you haven't even kissed! You've got it bad girl! It's written all over your face. What happened to my "black or white – no time for grey areas" friend?'

The smile remained firmly etched onto my face, like the proverbial Cheshire cat, my phone gripped tightly in my right hand.

'What are you going to do? One thing is for sure, if Rob sees you walking around with that smile, even he won't miss it.'

'I know,' I said, solemn all of a sudden. 'I have to leave.'

'What! You can't be serious?' she shrieked, her voice loud enough to attract several stares from neighbouring tables. She continued in a hushed whisper, 'Lucy, you don't even know this man. You can't leave your husband of seven years for someone that you barely spent seven hours with.' Her eyes narrowed, and she ran her fingers through her curly hair.

'You're missing the point, Clara. I'm not leaving Rob for a man I spent less than seven hours with. I'm leaving him for me. Admittedly, it's taken meeting someone else that I am completely infatuated with to realise it. But regardless of whether I ever see John again, I cannot stay in this marriage. If I never see John again, I need to leave Rob. I'd rather be on my own than where I am; unhappy, a slave to a vow. I have to get out before I suffocate. It's all I can think about since that weekend in Bristol.'

'Well, I'm not exactly surprised that you're thinking of leaving, it's been obvious to us all for ages that there was something desperately wrong. You spend no time together; you never talk about him. You are as well to be on your own, for all you get out of that relationship. I just can't believe that you are so mad about that guy we met. I just didn't see it coming. I mean, he's a farmer! From the arse end of nowhere in Ireland!'

'I know. Neither did I. I wasn't looking at all. But it hit me with the force of an oncoming train.'

'Are you sure it's not just the seven year itch?' She leaned curiously over the table.

'It's one hell of a fucking itch if it is.' I laughed harder and longer than I should have, relieving some pent-up tension. Once I started, I couldn't stop. People were beginning to stare. I took a couple of deep breaths and composed myself, but I couldn't wipe the smile. It felt so unbelievably good to tell someone. I trusted Clara with my life.

'Just be careful, Lucy. It's not just your life you're messing with.'

'I know. And believe me I'm not going to embark on something until I am well and truly out of that house and gone. And whether it works out or not, it gave me the kick up the arse I needed to leave. So, for that I will always be grateful, regardless. I'm done wasting my life. I could get hit by a bus in the morning.'

'I don't want to see you get hurt. Be careful,' Clara said solemnly. She actually looked worried for me.

'Don't worry about me. It's not like things could get any worse,' I reassured her.

Chapter Seven

WEDNESDAY 18TH JULY 2012

'I need a favour, Clara.' I went to her at her desk when my eleven thirty patient failed to show up.

'Of course, what is it?' She lifted her head up from the screen and pushed her glasses up on top of her glossy black spiralling curls.

'You know how we've got Lizzie's hen night on Saturday?' I reminded her.

'Yeah, I already said you can stay at mine, no problem.' Puzzled eyes darted over my face.

'I know you did. Thanks, I'm definitely going to take you up on it. The thing is I need you to be my alibi during the day on Saturday too,' I pleaded.

'Of course. Where are you going?' she asked.

'Dublin.' That got her attention.

'For the day?' Widening oval eyes stared incredulously back at me.

'For the day,' I confirmed.

'You've gone mad in the head. Well and truly lost it my dear! Over a ginger dude from the arse end of nowhere in Ireland. I think you might be having a midlife crisis, but I'm all for it. About time you lightened up!' I knew she wouldn't let me down.

'You're the best.' I leaned over the desk to give her a hug.

'Just be careful. I hope you know what you're doing,' she warned.

I didn't know what I was doing. I was starting to wonder if my feelings for John were as real as I thought they were. He seemed too good to be true. And my mother always told me if things seemed too good to be true, they usually were.

John continued to phone me each day. The calls had become longer, the conversations deeper. I was more emotionally involved than I cared to admit. The armour lowered consistently, inch by inch. John knew me better than my husband did – without a doubt. Before I'd even spoken, if I only breathed down the phone, he could ascertain what kind of mood I was in.

We talked for hours and never ran out of things to say. He opened up about his past; told me he'd never met anyone serious before, though he'd apparently been ready for a while. About his career, how he had progressed from a college degree in sport science, to a farmer running his own show. He told me had another business as well, but he didn't elaborate; he said he'd show me one day. It piqued a little curiosity within, but I didn't have time to consider it because there was always so much to talk about.

We took it in turns to ask each other the daftest questions, like if you could only have one more meal on this earth what would it be. We talked about music, films, running (his love of it and my loath of it, although I loved the calories it burned) and books. I was an avid reader; I could read a book in a day if it was really good. John hated reading, he said he couldn't think of anything worse. He preferred films. On the rare occasion we actually did fall silent, I simply enjoyed listening to his quiet breathing over the phone line, enjoying the knowledge that he was there.

We got to know each other better than two people that were doing the regular dating thing, primarily because we couldn't do that, not just because of my marital status but because of the distance. So we talked instead, sometimes for an hour or two. He had become one of my best friends already, my closest confidant.

For a week, we'd been toying with the idea of meeting up for the day; either him flying to London or me flying to Dublin. I made it quite clear there would be no overnights. It wasn't him that I didn't trust; it was me.

There was an early morning flight out of Southampton that would have me in Dublin at eight in the morning. John was going to drive from Mayo, spend the day with me, and I would fly back to Southampton that evening, and go to Lizzies hen night as arranged.

Once we had a plan in place, I was counting down the hours until I saw him again. How did this happen to me? The excitement was physically unbearable. The weight was falling off me at a rapid rate. Not only could I not sleep, but I could barely eat as well.

My brother's wedding was ten days away and I couldn't wait to reclaim my life afterwards.

Chapter Eight

THURSDAY 19TH JULY 2012

Nineteen has always been my lucky number. It wasn't so lucky for Betsy. While I was working, a patient reversed his car out of the practice car park, straight into the back of my car.

I dropped my car at the BMW garage and was lent a brand spanking new BMW One Series while mine was repaired. It was gorgeous, but that was the whole point; to suck you in to a hire purchase agreement you would never normally consider, unless of course you had driven the car, become profoundly attached to it, and somehow convinced yourself that the ridiculous monthly repayments weren't actually that bad after all.

The smell of the brand-new leather, the feel of the power at the wheel, the quiet hum of the engine, the metallic graphite grey paint, what wasn't to love?

The one-thousand-pound excess – what was not to fucking love.

Admittedly, I was thinking about John, just for a change, not concentrating as I should have been. On approaching a small roundabout, I watched the traffic from the right as I waited for an opening to pull out. After several seconds, I saw my chance and put my foot on the accelerator. A deafening bang alarmed me, but not as much as the fact that I couldn't actually go more than a foot forward. I pressed hard on the accelerator once again. I kid you not.

Sadly, I hadn't taken into account the car in front of me had not taken the opportunity to progress out onto the roundabout. Not only had I driven into the back of it once, but I had done it a second time for good measure. Fuck.

A middle-aged, angry little man thundered out of his Vauxhall Clio and stormed over to me. I let the window down with a wince and inhaled deeply to prepare for the onslaught of abuse that was surely coming my way.

'What the fuck were you thinking? Were you even looking at all?' he shouted.

I presumed it was a rhetorical question and didn't bore him with my potential new lover and impending divorce.

'What am I meant to do with this now? How much do you think it's going to cost to get this fixed?'

I let him vent before I replied. 'I'm really sorry. This isn't even my car, it's a hire car. I'm so sorry.' I repeated myself about twenty times while he stood there shaking his head and pointing at the back of his car.

I didn't dare get out and look at the damage to the BMW. He mustn't have had any insurance because eventually the angry little man got back in his car and drove off. There was a tail of traffic forming, and frustrated commuters beeped their horns at the delay.

I shakily drove the rest of the way to work, turned off the engine and put my head in my hands before I started to cry. I mean really cry. It wasn't the car. It was everything. My head was wrecked from over-analysing everything. I'd barely slept a wink in weeks. It was the straw that broke the camel's back. The guilt. The feeling of despair, of being trapped. Claustrophobia. The longing for what I never knew existed until recently. The uncertainty was something I couldn't bear, but had to endure.

One of the other dentists arrived and made me a cup of tea. He took the newly damaged BMW away to his mate's garage and brought it back at lunch without a scratch on it, all for one hundred and fifty pounds. If only the rest of my life could be sorted out so easily.

That night, I parked up at Southampton seafront overlooking the harbour and described my eventful encounter to John. I fully blamed him for my accident.

I'd become one of those ditzy lust-struck women with no rationale.

Once he ascertained I wasn't hurt, he howled with convulsive snorting laughter. How I'd actually tried to go, not once, but twice. As an afterthought, he added seriously, 'Remind me not to let you drive my car any time soon.'

Chapter Nine

SATURDAY 21ST JULY 2012

I hardly slept between excitement and fear of the alarm not going off. I stayed at Clara's as it was easier to go from there than from my house. She made salmon and salad for dinner and we washed it down with a couple of glasses of white wine. It was better than any therapy. She continuously asked me if I was sure of what I was doing. I wasn't.

If I had to hear about the seven year itch one more time, I would crack up. If it was an itch, there was only one person who could scratch it, and no prizes for guessing who that would be. In a way, it was comparable to an itch; I couldn't escape it, and there was absolutely no relief from it.

There was no need for the alarm, I was up long before the crack of dawn. I dressed in dark blue jeans, a white vest and a navy blazer.

As I passed through airport security, a flicker of madness threatened to overwhelm me. What if all of this was in my head? What if I'd built him up to be something he wasn't? What if he was an axe murderer?

No. I was acting purely on gut instinct, and my gut urged me to go with this.

I boarded the Flybe propeller plane and put my headphones in, unable to face anyone talking to me. The butterflies in my tummy were very real. In an hour I would see John. I closed my eyes, concentrated on regulating my breathing and tried to relax.

Things had been awful at home the past couple of weeks, all my own doing of course. Instead of ignoring the big wedge between myself and Rob, I'd since welcomed it, encouraged it even. Instead of trying to coax conversation out of him, I avoided him.

I felt cruel. It wasn't in my nature; I didn't want to be that person. He must have noticed the subtle changes, and I hated doing it, but I thought if I increased the already vast distance between us, when I did leave, he wouldn't feel it as a loss as such. I wasn't sure if that even made sense, but it was the only thing I could do that wasn't drastic.

As soon as the wedding was over, I vowed to talk to him properly. But I didn't want to spoil my brother's big day with any awkwardness. The wedding felt like a lifetime away, I just wanted to get it over with rather than spend every day dreading it, knowing how awkward and awful it would be. I'd tried to rehearse in my head what I'd say to Rob, but I just couldn't think of any way of putting it that would make it easier. The fact of the matter was that I wanted a divorce. And the sooner the better. In my mind we were already separated.

A part of me wondered whether he might secretly want a divorce too, now he had his passport, hence the complete and utter lack of effort for the last few years. Or maybe this was what a normal relation-ship was to him. I honestly didn't know.

The plane descended to a bumpy halt in Dublin, right on schedule. The sun shone hazily through the clouds; the temperature distinctly lower than it had been in Southampton. I ran my fingers through my long dark hair and sent up a silent thanks to whoever was up there looking down on us that it wasn't raining. We disembarked the plane and I merged into the swarm of passengers exiting through passport control. Hard to believe I was actually in Ireland. Last time I'd been here with the girls, we'd taken in the usual tourist sites; Stephens Green, The Guinness Factory and The Open-Top Bus Tour.

I strode towards the exit signs with an air of confidence that I truthfully didn't feel inside As I crossed the automatic double doors, I caught a glimpse of him. Seeming to sense my presence, he looked up. We both grinned, almost shyly.

The draw was instantaneous once again, a physical pull I couldn't deny. 'Welcome to Ireland,' he said warmly, planting a tingle inducing kiss on my cheek.

'Thanks.' I drank in every detail. A football shirt sculpted his broad shoulders, dark jeans hugged his waist. He was as handsome as I remembered. Not in an obvious, in your face kind of way, but in a subtle understated way. He had class, an air of quiet confidence, and he radiated an almost intimidating assertiveness. Like he knew exactly what he wanted, and was willing to work exceptionally hard to get it.

Nerves crept in as I drew in a lungful of Irish air. John took my hand reassuringly and led me out to the carpark where he fed several euro coins into the parking metre. He led me over to a gleaming black A5. I had no idea he was an Audi Wanker, and as I pulled him up on it, he laughed out loud.

'I've been called many things before in my life,' he mused. 'But never before have I been called an Audi Wanker.' He wasn't offended.

'Seriously! It's a real thing!' I assured him. 'Google it and you'll see everyone complaining about Audi drivers, although maybe it's just a British thing.' I shrugged, playing it down.

It broke the ice; we were still laughing as we pulled out of the airport. He assured me after the week I'd had, I was in no position to be judging other drivers, regardless of their choice of car.

Within a few minutes, he had me at ease and conversation flowed naturally. John was everything I thought he was and more; funny, witty and sharp. And gorgeous, did I mention that he was absolutely gorgeous? I kept stealing tiny glances in his direction, trying not to get caught, but it appeared he had the same idea. I couldn't take my eyes off him, the same as the first weekend, but now the draw was even more powerful. After hours talking on the phone, I knew he was so much more than gorgeous. He was considerate, smart and currently one of my closest friends.

John expertly parallel parked his wheels into a tight space outside a tiny café in a little village in the outskirts of Dublin. I specified I did not want to go anywhere near the city centre for fear of bumping into someone I knew. I'd met a lot of people through my job and my social circle was wide. It would only take bumping into a patient on a weekend away or a friend of a friend away on a hen or something similar. Not a situation I needed to be in. My nerves were shredded enough as it was. Plus, I wanted to be somewhere quiet with him so I could enjoy him all to myself for the few short hours that we had. I wanted to savour every detail. He was a drug to me. I couldn't get enough.

We found a booth and the owner of the café arrived to serve us herself, making polite conversation about the weather. It dawned on me that I still had my wedding ring on and she assumed John was my husband. It was a lovely thought.

I ordered tea and a scone and he ordered the full breakfast. I couldn't eat a lot even if I wanted to, my stomach was fragile with excitement and the guilt of what I was doing.

'What would you like to do, Lucy? Is there anything you want to see while you're here?' I couldn't help but notice his deliberate innuendo, he was constantly teasing me, a glint of supressed laughter in his turquoise iris's.

'I just want you to myself for the day. I put my trust in your capable hands.'

'Sure, I'm only an auld farmer from the west,' he joked. 'I'm as lost as you in the big smoke.' He winked at me, enjoying playing his role as a hay sucking country bumpkin.

'Very funny, smart arse.' I laughed. 'What have you got planned for me?'

'If we leave Dublin by one o'clock, I could have you back in the wild west by four, which would leave a full hour alone with you at my house before the girls need milking.'

He joked about stealing me away but the truth was I would throw caution to the wind and go willingly, in other circumstances.

'The girls?' I nearly spluttered a mouthful of tea through my teeth.

'Sure, you know how it is. You didn't think you were the only female in my life?'

'You speak of them a little too fondly.' The laugh burst from my throat, but there was something lovely about the way he referred to his cows.

He paid the bill, left a generous tip and ushered me back to the car, eying my choice of footwear.

'They cannot be comfortable,' he stated, looking at my favourite cream five-inch heels.

'No pain, no gain.' My mother's motto had stuck with me.

'Can you walk in them?' he asked seriously.

'Absolutely. One of many talents.'

'Great. I'll take you somewhere you'll love.' He oozed confidence.

We drove through the quiet country lanes, barely meeting another car. He dropped his left hand onto my lap, which sent tremors from my neck to my toes. I memorised every detail so I could replay it in the early hours of the morning when sleep eluded me.

We arrived at a gorgeous viewing point, a waterfall descending into a deep grey rock pool below. John opened the car door for me.

'I've another pair of runners in the boot if you want to try them?'

'I wasn't exaggerating when I said I could walk in these shoes.' I'd had plenty of practice traipsing round bar after bar in them. I could last the entire day without breaking a sweat.

He took my hand again, and we strode purposefully towards the waterfall. We had it to ourselves for the moment. It was so peaceful, the only sound was the gentle cascading water into the pool below, the rhythmic trickling reassuringly therapeutic.

John found the stump of a huge old oak tree a few feet from the rocky ledge. He sat, pulling me down onto his knee smoothly, wrapping his arms around my waist from behind. The weight of my body descended onto his lap. As we watched the water gravitating downwards, I felt my internal gravitational shift. I was acutely aware of the proximity of his body, enjoying the physical warmth of his every inch. He smelt of sandalwood soap and freshly cut grass. My body hummed with hot, fierce desire.

I inched my face to his, wanting to make the most of every second that I could physically lay my eyes on him, and imprint every detail in my mind. He met my gaze with a deep burning one of his own. This time it was me leaning in towards him, desperate to taste him, needing to feel his mouth on mine. Our lips met, his warm wet tongue gently explored my mouth, and multicoloured vivacious fireworks exploded inside me. It was the most sensual kiss of my life, made so much sweeter because I'd longed for it a million times over. My hands ran the length of his broad back and lean torso, moulding every inch of his upper body. Another car arrived and we jumped apart guiltily, our perfect moment temporarily interrupted, but etched into me as fresh as a soldered wound. I was in no doubt that I was capable of falling head over heels in love with this man.

Back in the car, I found myself leaning across the handbrake, yearning for more. It had been so long since I'd felt any physical desire, I'd began to wonder if it had left me indefinitely. I was in no doubt anymore. Every organ of my body was on fire, every single cell and nerve end blissfully aware of him.

We kissed in the car like a couple of teenagers, our tongues darting back and forth dancing, tasting each other, unable to get enough. He felt so good, I physically fought the urge to climb over the car and jump on his lap. It was a good job there was no overnight, because the way the day was starting out, I wouldn't be able to control myself past lunchtime, and that was without any wine.

'You look like the cat that got the cream,' he broke the kiss, and his eyes roamed over me.

'If only.' I sighed, longingly.

'I've never wanted anyone in my life as much as I want you right now.' Sincerity exuded from those soulful eyes.

'Ditto, my friend.' I placed my hand on his leg as he negotiated the gearstick into reverse. 'It will be worth it, when the time is right.'

One thing was certain; this was the real deal. I would move mountains for the chance to see how a relationship might develop with John Kelly. He might have posed as a naïve dairy farmer from the west of Ireland, but I suspected there were many more dimensions to him than met the eye. I was dying to see them all.

He drove us to a nearby hotel with a long gravel driveway and delicately tended to gardens. The sign on the gate said Powerscourt. At the entrance the doorman took the keys and parked the car, while we were shown into the bar. I ordered a glass of prosecco and he ordered a pint of Guinness.

'Will you be joining us for lunch today, sir?' The waitress looked straight at John without acknowledging my presence.

'Absolutely,' he replied, placing his arm lightly around my waist drawing me into the conversation. 'Perhaps in about half an hour?' He looked at me questioningly.

'Great idea,' I said brightly. She nodded curtly and left us at the bar to admire the enormous sash windows overlooking the beautiful grounds.

'Am I invisible?' I pulled a face at her retreating back.

'She's just peed she can't be drinking prosecco instead of serving it.' He was probably right. In fact, I'd probably feel the same. But because I was so obsessed with John, I assumed every other woman in the world would want him too. And who could blame them, he was absolutely gorgeous.

That was the thing about finding somebody so special. It was a double-edged sword; because he was so exceptional to me, I was frightened to fully enjoy him for fear of losing him already. Did everybody feel like this in the beginning or was it just me?

In all my life, I'd never been exposed to any true love stories that lasted. From what I'd witnessed, it only ever happened in fairytales. I tried to kick the cynicism because I was in danger of allowing it to steal any future happiness away from me. I'd drive myself crazy if I didn't stop over-thinking things. I dragged myself away from my tortured thoughts and back into the moment.

'I hope you don't think you're wining and dining me, and taking advantage of my innocent nature?' I took a sip of my drink, aware that we were once again in a hotel together.

'I told you already; you're in safe hands with me. I promise you, when the time comes you won't be in any doubt of my intentions,' he said in a low voice, deliberately running his eyes over the length of my body. 'Relax. Enjoy the afternoon. I promise you I'll take care of you and deliver you back at the airport in one piece, this time. Next time I get you over here though, I can't promise I'll let you go again. It took me thirty years to find you.'

Lunch was fabulous, we had a goat's cheese tartlet to start; I had monkfish for a main and he had a fillet steak. Afterwards we shared the dessert platter; six delicious treats, each one more mouth-watering than the last.

It was nothing like a traditional first date, it was so much better because we already knew each other so well. The situation had forced us to be brutally honest with each other from day one, which would form a solid foundation for a proper relationship, if only I could make myself available to him. I had to. The itch had become a full-blown rash.

He stroked my fingers as we talked. I knew it would break my heart to leave him again. The day exceeded even my wildest dreams. I was, without a doubt, crazy in love with him. He breathed life into every love song I'd ever heard; all that was previously tacky now became relatable. What had happened to me?

I excused myself to go to the ladies' room. As I washed my hands in the sink, I glimpsed my reflection in the mirror. I looked ten years younger; my cheeks flushed from laughing. I dared to smile at myself for a split second, before the devil on my shoulder tried to ruin everything, tormenting me with one word – adulterer.

Ok, it was bad, I know. I wasn't sure what was worse, actually being in love with someone else, or the physical act of kissing another. There had been nothing physical at home for a long time, and there had never been real love. I was terrified this chance would slip through my fingers before I got the opportunity to find out if it was everything I hoped.

It was less than ten days until the wedding. I'd have to suffer my conscience for another few days before I could try to put things right. I left the ladies' room more sombre than I went in. John picked up in the change of temperament immediately.

'Everything ok?' His eyebrows knitted closer.

'Yes. No. I don't know. I've had such a lovely day. I can't bear to leave. Here with you, I forget that there's anyone else in the world but the two of us. Then when I'm alone again, I literally batter myself black and blue for what I'm doing, for the way I'm feeling.'

'Lucy. You've been an absolute lady. The situation is far from ideal. For any of us. How do you think it makes me feel knowing that you go home to him every day?'

'You know it's not like that.' I took his hand, desperate for him to understand, to know I wasn't having my cake and eating.

'I know, sweetheart. I'm only saying it's not what any of us would have chosen. It's just the way things have worked out. And please God, they will work out. Not long to go now, just hang on in there.' He squeezed my hand reassuringly.

I hated not knowing when I would see him again. But the trip had been so worth it. I was in absolutely and utterly no doubt about how I felt about him. And he left me with no doubt that he felt the same. He soothed my soul and simultaneously set my heart alight.

The drive back to the airport was subdued. Neither of us could make the other feel better about our impending goodbye. The next few weeks and months would not be easy. But nothing worth fighting for ever was I suppose.

At the departure drop off, he got out the car and embraced me into his strong chest. 'I'm only ever a phone call away. And if you need me, I'll be there in a shot.'

My eyes welled embarrassingly with unshed tears. When did I become one of these weepy, lovestruck women that couldn't think straight?

He kissed me deeply and held the small of my back, pressing me into his lean frame.

'I'll call you later.' I walked reluctantly into departures and looked over my shoulder to wave at him, and for one final glimpse.

He got into his car, banged his hands off the steering wheel and raised them up to his temple in an exaggerated motion of horror and mouthed at me, 'Audi wanker!' We both laughed out loud as he pulled away, blowing me a kiss.

Chapter Ten

THURSDAY 26TH JULY 2012

One more sleep until the long-anticipated wedding. Rachel, my best friend, arrived from Edinburgh with my cousins. I had the Moet chilling in the fridge and the Grey Goose on standby. I needed my friends more than ever before, craved their familiar presence as I prepared to turn my life upside. As soon as the weekend was over, I would approach Rob for a divorce. It had been a long few weeks, but I was on the home run.

Bridezilla was staying at the venue tonight, thankfully. Probably so she could order all the staff around. I was just delighted she wasn't my problem that evening. I had enough of my own already. At least Rob was staying at my brothers, so I was free of the awkwardness for the night.

A nervous excitement bubbled within. Not about the wedding, but about what I knew was to follow. Nervous about broaching him with my request, unsure of how he'd take it, how everyone would take it. Excitement at the prospect of my impending freedom.

I spent the previous month weighing up my actual happiness, my future on the scales versus everyone else's opinions. There would be a few raised eyebrows, but I was so mad about John Kelly, whatever I had to go through would be worth it. Was I setting myself up for an epic fall? Possibly. But I couldn't live with myself if I didn't summon enough courage to at least try.

Chapter Eleven

FRIDAY 27TH JULY

I didn't go to bed until six in the morning. We were supposed to be at the hotel with Bridezilla getting our hair done at nine, but I'd forgotten that while I was drinking champagne with the girls, singing Florence and the Machine's "Shake It Off" far too passionately for a Thursday night, in an end-terraced house, in a family occupied estate.

Reluctantly, I dragged myself into the shower, threw a bag together and got into the car with Rach. We made our way to the venue, a trendy Novotel by the airport. I probably shouldn't have been driving, but with fourteen missed calls from Bridezilla, there wasn't really any other option.

Heidi was her usual pleasant self when we arrived.

'What time do you call this, Lucy? For God's sake! And there's no sign of that bloody hairdresser you booked either. Where is she?'

'Calm down, Bridezilla,' slipped out before I could check myself. Thankfully, she laughed. Either she'd been drinking or the excitement of the day had gone to her head.

'She's on her way. She text me already to say she was a bit lost. I had to give her directions.' What she really text was that it was her birthday the day before, she'd had a few too many that night and was running late. She was in good company.

The morning passed in a blur of make-up and champagne. The first glass was slow to go down, but I soon regained my composure and snuck a quick selfie for John. I couldn't really talk to him properly last night with the girls there. I missed the comfort that talking to him gave me.

In different circumstances, it would have been great to have him here today. I wondered if my family would like him. Would we ever get the chance to find out? I wished for the millionth time things were different.

At the church, the organ played softly in the background in anticipation of the first glimpse of the bride. It was surprisingly nice to see so many familiar faces: uncles, cousins, family friends and school friends. In truth, I hadn't actually given the wedding much thought since I'd met John. Even I had to admit, my head had been well and truly up my own arse. I mentally scolded myself for being a terrible sister, silently promising to do better.

My mother sat in the second row of pews in a lilac, slim-fitting Coast dress with a dainty cream head piece fastened to the side. She was ridiculously good looking for a fifty-year-old woman, and my friends regularly admired her youthful appearance and sense of style, not to mention her fondness of a glass of white wine. She was my best friend, and I was grateful for her every day of my life.

Her partner, on the other hand, was a complete dose. None of us had any idea what attracted her to him in the first place. There was something slippery about a six foot, overly confident salesman with ideas way above his station. My grandfather described him as having 'notions'.

Trevor didn't drink. I mean at all. Which wouldn't be too bad that's if you could get past wondering if he was a previous alcoholic or if he couldn't trust his own behaviour with a drink? No, the real problem was he hated to see any of us enjoying ourselves or having a drink. He would regularly say to my mum in a sneering, patronising tone, 'You're not having ANOTHER glass of wine, are you?' The poor woman was made to feel guilty every time she wanted to let her hair down.

None of us could understand it, my mother was nobody's fool. She was the most loving parent I could have wished for growing up, a little over protective at times, but definitely nobody's fool. She had a hard edge to her when it suited her, and growing up, we often joked about her Glaswegian Kiss, should anyone dare to cross her. But she had been with this miserable, long streak of a man for five years and none of us could understand it. Each to their own, as I found out the hard way.

My mother shot me a conspirational wink as the ceremony began. My brother stood at the top of the aisle with his floppy blonde hair grazing his eyes, looking exceptional in his tuxedo.

I scanned the pews, looking for Rob. There he was: two rows behind my mother, wearing a grey Gap suit from last year. I needn't have worried about making eye contact with him – he was staring into space as usual. Eventually, the ceremony drew to a close at long last and Simon and Heidi were pronounced Man and Wife.

Heidi had decided each bridesmaid would host a table at dinner, which suited me down to the ground. I got to spend the day with my best friend and cousin. Rachel swapped seats with Rob, reminding him she very rarely got to have dinner with her bestie. She'd saved me a few times this day already, and for that I was eternally grateful.

The food was fabulous and the sweet table was even better. I was an absolute devil for Haribo. You'd think, given my job, I'd know better. Champagne flowed freely, no expense spared, and the sun shone gloriously all day, allowing the guests to make the most of the outside patio bar and gardens until late in the evening. Despite the previous late night, I managed to stick it in the residents' bar until five o'clock in the morning again, with my trusty sidekick, Raquelle, who could always be relied upon for 'one more for the road.'

As the sun came up on the 28th of July, Rachel and I toasted new beginnings, quietly reflecting on the previous few months. It was surreal how everything had changed so dramatically in such a short space of time.

I reluctantly made my way to bed, doubting I would be able to sleep at all. I was happy for my brother, the day had been everything they had wanted and more, and even though I moaned like hell about Bridezilla, it was an honour to be a bridesmaid at my brother's wedding. I could only say that when it was over. I waved them off on their two-week honeymoon to Mexico the following day, and then I decided I would sort my life out. Or wreck it, depending how you looked at it.

Chapter Twelve

MONDAY 30TH JULY 2012

'What do you mean you want a divorce?' Rob was completely and utterly shocked to the core. Which in turn shocked me to the core. How could he be so fucking clueless? After everything. Years of just nothingness. Surely he must have had some inclination.

'I'm not happy, Rob. And I haven't been for a long time. I'm sorry.' I stood on the landing in the hall outside his bedroom as he sat on the bed where he slept alone every night. I wondered if he was living on a different planet to me. 'I don't know what more you could want.' He threw his arms up in temper.

It was so incredulous, I almost laughed. Almost – it was far too serious a matter for that. I took a few deep breaths, battling to maintain my composure.

'We live like brother and sister. In fact, brother and sister have more in common than we do. It's been years since there's been anything between us. We're stuck in a rut that's so deep; we're suffocating in the soil that's beginning to cover us. I'm sorry. I'm not going to change my mind; I want a divorce.' I couldn't make it any clearer.

He opted for a different approach.

'The grass isn't greener on the other side, Lucy. We have a good life together. I admit, it's not the most exciting life, but no marriage is exciting after seven years.' It was a poor attempt to persuade me.

'We have a good life because I work hard for it,' I said to him quietly.

'There you go again, throwing it in my face because you earn more money than me. I knew you'd bring that up,' he retorted, throwing his hands dramatically into the air.

'I'm not taking about money.' It was more about lacking in ambition than lacking in finances. 'I'm talking about the way I make sure dinner is done, that the house is clean, that your shirts are ironed, that the bills are paid, that we socialise at weekends, that we go on holiday. You never actually WANT to do anything. I always have to instigate everything. I'm your mother and your PA rolled into one, organising your life and picking up after you.' He flinched, but it was only the truth. I'd kept it bottled up for too long and it all rolled out at once.

'Well, what if I don't want a divorce?' He crossed his arms over his chest. 'I'm quite happy with the way things are.'

'Of course you're fucking happy.' I blew out a breath; heat crept into my cheeks. I rubbed my temple as a vein pumped furiously. 'Why wouldn't you be? You've a great life, watching Sky fucking Sports all weekend, throwing your empty cans of Stella at your arse while I run around after you wondering quietly if you should be STUDYING,' my voice cracked, tinged with hysteria.

It was futile, he refused to even acknowledge our problems.

'I need to get out of this house, and I need to get out of this marriage before I say or do something I regret. I don't want this to be any harder than it's undoubtedly going to be, Rob, but it's over between us. I'm sorry if it's not what you want to hear. But I have to do what's right for me for a change.'

Anger seeped from my body as quickly as it came, replaced with a deep sense of sadness at the entire situation. Nobody set out to get divorced. A sinking sense of failure enveloped me, even with the knowledge that it was the right thing. Eventually, Rob would realise it was right too, when he found someone that would really and truly love him and he would really and truly love in return. I slumped on to the couch downstairs and sobbed my heart out. Cried for myself, cried for

Rob, cried at my lost youth, at the fact I'd got married so young in the first place. That I would have this hanging over me for the rest of my life.

It was something I couldn't undo. I hated hurting him, and I hated that I was the one giving up and breaking the vows. It certainly wasn't my intention. If I could go back in time, I wouldn't have rushed in and married him in the first place.

As the sun set, I reflected on simpler times, wondering how we had ended up living as two complete strangers. It was only a matter of time before one of us fell in love with somebody else, because we certainly weren't in love with each other.

My mother warned me years ago that somebody else would turn my head. I immediately dismissed it, the last thing I ever wanted was another man. I thought it was ridiculous at the time, reluctant to take romantic advice from her. She had dreadful taste in men. But my God, she was right. She knew me better than I had given her credit for.

Rob didn't emerge from his bedroom after our conversation. The guilt ate away at me, but at least it was out in the open. I decided to leave him to think things over for a few days and see how he felt when the dust settled.

I was too immersed in my own thoughts to talk to John that night, wishing to grieve the end of an era in peace. He might misunderstand my sorrow. It wasn't that I didn't want to leave, to begin a new chapter of my life. It was just that I felt awful, my happiness was costing Rob his.

Chapter Thirteen

SATURDAY 7TH AUGUST 2012

I waited on the couch for Rob to return, he'd been looking at flats in Basingstoke where he could commute to London for work. Construction workers earned way more in The Big Smoke.

It had taken a lot of persuasion to get him to agree to even view the apartments, but I warned him I'd given notice on our rented house in Winchester. We had to leave by the end of August, which didn't leave a lot of time to get organised. I rang the letting agents for him, gave him the deposit and agreed to pay the first month's rent cash in advance to secure a property, if he found one he liked. Short of actually viewing them myself, I could do no more for him.

The viewings were at lunch time, and it wasn't like Rob to be far away from the couch at the weekend. I had to assume that he was deliberately trying to teach me a lesson by not coming home. It wasn't like he really had any friends he could be with. He'd never wanted to make friends, never tried to socialise with anyone in fact. It was one of our many problems, I loved to be with people and be out socialising, he had zero interest in socialising with anyone at all, including me.

He had work colleagues, so I assumed he was with one of them. I worried that something had happened to him, but that was what he wanted; to punish me. To hurt me like he was hurting. I got it. It was only what I deserved and better than no reaction at all. He understood that this was happening, whether or not he liked it.

I looked down at my phone and as I picked it up to check the time again. It rang loudly in my hand. It was John.

'Hello?'

'How's Lucy?' His gentle voice soothed my soul.

'I'm ok. You?'

'You sound deflated.' His intuition was rarely wrong.

'It's nothing, just been a bit difficult today. What did I expect?' I knew it wouldn't be easy.

'What happened? Did he hurt you?' John automatically jumped to my defence.

'Not at all. I expect he is trying to punish me though.'

'Lucy, you are not his mother. And you're only his wife in writing. He's a grown man, he needs to accept responsibility for himself. Run yourself a bath, pour yourself a glass of wine, and get into bed. Don't wait up for him. What kind of state do you think he'll be in when he gets home? I'm damn sure he's not out drinking tea somewhere. I worry about you.' A low sigh whistled over the phone line. 'I wish you'd let me come over.'

'That would only add fuel to the fire. This is something I need to sort out myself, but thank you.'

I wasn't used to anyone fighting my battles for me; it was nice to know I had someone in my corner. But so far, I'd mentioned nothing about John and right or wrong, I hoped to keep it that way to get the divorce across the line quickly. It wasn't like we were physically involved in another relationship, and it wasn't like we were going to bump into him in the local pub. The last thing I wanted was Rob to get wind of the driving force of my actions, then deliberately drag things out longer than necessary out of revenge.

The front door banged loudly, and I heard Rob cursing as he struggled to kick his shoes off.

'I've got to go; I'll text you in a bit. Don't worry, I'm fine,' I assured him.

'Ring me if you have any problem at all. I can be there in a matter of hours.' 'Thanks. I appreciate it.' I hung up before Rob made it into the sitting room. 'Ah there she is,' he bellowed, as if he had an audience. 'My lovely WIFE.' He practically spat at me. I could smell the Jack Daniels off his breath as he staggered closer to me. One thing he could never do, regardless of his intentions was physically intimidate me.

'Here I am indeed. And in a better state than you, thankfully. How did you get on today?' I had no time for this mental bullshit tonight. He could never beat me up more than I do to myself regularly. I was an expert at it at this stage.

'Why do you care, darling?' He was feeling brave, his tone dripped with sarcasm as he actively sought an argument.

'That's a really good question, and one that people keep asking me. But I want to know that you're ok. Believe it or not, I didn't want it to come to this. But it's not exactly just crept up on us out of the blue now, has it? We've been living separate lives for years and you know it.'

'So you keep telling me.' He rolled his eyes and flopped down at the opposite end of the couch.

'So, did you take any of them or not?' I asked.

He hesitated for a few seconds before wavering, remembering I'd offered to pay his rent in advance.

'I provisionally took one, but I didn't sign yet. They wanted photo ID and bank statements, which I didn't have with me.'

'Well, I suppose that's one less thing to worry about.' I tried to reassure him, though he didn't look convinced.

'I'm sorry, Rob.' I apologised to him for the hundredth time this week. 'I really am, but there's a whole wide world out there and you will realise we haven't been living in it, not really.'

'So you say. You know this isn't what I'd choose, Lucy.' He was testing the water again.

'I know, Rob. Please let's not keep going over this. I won't change my mind. Don't do this to yourself. Try to see it as an opportunity, a new chapter. Use it to do something that you want to do before 'you' became 'us'.'

'The thing is, I can't really remember anything that I actually ever wanted to do before.' That didn't surprise me in the least.

'Now is the time to think about it. Do something that makes you happy.' 'What are you going to do?' His tone was almost child-like.

'I don't know.' I answered truthfully. But at least I had options. I could stay with my family for a while or I could go back to Edinburgh. I could have a place to stay and a job with just a couple of phone calls.

'But without a shadow of a doubt, this is the right thing. Try to get some sleep,' I said to him as I left the room.

'As if,' he scoffed.

He'd always previously slept like a baby. I used to hear the snoring through the thin plasterboard walls, while I lay awake, over-thinking everything. But since I asked him for the divorce, I'd been sleeping like the dead. An immense weight lifted off my shoulders.

I scrapped the bath for a quick shower and took a cup of tea up to bed with me.

Lucy:

All ok. Call you in the morning.

John text back immediately. He must have been on standby in case the shit hit the fan. I'm not quite sure what he was planning to do from there but it was a lovely thought all the same.

As long as you're ok. Sweet dreams.

Chapter Fourteen

FRIDAY 31ST AUGUST

Living in the same house as Rob proved to be too tough. I left before the lease was up.

Things had become petty. He wanted to argue every day over the most ridiculous things in order to hurt me. Ruth offered me a room to rent while I sorted my life out. I didn't have to make any rash decisions, and I was out of that toxic environment. It was only a few minutes away from where I used to live, but it was far enough for now.

I put the car into first gear and pulled away from the house I'd called home for the previous two years. In the rear-view mirror, I saw Rob at the green rusty gate, gazing at the house solemnly, his suitcase with the last of his belongings at his feet. It was surreal. The end of an era. That red brick terrace had seen the worst of us over the last couple of months.

John was relieved I was out of the house; worried things would get ugly. They wouldn't have, not physically anyway. Rob wasn't like that. I couldn't blame him for being furious with me. At least if I left, he could begin his new chapter as well.

It seems so odd that you spend years of your life with someone, then all of a sudden, it does a full one-eighty to nothing. When it's over, it's over. I told Rob if he ever needed anything, I would try my best to help. I wanted things to be as amicable as possible, grateful it was quick and that we hadn't been tied to a mortgage.

After handing back the keys to the landlord, that was pretty much it. All the worrying, all the wondering, all the work it had taken me to break free, and now I was.

The sadness I'd harboured in the first couple of weeks had disappeared. The guilt remained, I was sorry Rob was unhappy, but in myself I was surprisingly fine for a woman that had just left her husband.

As I drove across town to my new short-term home, the hands-free rang, penetrating the silence. I pushed the green phone on the steering wheel to answer.

'Hello?'

'How did it go?' John's Irish lilt deliciously reverberated around the inside of my car.

'It's done, anyway. The end of an era. I won't know what to do with myself when it finally sinks in. I'm in shock that I managed to work through it, but we got there in the end.'

'It's been a tough few months, girl. Change is always hard. And you've got a big heart. I know you hated doing what you did.' The affection in his tone made my heart swell.

'Now, just don't go too wild with your new-found sense of freedom.'

It was intended as a joke, but I detected an undercurrent of insecurity in his voice. He'd commented before, that when I managed to leave, I might want to spread my wings a bit. It was something that secretly worried him.

'Don't be daft,' I reassured him. 'There's only one man I want to spread my wings with, and I'm almost there. I've crashed cars thinking about you,' I reminded him.

'Oh yeah, I'd forgotten about that.' He was openly relieved. 'I've been getting such a slagging from the lads lately. They're practically holding a funeral, grieving my single days as though I'm written off already, but honestly Lucy I don't want to put any pressure on you, but I haven't looked at another woman since I met you.'

Well, that was music to my ears. I hadn't wanted to put any pressure on him, hadn't wanted him to feel weighted that I'd left my husband for him, to be overwhelmed by the enormity of the situation. He'd played a huge role in me leaving, but I said from the very beginning that even if it never worked out with John, if I never laid eyes on him again, he had done me the massive favour of opening my eyes to what it could and should be like to be in love.

'So, is it too soon to tell you I bought you a present?' he said optimistically.

'If it's an engagement ring, you can keep hold of it for a bit longer, I'm not quite ready for that yet!' I teased, spluttering out a laugh in the process.

The tan mark was still very visible on my left hand at the ring finger, a permanent reminder of my recently updated status. I winced each time I caught sight of it and prayed for continuous good weather.

'It's a flight to come here, next weekend,' he said.

'Ah.' He didn't waste any time.

'I know you said you wanted to wait until the house was gone, and now it is, I didn't want you to have any time to make up another excuse.'

I didn't answer immediately, turning it over in my head. I'd wanted the rented house in Winchester completely emptied and to draw a line under everything formally before I embarked on something new. Now it was. The Decree Nisi had been approved, it was only another six weeks before we could apply for the Decree Absolute.

He took my hesitation as a negative. 'Oh Jesus, Lucy, I'm sorry. Was I out of order? I wanted to do something nice for you. And I'm desperate to see you. But look if it's too soon you don't have to use it.'

I considered it for a few seconds. 'Ok.'

'Ok? As in ok, you're coming?' he reiterated.

'Yes. I'm coming,' I confirmed before I could over-think it. 'I suppose it's about time I saw those girls of yours for myself.' I referred to the cattle that he spoke of so affectionately.

'Well, they are dying to see you. And so am I.'

Clara and Ruth were waiting in the Slug and Lettuce for me. They insisted I'd need a drink to celebrate my new-found freedom. I wasn't sure it was right to be celebrating, but I was in definite need of a glass of wine or five.

I couldn't believe I'd done it. I was a free woman. That tension in my neck from continuously treading on eggshells began to ease. I forced myself not to wonder where Rob was, if he was on his own. I hated the thought of it, but was relieved it was no longer my problem.

The Slug was busy as usual, packed with girls in tiny shorts and stilettoes. I felt decidedly old for twenty-seven. I looked down at my light blue Superdry skinny's and pink vest top and decided I better go shopping sometime soon. I didn't want old clothes reminding me of old times.

I bought a bottle of Pinot Grigio and some nachos for the table. The girls welcomed me warmly with hugs and kisses. Clara scrutinised my face intently, waiting for me to break down and cry, but I felt sound, steady as a rock.

'So how does it feel?' She pushed her glasses further up her face to get a better look at me.

'It feels strange, I won't lie, but also exciting. Like my life is my own again. Anything could happen. Don't get me wrong. You know what a control freak I am, the unknown is kind of terrifying too…'

'Well, anything could happen, Lucy. It is exciting. I'm glad you're ok. It was too much, too young. So much responsibility from such a young age. So, now you've officially left, when are you going to see lover boy? You could do with dusting the cobwebs off.'

She didn't realise John was already one step ahead of her.

'Funny you should mention it. He rang earlier. He booked me a flight for next weekend.' I loved their widening eyes as I dropped that bomb jovially into the conversation.

'Well, he's keen, we'll give him that.' Ruth raised her eyebrows, taking a huge slug of her wine. 'In all honesty, Lucy, if it was anyone but you, I'd say you were having a midlife crisis. But you're probably the most sensible person I know. Have some fun for once. Whatever you do, don't get serious too quickly. You need to be carefree for a while.'

'You're too late, Ruth,' Clara exclaimed. 'She's already in love with him.'

'You are not?' Ruth turned to me accusingly for confirmation.

I looked down at my glass and said nothing.

'You can't be serious?' Ruth questioned again.

'I'm not saying anything, it's too soon. But I have turned into one of these crazy bitches who checks her phone five hundred times a day and then when it finally does ring, I can't bring myself answer it, because I don't want to look like I've been sitting by it waiting desperately all day, even though that's exactly what I have been doing. It actually kills me to ignore it, but I do. Then I spend an agonising thirty minutes watching the clock, waiting until it's an acceptable time to ring him back and say I was busy, or out for a drink or some other nonsense. I hate playing games, but I'm terrified of scaring him off too.'

'I think if anything was going to scare him off, it would be the fact that a woman he met when extremely drunk on a stag weekend, left her husband of seven years to be with him.' Ruth kept it real as usual.

'What I haven't told you is that he's never had a relationship that lasted more than three months.' Now the cat was out the bag about how I felt about him, I decided to confide in them completely.

'And?' Clara said. 'He obviously never met the right one. Or are you telling us they always get rid of him after three months?' She flicked her spiral curls from her face.

'No, I think it's generally him. He told me if he saw something in them he didn't like, that would be it. He said he could never see past that one thing then, whatever it was, no matter how trivial. But girls, what if he sees something in me after three months? And he gives me the p45? It would be awful on so many levels, utterly humiliating and probably exactly what I deserve, after my less than perfect behaviour. Karma you could call it.'

'Don't be daft,' Clara assured me. 'If you want my opinion, I'll give it to you.' She looked at me for confirmation that I was ready to hear some brutal home truths.

I wasn't ready, but if my best friends couldn't be honest with me, then who could?

'Give it to me.' I knocked back my glass of wine and poured another.

'I think it's an infatuation, Lucy. I think you want him because you can't – sorry couldn't have him. You have chemistry, no doubt about it. You'll go to Ireland next weekend, have loads of filthy sex and then eventually, whether it be a week, a month or a year down the line, the novelty will wear off. Let's face it, you can't seriously see this working out long term, can you? You are an ambitious city slicker who loves to shop in the biggest malls and drink cocktails in busy bars. You thrive on the hustle and bustle of the city. He's a farmer from a tiny farming town in the west of fucking nowhere with no shops, no bars, and the only opportunity you may get, and that's if you're lucky, is to buy another cow from the mart.'

Fuck, that was honest. I hadn't thought about the specifics of the situation that far in advance. I'd been so focused on breaking free, consumed with thoughts of a short-term nature, I hadn't got past the divorce in my mind.

'Look, girls, I don't know about any of it to be honest.' I ran my fingers loosely through my hair. 'I have this feeling in my gut that keeps telling me to go with it, see what happens. I'm beginning to sound like my mother.' I put my head in my hands and the girls sniggered, knowing what a fatalist my mother was.

'Are you sure it's not just wind?' Clara spluttered. She didn't believe in gut feelings and fate.

'Don't over-think it,' Ruth advised me. 'Visit John, enjoy yourself and what will be will be.'

'Oh my God, Lucy, I'm not sure you're ready!' Clara's hands flew dramatically up to her perfectly made-up face.

I waited for the punch line.

'I mean, do you even own a pair of wellies?' She threw her head back, dissolving into cackling laughter, and gestured towards my beautiful gold high heels. 'Those heels are going to sink into the first pile of cow shit you trip across honey; don't say I didn't warn you!'

I couldn't help but laugh. It was kind of funny.

'Have you ever even been to a farm?' Ruth teased. 'You know it's full of animals that stink of shit and demand more care than a new born baby? And just when you finally form some sort of bond – boom! They're taken away and carved up for dinner!'

Wow, Ruth wasn't painting a pretty picture at all. A sliver of alarm ripped through me. I'd never thought about it that way, but then I was a total hypocrite because I wasn't exactly a vegetarian. I simply chose not to think about where the food on my plate came from.

'Do you even know what slurry is? Never mind *Sex in the City*, it will be *Treks in the Shitty*!' Clara cried.

'And there's no Harvey Nichols, Lucy. So I don't know what you're going to do with yourself for the entire weekend,' Ruth added.

'Ooh, I'm sure lover boy will have thought up a few activities to entertain her. She's about to find out if the rug matches the carpet!' Clara slapped her thigh in glee.

I couldn't help but laugh along with them. It was funny. I had no idea what to expect, and I hadn't had time to think about the specifics of it yet. Only that I desperately wanted to see him.

'What will I pack?' I asked them with a frown.

'The sexiest underwear you own and make sure its green to match your new Hunters!' Clara screamed, releasing another huge belly laugh.

The laughter helped the tension of the last few weeks evaporate further. It would take a long time to let it all go fully, to forgive myself for my own failures. But that's exactly what I planned on doing.

Chapter Fifteen

SATURDAY 8TH SEPTEMBER 2012

The Aer Lingus flight touched down in Knock Airport at lunch time. John said I was the only woman in the world could describe a plane landing in a manner that was explicit. He must have had sex on the brain. I did too. I wondered, increasingly so, what it would be like. I hadn't been with many men and was slightly concerned about my lack of experience and, let's be honest, complete lack of interest in that department until recently. What woman was one hundred percent confident in her own body, regardless of what size she was or how much weight she'd lost?

It had been a fast week getting organised; waxing, nails, hair. I bought eight sets of new underwear (none of which were green, coincidently), three jumper dresses that could be dressed up or dressed down as necessary, a little black dress, two new pairs of jeans, a short-sleeved crisp-white shirt and four new vest tops.

It was partly for John's benefit but more so for myself. I wanted to feel good. Out with the old and in with the new.

Knock was the tiniest airport I'd seen in my entire life. John waited, hands folded across his chest in anticipation as I breezed through passport control. The man sitting behind the desk barely glanced at my passport, welcoming me to Ireland.

It was so surreal. I'd spent every minute of the day wishing for this, and there we were. Me separated, only weeks away from an official divorce and him still interested, despite the complications. He was still as strikingly understated as ever, dressed in light blue jeans and a grey hoody.

'I see you dressed appropriately for the occasion.' He kissed me full on the mouth this time, my tummy flipped as he took a step backwards looking me up and down from head to toe, taking in my white jeans and gold stilettoes. He shook his head, laughing.

'You realise I live on a farm?' he asked.

'Yes, but you don't sleep in the barn, do you?' I answered sharply, stirring a hearty laugh from him. 'Put your claws away, girl, I'm only saying you look fantastic, if a little impractical.'

'I thought I was coming to visit, not to do the farming for you,' I said with a helpless shrug.

'You are in for a lovely weekend, make no mistake about it, but it's important you see the reality of life here as well. You'll be getting the full tour of the farm. You'll love it, trust me.'

I glanced at him doubtfully. It was a good job I did trust him. My safety was completely in his hands now. I was in his territory, and he was very comfortable with that. He oozed confidence in the way he strode to where he had double parked the Audi outside the front door like he owned the place. I had longed for a man that could take control. Be careful what you wish for. You might just get it. He opened the passenger door for me and I slid into the black leather seat, fastening my seatbelt tightly. John said he lived about twenty minutes from the airport. I tried to relax and take in the scenery.

'I'll bring you the main road home.' He shot me a cheeky wink.

I glanced at the scenery doubtfully. If this was the main road, I'd hate to see the back road. A narrow winding country lane stretched before us. At the steepest bends, I glimpsed a magnificent lake, so still, so peaceful looking. It dawned on me that the tranquillity could be attributed to the fact that there was not another soul in sight. The entire landscape appeared like a picturesque postcard.

Conversation was minimal, me busy taking in my surroundings and

John deep in thought, or perhaps he was just concentrating on the road. I rested my hand lightly on his thigh and he smiled at me.

'Are you excited to see your new home?' he joked as though it was a forgone conclusion.

'Hmm,' I muttered. I couldn't see myself as much of a country-woman, but I would not negotiate terms anytime soon. I planned on enjoying the weekend, happy to be with him instead of admiring him over FaceTime.

'Wait until you see the town, you're going to love it.' A twinkle of mischief lit up his eyes. We'd already been driving for over half an hour, which was longer than he said, and I still hadn't seen anything that looked remotely like a town.

Up ahead I saw signs for a place called Ballina. I was trying to work out the difference between miles per hour and kilometres, whichever way you looked at it, he was still speeding and the airport wasn't as near as he'd led me to believe.

'Someone's been telling porkie pies.' I looked at my watch pointedly.

'Sure, it was the traffic that held us up. It's normally a lot quicker than this.' That man had an answer for everything.

I couldn't help but laugh. John was like no one I'd ever met before; his sense of humour was warped.

Ahead I noticed a few detached houses lining each side of the road and things started to look a bit more promising. A petrol station, a corner shop, a butcher, a pharmacist and a bookies.

'Welcome to Ballina,' he said warmly.

'This is it?' I put my hand over my mouth to stifle a giggle. He had to be having me on?

'This is it. There are more shops down there.' He pointed towards the river.

I saw a Tesco's, a florist, and Penny's. If I'd have blinked, I would have missed it. Oh dear, it was quainter than I thought. A few people roamed the streets, but it seemed pretty quiet generally.

'Busy today,' he said, as if he could read my mind. 'Saturday you see, the markets on as well.'

I didn't see a market. It certainly wasn't going to give Camden a run for its money.

We passed through the 'town' and out into quieter streets and the scenery became more rural again.

'Is it far?' I asked.

'Ten minutes.'

'Is that a real ten minutes, or an Irish ten minutes?' I asked. He chuckled but failed to answer the question.

Eventually, I saw a sign that said Killala. He indicated right. We turned into a by-road and followed it along for about half a mile. I glimpsed the crashing waves of the wild Atlantic Ocean at certain bends in the road. Three big detached stone fronted houses loomed ahead, each with their own separate stone wall, one house set back further than the next. He indicated, and he pulled into the third one. It was impressive.

The gravel crunched under the tyres as he reversed into a parking space next to a gleaming green tractor.

'My other wheels.' I don't know why I was surprised; I knew he was a farmer.

'Welcome home.' He leaned across the car, planting a tender, lingering kiss on my mouth.

The nerves gnawed at the lining of my stomach; excitement hummed through my blood. We'd waited so long to be alone together; I was desperate for it to be as good as we'd both anticipated with the chemistry heightening for months. One way or another, it was heading for a conclusion very soon.

He opened the car door for me. 'Mind you don't go over on your ankle in those stilts you're wearing.'

I held onto his arm as he led me up the length of a cobbled pathway to a heavy, black front door. The windows were set symmetrically, two on either side of the door and a big corner window on each end of the house. The door was unlocked.

A spacious, light-cream hallway with a double height ceiling and a cream wooden centre staircase welcomed us. John led me by the hand through to the next room – an enormous kitchen. Again, the walls were cream with ivory, wooden cupboard doors and a slightly darker beige granite work top covering a huge island in the middle of the room. The island had three cream leather stools at one end, the other housed a wine-rack stocked with twenty-five bottles of various red and white wines.

This house was like something from Grand Designs.

'Your house is beautiful.' It wasn't what I'd expected at all.

'No, you are beautiful. This is just a house.' He pushed me gently back against the island, sliding his hands inside my jacket and around my waist. Millimetres away from my face, he leaned in to kiss me deeply, slowly but fiercely, pushing his mouth on to mine. I rested my hands around his broad shoulders and pressed my body against his, exhaling as I handed myself over to him, revelling in the feeling of his hands on my seriously neglected body.

The front door banged loudly, and he rolled his eyes up to the sky and tutted.

'Hello?' A woman's voice echoed through the spacious hallway.

Startled, we jumped apart. In walked an absolutely stunning woman in tight navy jeans, knee-high boots and a slim-fitting cream jumper. She had dark short bobbed hair and her face was made-up with a hint of blush and mascara. She could pass as a model from an autumn clothing catalogue.

'Sorry to just barge in on ye and ye just home.' Her accent was as equally beautiful as the rest of her, although she clearly wasn't a bit sorry for the intrusion. Excitement shone all over her face as she took us both in arms around each other.

'When I saw the car home, I just couldn't help it. We're all so desperate to meet this new woman of John's that we keep hearing about!' She examined me curiously as she crossed the room and shoved John out of the way, enveloping me in an unexpected bear hug.

'Welcome home.'

She was the second person to welcome me home to a place that wasn't actually home. I stood rigid, slightly confused with no idea who this woman was, holding me tightly by the shoulders while she scrutinised my face.

John sniggered, enjoying my obvious discomfort.

'Oh my God. I am so sorry! I forgot to introduce myself. I'm

Trisha. I'd forget my head if it wasn't screwed on. I live next door.' She let go of me then.

'Trisha, it's lovely to meet you.' I genuinely meant it. She seemed absolutely lovely, if a tad over familiar.

'We have heard so much about you, lady! I just couldn't resist sticking my head in for a quick nose to see what all the fuss was about. We've never seen him like this about a woman before, he's the talk of the town.' John lowered his face slowly into his hands in embarrassment.

It was my turn to enjoy his discomfort. I smiled widely at Trisha and pulled out one of the leather stools. 'Tell me more.'

She slid in without hesitation and said to John affectionately. 'Put the kettle on will you, you miserable git.'

Trisha stayed for an hour and a half. I learnt that she was a primary school teacher with a three-year-old son, whose partner worked away a lot. She'd been at school with John and had known him her whole life. I got a lot of information in a short time, not getting a word in edgeways, but loving it. She was so lovely; open, honest and unafraid to laugh at herself.

It wasn't exactly how I envisioned the afternoon going, but it was a brilliant second. I'd found a friend, at least.

John wasn't backward in coming forwards. As soon as she had finished her second cup of tea, he said politely but firmly, 'Now Trisha, don't you have somewhere else you need to be?'

'Oh sorry.' She stood up quickly and brushed some stray biscuit crumbs off her lap, onto John's immaculately clean tiled floor. He watched on with raised eyebrows. Apparently, he was a fellow neat freak.

'I'm taking up your entire weekend here, telling you my life story. I'll see you before you go back, ok?' She gave me another tight hug before she whirled out as quickly as she had whirled in.

'I'm going to have to start locking that front door,' John said grimly. 'Where were we?' He crossed the floor to reach me and resumed his position, his warm full lips over mine. His fingers ran through my loose hair, tracing my neckline, gently edging down towards my bust.

Once again, we were rudely interrupted as his mobile phone rang loudly on the counter.

'For fuck's sake,' he exclaimed. 'It's a fucking conspiracy! Yes?' he answered the phone brashly. I couldn't hear the other person and I only caught half of what he was saying, between his accent and the speed in which he replied, but I gathered it was his mother.

'Yeah. She's here.' Pause while the other person spoke. 'Yeah, we will. Later. Definitely. Yeah, I told you I would, didn't I?' He rolled his eyes with a smile. 'Yeah. We'll see you in a bit. I'll tell her.' He winked at me. 'Mam is looking forward to meeting you.' He threw the phone back down on the counter with a smirk.

'Did you tell her everything?' I'd asked him to be honest with his family about my situation and the circumstances. Honesty's the best policy. John assured me his parents wouldn't care, as they were more like friends to him than parents. He spoke of them fondly. But I was acutely aware that I was in a predominantly Catholic country where some ideas were at least fifty years behind the times. Divorce only became legal a few years before my visit.

'They know. They can't wait to meet you. My sister thinks you could be the one,' he teased.

I was flattered, but didn't have time to over-think it as he pulled my hand and proceeded to finish the tour of the house. Pushing back sliding doors at the far end of the kitchen, he revealed a brightly lit sunroom. Floor to ceiling church windows overlooked a rocky beach, a mere stone's throw away. The wild Atlantic Ocean crashed powerfully, foam ripples lapped at the shore before bubbling and fizzing back out with the tide again.

It was rustically beautiful, so wild. I could have stared out of the window for days, so therapeutic it was watching the swell of the ocean.

'Wow.' I turned my head reluctantly away from the view to take in the rest of the room.

An open fire took centre place, and a custom-made beige sofa extended the length of the opposing back wall. I sat down for a minute, absorbing the peace and tranquillity. I felt a million miles away from the city I'd left only this morning.

'You like it?' He leant against the fireplace and tilted his head to the side in question.

'It's unreal. You never said.'

He shrugged.

To the left of the house, the side where there were no neighbours, stood an enormous barn, and a separate shed. Cattle grazed in the distance; the famous girls.

'I'll show you the rest.' He steered me back to the hall, and off another doorway leading into a second sitting room. A sixty-five-inch television was mounted on the wall and an LED fire below it. Other than a brown leather suite of furniture and a bookcase, the room was a pretty bare.

'Meet Steve.' He gestured to the wall behind me where a stag's head was mounted on the wall, and grinned at my disgust as I backed away from the unfortunate thing.

'Steve has to go. Gross.'

We continued on with the tour, both well aware where it would end.

The downstairs bedroom was unsurprisingly cream again, with a plain bedspread and blackout blinds on the windows in line with the décor of rest of the house. He closed the bedroom door and opened the final door off of the hall. It was a wet room, bigger than my bedroom at home. A shower boasted mood changing LED lights above it. It was very tasteful, but plain.

'Everything is magnolia. I figured one day when I eventually met someone, they might want to put their own stamp on it anyway. It keeps it bright, easy to maintain.'

He led me up the magnificent centre staircase and I looked up to see four VELUX windows directly above us, allowing the natural daylight to stream in, illuminating the hallway. We stood at the top, leaning our elbows on the bannister for a minute while I took it all in. The same wall lights were positioned in the same spots upstairs as downstairs. He was methodical in his approach; I'd have to give him that.

Behind the first door on the right was a bright and spacious double bedroom with an en-suite in the same style as the downstairs bedroom and wet room. The second door opened on to a very similar setup. He shrugged his shoulders as I laughed quietly.

The last door on the left could only have been his bedroom. Butterflies fluttered wildly within. He placed his hand reassuringly on top of mine as I hesitated briefly, fingers on the handle. Together, we opened the door.

A four-poster queen-size bed rested against the back wall, dressed with cream sheets and a darker faux fur throw. Two huge cream Victorian looking lamps stood proudly on each bedside locker. However impressive the bed was, it was not the main attraction. A floor to ceiling window captured the same view as the sunroom below, but the extra height meant the view was even more mesmerising, if that was possible.

'Wow.' My feet sank into the deep piled carpet as I crossed the room, eager to get a closer look. He followed me, resting his arms around my waist from behind, we looked out on to the ocean together. He nuzzled in at my neck and I turn to meet his kiss. 'It's absolutely stunning,' I whispered.

He didn't reply. Instead, he led me to the bed, pushed me back gently onto the plump pillows and looked questioningly at me, silently searching for permission. I nodded, slipping off my blazer and sandals.

He pulled off his top to reveal a tight, toned porcelain body. I memorised every inch of him as he kicked off his clothes, expertly climbing on top of me, resting the weight of his body on his elbows, his face an inch from mine. He smelt of sandalwood again and something else I couldn't put my finger on. The scent of him was intoxicating, drawing me in, desperately wanting more. He tugged off my white jeans, discarding them on the floor and left me lying on my back in just a vest top and white lace underwear. A low whistle of appreciation chased away my remaining nerves. The glinting hunger in his eyes apparent.

John pressed tiny kisses against my neck and teasingly ran his hands over the length of my body, pulling my top over my head. He murmured throatily, 'I waited a long time to have you here.'

'I hope it will be worth your wait,' I whispered back, shyly.

'It already has been.' His eyes deliberately roamed my tanned cleavage and exhaled slowly, pupils burning through mine, savouring every inch of me. He ran his fingers over the lace and pulled my bra down. I was supported, but very much exposed for him to tease with his tongue. My back arched in pleasure. I silently begged him to give himself to me, aching to feel him.

He pushed in on top of me, pulling my new underwear to the side, too impatient to remove it; his desperation matched mine. Intense eyes gazed at me as he entered me, we'd both waited long enough. Moving together back and forth, the rhythm picked up, the two of us panting, clawing each other desperately, bucking hard and fast until we finished together, sweating and exhausted.

He rested his head on my chest until the hammering of our hearts slowed down to a regular beat and looked at me with those soulful blue eyes.

'How was that for you?'

In truth, it was unreal. I'd never wanted anybody like that in my life. I never physically needed anybody like that before. The desire was feral. It was raw, and it was real.

'It was incredible.' I bit my lower lip. 'It feels like more.'

'I agree,' he murmured, rolling behind me to spoon me and play with me some more.

He ran his finger up and down my inner thigh, teasing me, torturing me. I spun round, pinned him down and unhooked my bra, letting one strap slip down before the other. Then I placed my fingers inside my knickers, deliberately lowering them, suddenly confident in the face of his obvious approval. I enjoyed the way he stared longingly at me; his breath caught in his throat. I pounced on him, like I wanted to in the car that time. We lasted longer this time, kissing, stroking and exploring each other's bodies, until we both finished again. I flopped down on top of him and we lay quietly satisfied. He kissed the top of my head tenderly and ran his fingers through my hair.

'You are something else,' he said, as I rested on his lust sheened chest.

When my trembling legs had recovered long enough to stand, I glanced around the room for the nearest bathroom. There were two doors aside from the one we had entered through. He pointed to the left-hand door. 'Bathroom.'

'What's behind the other door?'

'Open it and see.'

I opened it cautiously, unsure what to expect. Shelf upon empty shelf stood in front of me. To the right side were several rails for clothes. It was a walk-in wardrobe and his clothes only took up a mere quarter of the space available.

I had no idea his house would be like this. I expected a crumbling, but quaint cottage with mountains of character, low ceilings and wooden beams. More cosy, less extravagant. I don't know why. All the talking we had done beforehand, so many nights on the phone until the early hours of the morning, he never mentioned his house was like something out of a magazine. He was so understated in every way.

'Come with me.' He led me to an en-suite with twin sinks and jacuzzi bath tub. The shower stood freely in the corner. He turned the mood lighting to a lilac setting and pulled me in under the warm running water, lathering my body with soap, massaging my shoulders as he washed me. The heat and his touch were better than any professional massage I'd experienced before. It was absolute bliss, a million miles from the real world. His firm hands kneaded my naked skin.

'Jeez, and I thought you were a mere Audi wanker. Turns out you're the house version as well.'

He laughed. 'I suppose it's not something you could explain without sounding like a complete prick. I know it's special. I built it with the hope of a family in mind. I just didn't meet anyone suitable. Until now.' He glanced at me out of the corner of his eye to gauge my reaction.

'Beautiful house or not, you still didn't find anyone suitable. Have you forgotten I'm a city slicker and you're a country bumpkin?' I stuck my tongue out at him in jest. We really were worlds apart in a lot of ways, despite the way I felt about him.

'Let's finish the tour and you can make your mind up when you've got the full picture.' He wrapped a towel around me and fetched another for himself.

'I thought we'd finished the tour with the grand finale there?' I teased.

'You haven't been outside yet.' He looked at the white jeans I was pulling back on. 'Have you anything darker with you?'

'In my case, in the car.' He left to get it, leaving me alone in his bedroom.

When he returned, I hung my weekend clothes in his wardrobe and pulled on my dark new jeans, flat brown leather boots and the white shirt.

'Better?' I looked down at my attire for confirmation.

'You look great. I'll give you one of my jackets. That should keep your shirt clean. And if you like those boots, I'd change them, they might look a little more practical than the skyscrapers, but they're going to get filthy out there.' He winked at me before continuing. 'I was prepared, even if you weren't. I bought you a present.' He seemed delighted with himself as he led me downstairs and back through the kitchen and out into a utility room that I didn't realise existed. A large box sat on the worktop, wrapped in pink tissue paper.

'What is it?' I absolutely loathed surprises, the secret control freak that I was. 'Open it and see. It won't bite.'

I unwrapped the packaging and pulled the lid off what looked like a giant shoe box. Inside were a pair of baby pink Hunter wellies. In a size six. OMG. I couldn't wait to tell the girls; they would wet themselves laughing. The funny thing was, I actually loved them.

'How did you know my size?' I asked in surprise.

'I asked Clara,' he said simply.

They fit like a glove and were surprisingly comfortable. He handed me a waterproof jacket which was about four sizes too big for me, and we set off out the back door crossing the field. A whip in the wind hinted at autumns impending arrival. We headed towards the beach at first; the grass turned to rock as we got closer. John held me tightly as I negotiated the few steps down to the rocky sand. The smell of the beach was wonderfully familiar, taking me back to my childhood days as if it were yesterday.

'This is unbelievable. Your own private beach. Does it ever get busy?' I asked him.

'Honestly? We rarely get the weather for it to be busy, and there are only a few points you can get down to this part of the beach. Mainly it's just used by Trisha and Jane.'

'Who is Jane?'

'She's going to be your other best friend,' he informed me with a small smile. 'She lives in the first house, next door to Trisha. She's a Guard.' 'A guard of what?'

A long rumbling laugh escaped his chest. 'A policewoman, I think, is the term you would use to describe her. You know, blue flashing lights and handcuffs etc? She's from Donegal. She's the only Guard that goes into work with a full face of make-up. She wouldn't look out of place in a nightclub, bar the uniform of course.' He grinned.

'I like her already.' She sounded like someone I could relate to. I went to work with a full face of make-up on, despite the fact most of my face was covered with a mask. And if she was anything like Trisha, I knew we'd become great friends.

'Her husband's also a Guard. His home house is only a mile away from here.'

'You mean his parents' house?'

'Yeah.'

'Gosh, imagine living only a mile from where you grew up. I can't imagine living on the Isle of Wight now, bumping into people I went to school with and seeing the same faces day in and day out.'

'Lucy, it's the same for me too. My parents live a stone's throw away from here, just around the next corner. For a lot of us, it's the complete opposite. We couldn't imagine living anywhere else. Don't get me wrong, I don't live in my parents' pockets; sometimes weeks pass by before I get a chance to visit them properly, depending on how busy I am here, but I honestly wouldn't have it any other way. There's a lot to be said for living in a small community,' he insisted. 'There's also a lot to be said for living in a city; culture, variety, opportunity.' We'd have to agree to disagree on this one.

'True. But everyone has to lay their hat down somewhere,' he said thoughtfully. 'I'd prefer to do it somewhere I know people. If I ran into a bit of bother, whatever it may be, you can guarantee that in this place I'd know someone that could help me. There's a lot of comfort in it.'

I couldn't imagine it. I hated the thought of every mistake I'd ever made being right on my doorstep, the entire town knowing everything about me.

We stared at the ocean once again, both lost in our own thoughts. I felt a million miles away from my past. John had been right about one thing. Nobody would ever find me here. It was so remote.

He led me towards the animals, where I was surprised to see a man and a teenage boy with the cattle.

'This is Hugh and his son, Sam. He works on the farm with me. This is Lucy,' John said, while I shook both their hands.

'Ah, the infamous Lucy,' Hugh said knowingly. 'We've all been waiting to meet you.'

'So I keep hearing.' I turned to John accusingly, but he blatantly pretended not to hear us, despite the fact he was less than a foot away.

'Well, what do you think of the place?' Hugh asked, chewing a bit of straw.

'It's absolutely beautiful.'

'It surely is. There's no place like it. We'll make a good Mayo woman out of you yet.' He smiled and turned his attention back to the animals.

'We'll see you later, no doubt,' John called over his shoulder as we headed towards the barn. It turned out the barn wasn't actually a barn. As we got closer, I could see the stables and four fine big horses in their paddocks.

'Did you ever ride?'

'No. I wish.' I had wanted to when I was younger, but my mum was such a worrywart she thought I'd fall off.

'I'll teach you,' he promised, stroking the horses affectionately. 'This is Maisy. She's a thoroughbred.'

I nodded like I knew what that meant. We continued the tour. There were hens and geese as well. Apparently, they laid the best eggs I'd ever taste. John brought me into what I thought was a shed, but it actually looked more like a work shop.

'This is where the real work gets done.' He gestured at numerous antique-looking pieces around him. There were vases and pictures and furniture and all sorts of objects I didn't recognise.

'What is this place?'

'This is where we make the money,' he said gratefully.

'I thought you were a dairy farmer?'

'I am. I was. Since things took off with the antiques a few years ago, I had to get some help in.' He referred to Hugh and Sam. 'I didn't expect it to go so well, but business is booming. I have an excellent eye for detail.' He looked at me suggestively.

'Oh, you do, do you? An excellent eye may be one thing, but a reluctant tongue is another. You never mentioned any of this to me.' I thought we'd talked about everything; I couldn't understand why he didn't tell me about any of it. I shared everything with him.

'I was going to tell you. I didn't want to bore the pants off you before you even got here. Antiques aren't riveting to most people. It started off as a hobby but it turned out to be a lot more.'

I noticed a laptop on an old mahogany desk in the corner and realised it looked familiar to me. This is where he did his FaceTiming from. No wonder I expected a quaint crumbly cottage with wooden beams.

'Most of the business is done online, but I could be in Dublin myself twice a week sometimes.' It made sense, his ease in the city and the car and house. I wondered why he didn't tell me, not that it mattered, but it was such an impressive achievement he was obviously good at what he did. He should be proud. If it were me, I'd be shouting from the rooftops.

My stomach rumbled loudly. I'd forgotten to eat with all the excitement of the day and it showed.

'Come on,' he said, 'I'll fix you up some dinner, you're going to need it for soakage, anyway.'

'Why? Where are we going?'

'You'll see.' He grinned elusively.

As it transpired, he was a dab hand in the kitchen as well as everything else. I don't know why I was surprised. I sat at the island sipping a glass of Malbec from his extensive wine collection while he chopped mushrooms and onions to go with the fillet steaks he was frying. It smelt delicious. Was there anything this man couldn't do?

It was surreal how much everything had changed in the last ten weeks. That was all it was, but it felt like a lifetime. If anyone had told me the night of Heidi's hen that I would meet a red-haired Irishman and leave my husband, I would have laughed in their faces. Yet, there I was. And it felt so right.

A niggle of worry slithered into my gut at the impossible prospect of a future together. I forced it to the back of my mind, determined not to ruin the trip over-analysing the future.

We ate at the island; the fillets were done to perfection, medium rare.

'Is there anything you can't do?' I asked him.

'I'm sure there are plenty of things I can't do. I just haven't found them yet,' he said smugly, with a wink.

'You're amazing.' I meant it.

'No, *you're* amazing,' he said, before adding, 'no, you hang up, no you hang up first.' Mocking me, with those teasing blue eyes, he had a unique method of making me laugh.

We cleaned the kitchen side by side as if it was part of our normal daily ritual. I forgot about anything else outside of the front door, like only the two of us existed. It was effortless just being in his company. No, it was more than effortless. I felt like I belonged.

We finished the bottle of wine in the sunroom overlooking the sun setting spectacularly over the ocean. It was a tiny slice of heaven nurturing my tortured soul, the weeks of stress and tension evaporating by the second. I rested my bare feet in his lap and we admired the scenery together.

'Don't get too comfortable, lady, I've got plans for you tonight,' he warned me.

'I think I like the sound of that.' I eyed his torso suggestively.

'Absolutely, you can bet your life on it, but first we need to make a quick trip out or else I will literally never hear the end of it. I hate having to share you, but my life won't be worth living if we don't call into the pub.'

'Ah.' The parents. I'd been looking forward to meeting them, though naturally a little apprehensive. He said they were fine with everything, but who would choose a divorcee for their only son? I hoped they were as easy going as he made out.

'The quicker we go, the quicker we can come home and open another bottle of wine to take upstairs with us.'

Now that I liked the sound of. 'What should I put on?' I glanced down at my white shirt and jeans.

'You're overdressed already, trust me, it's not that kind of pub.'

I pulled on my flat brown boots and blazer and we set off on foot to the pub. Thankfully, it wasn't raining. There were no pavements, we literally walked in the middle of the gravel road. John assured me minimal traffic passed this way. It was a dead end at the bottom. I had to tread carefully not to fall into one of many potholes that decorated the road.

The pub was about half a mile away, and we walked briskly. I soon saw signs for 'Kelly's' and my chest tightened with mild apprehension.

John swung open the heavy black door and ushered me inside. Every single person in the pub turned to look at us. A woman in her fifties stood behind the bar pouring a pint of Guinness, concentrating intently on what she was doing. As she glanced up, her face broke into an almighty grin. John was obviously the blue-eyed boy, and why wouldn't he be? He was the most incredible man I'd ever met in my life. She welcomed us home graciously.

John's father stood proudly at the bar, sipping something small and potent looking. The resemblance between them made him obvious to pick out; the same red hair and chiselled chin. When he turned to us, there was a kindness in his smile. He took a step backwards to weigh up the package.

'Dad.' John shook his hand and grinned sheepishly. 'This is Lucy.'

'Hi.' I put my hand out to shake his hand, but he pulled me into a big bearlike embrace.

'Lucy, it's a pleasure to meet you. I'm Graham. So, you're the young lady that's putting manners on my son, is that right?' There was such unexpected warmth in his voice, it made me emotional. I felt I didn't deserve it, given the far from ideal situation I'd only very recently extracted myself from.

'Well, I'm not exactly sure that's what you'd call it, but I'm trying.' He let out a deep hearty laugh, insisting on getting us both a drink.

The pub was small and cosy. Short bar stools scattered around the edge of the room and a pool table took up a sizeable proportion of space. Three men on stools propped up the bar and I could see Hugh, the farmer I met earlier about to take a shot to pot the black ball, the game almost over. He raised his hand in acknowledgement and I smiled at him.

'This is Mary, or Mama Bear, as we do call her.' John introduced me to his mother, who had come out from around the back of the bar to give him an affectionate kiss on the cheek and a hug.

'How are you? Lovely to meet you,' I said with more confidence than I felt.

'Hmm. I'll decide if it was lovely to meet you in a couple of hours' time, lady.' She was joking, but if there was an element of truth in the statement who could blame her. Her son was the most amazing man I'd ever met. She was bound to be protective of him. There would be something wrong if she wasn't.

'What do you think of Ireland?' she asked me curiously, probably wondering if I'd stick it long term.

'It's beautiful,' I said honestly. 'Different.'

I sipped on another glass of red, frightened to change my poison at this stage but knowing I couldn't drink wine all night either, not unless I wanted to see my steak again.

John's parents were lovely, they made me feel comfortable very quickly, once they slowed down enough for me to understand what they were actually saying. I had to lip read and listen. But despite all that, I relaxed in their company. They were exceptionally witty, which must be where John acquired his distinctive sense of humour from.

For some reason, I found myself telling Graham about the last few weeks and how I was as surprised as anyone else to be here, after everything.

Papa Bear raised his eyebrows at my mention of the D word. Surprised at my openness, he was initially uncertain whether to comment that he was even aware of the situation.

'I know you know about the divorce, so don't be polite. I asked John to tell you everything, to be open from day one.' I had no problem talking about it. In fact, I thought it better to address it early on, before anyone around us asked any awkward questions.

'Ahh, well in that case, I might speak freely then, if I may?' he said, in a light tone. I got the feeling he was going to speak freely, regardless.

'Of course.'

'It sounds to me like you've had a hard few months, maybe even years, but things are on the up now. Trust me,' he said, nodding at John. 'He's got it bad.' He winked at me knowingly and I felt this could be the start of a firm friendship between us, seeing exactly where John got his rock strong solidarity from. They were good country people, straightforward, no bullshit. There was something very refreshing about them. No airs or graces, nothing pretentious. John was right.

'Who wants to play pool?' I saw the table was free.

Surprise lit in John's eyes. 'Sure, you might break a nail, sweetheart,' he mocked me. I laughed, rubbing my hands together in delight as he set up the balls for the game.

'Mind if I break?' I chalked my cue.

'Be my guest.' His tone harboured a hint of arrogance, so sure he had it in the bag.

More locals entered the pub. Everyone seemed to know one another, acknowledging each other with a friendly insult. It seemed in Ireland the stronger the insult you issued, the more highly you thought of the person.

I bent over the pool table, deliberately allowing John a view of my butt in the tight jeans I had on. If all else failed, a distraction technique always helped. I broke, expertly potting two reds with the first strike. John raised his left eyebrow in question. I went on to pot each and every red ball in turn, much to his surprise and mine. It had been years since I played. I just couldn't get a clear shot on the black, so reluctantly, I had to let him take his turn.

'You're a dark horse,' he said, potting four yellows in a row. 'What other hidden talents could you be hiding from me?'

He missed the fifth yellow and handed me the cue again. I potted the black, winning the game. We had a pool table in the garage as kids and used to play all day every day when we weren't at school.

'Best of three?' He frowned, unused to losing.

'Maybe later?' I knew it would irritate the life out of him, being left on the back foot. I couldn't be confident I'd beat him again. Better to quit while I was ahead.

Several drinks later, I had a long hard object in my hand, and it wasn't what I had been expecting only a couple of hours previously.

'Give it a good hard swing, Baby Bear.' I'd been nicknamed in the first half an hour. 'Let's see what you're made of,' Papa Bear (he too had been nicknamed), egged me on rubbing his hands together before clenching his fists in excitement. Hugh nodded encouragingly as John stood well back and watched without comment.

The stick I clasped in my two hands was apparently called a hurly stick. I raised it above my right shoulder and swung it with everything I had, knocking three drinks over and almost giving John a nose job in the process.

'Holy fuck, John, don't piss this one off! By God, you'll know about its son.' Graham seemed impressed at my effort, nevertheless.

'Sorry guys, so sorry about the drinks and the glasses.' Mortified, I headed to the bar where Mama Bear was pouring two more pints of Guinness having witnessed the disaster I caused. She pointed me in the direction of the toilets.

I entered one of the three cubicles, wobbling slightly as I went to sit down. I was drunk. I needed to go home. I laughed at the irony of it. Home. I'd only been here a few hours and the Irish lingo was rubbing off on me.

I liked Ireland, but if John lived in Saudi Arabia, I'd have gone there too. Bar the fact I would be breaking every rule in the country, between my old fondness for a glass of wine and new fondness for the extra-marital activities he'd introduced me to this afternoon. Did women still get stoned in those awful countries? Jeez, they'd have a field day with me. The Decree Absolute was surely in the post at this stage, though.

In the mirror above the basin, I noticed the flush in my cheeks, the sparkle in my eye, and I couldn't help but grin. If someone had told me I'd be in a tiny pub in the arse end of rural Ireland, having one of the most memorable nights out I'd ever had in my life, I wouldn't have believed it, but it was the company. One man in particular, but his parents came a very close second.

My idea of a great night used to be a trendy bar in the city with over-priced cocktails and dodgy lighting. And it wasn't just the lighting that was dodgy, the clientele could be questionable too. The contrast was stark. I was well accustomed to being chatted up by pretentious pricks who thought they could flash a gold card under your nose, throw out a few crappy one liners and call you frigid if you didn't immediately drop your knickers.

I returned to the bar and resumed my position between John and his father, taking a small sip of my half full glass of wine before announcing, 'I feel drunk.'

'And isn't that a great way to feel, Baby Bear?' John's father smiled. 'You couldn't come all the way to the west of Ireland without sampling a few of the delicacies.'

'Oh, I certainly sampled a few today.' I winked at him, and he let out a bellowing laugh. John rolled his eyes and shrugged his shoulders, but I could see the smirk on his face as he remembered.

'I don't doubt you did, my girl.' Slapping John hard on the back, he said, 'You are one lucky fucker, son. It's food for the soul; the equivalent of doing a four mile run, only much more fun. And more importantly, its healthy for any relationship. When you're at it, keep at it. It's the only advice I can give you.'

'I don't know when she last went to Specsavers,' John replied, 'but I'm hoping she doesn't decide to go anytime soon.' Ever the joker. Funny, charming and fabulous. Was it any wonder I became increasingly besotted with each second that passed?

'We'll make a move in a minute. It's past Lucy's bedtime. She needs some rest,' John told his father. 'I'm going to check Mam is ok.' He left me in the capable hands of Papa Bear. I found myself yet again admiring John from behind; full broad shoulders, narrow waist and his firm hard bum. For a man so tall and broad, he moved with grace and presence.

'You are in love with that boy,' Graham said, searching my eyes for confirmation of the obvious truth. A truth that I was nevertheless, still trying to hide.

A hot blush invaded my neck, spreading like wildfire, giving me away, even though we had been talking about something far more personal and potentially embarrassing only moments earlier. I paused, trying to think of a suitable response before trying to make light of it.

'Don't tell him, for God's sake. His head is big enough as it is.' I attempted to distract him with my feeble humour, looking down into my wine glass before taking another sip.

'I can see it as clear as day. And I can see he definitely feels the same.'

He had my unwavering attention. Straightening my drunken self on the stool, I leaned closer, straining to translate every word.

'I'll tell you something, girl. We've seen a few pretty girls in this pub in our lifetime. He brought the odd one down now and again. They'd come and then go just as quickly again. Not one of them lasted more than a month or two.'

I wasn't sure where he was going with this, but even in my tipsy state I realised it was important.

'But not one of them did he look at the way he looks at you. It's remarkable really,' he mused stroking the side of his head in apparent wonder.

I beamed from ear to ear.

And almost as an afterthought, he said, more to himself than to me, 'Interesting times.'

Chapter Sixteen

SUNDAY 9TH SEPTEMBER

A stampede of wild jungle animals trampled over my alcohol-poisoned head, and I had that momentary panic of 'where the fuck am I', before opening my eyes to find John next to me. Unwelcome flashbacks of the night before assaulted me.

The fresh air hit me (never mind the copious amounts of wine), resulting in me projectile vomiting into an unsuspecting blackberry bush on the walk home. John had been a gentleman, of course, holding my hair and back, and reassuring me that he'd never seen anyone vomit in such a ladylike manner. He was probably ripping the piss out of me, but I was too drunk to notice or care at that stage. Just desperate to get to the safe haven that was his house.

I groaned internally, cringing at the hazy but persistent snippets resurfacing. Something else was struggling to reach the surface of the shambles of my limited brain. I must have killed thousands of brain cells in my twenty-seven years, with a variety of Pinot Grigio's and Pinot Noirs depending on the season. I preferred red wine in the winter by an open fire, and a refreshing glass of cool white wine on a warm summer's day. A wine for every occasion. Is it any wonder the girls called me a wino? I couldn't wait to see how much they drink when they'd been married for seven years.

I scrunched my eyes tightly, trying to block out any other possible distraction, and fought hard to piece together the missing parts of the previous night.

It struck me in a flash; Papa Bear. I had a horrible feeling I proclaimed my love for his son. How cringeworthy. No, wait, that wasn't exactly right. I tapped my fingers repeatedly on the side of the bed, a horrible habit I caught myself doing whenever I felt anxious. The rhythmic drumming of each finger allowed me to feel some sense of control when that awful rush of anxiety invaded, which frequently occurred after consuming one too many fermented grape juices.

The memory returned in fragmented pieces. There had been others, but he'd not looked at them the way he looked at me. I beamed like an idiot, despite my alcohol induced war wounds, and wriggled closer to John, who lay on the other half of his enormous bed. Tucking my knees in behind his, I placed my arms round his waist and buried my face into his back. He exhaled a small sigh and locked his fingers through mine.

The last twenty-four hours had been an eye-opener. I was head over heels in love with him, but that was nothing new at this stage. I'd felt it almost instantly. But in the darkness of the long nights when I was home, I knew the rational part of my mind would question if this was real? Was he too good to be true? How could I be in love with someone I'd only known a few short weeks? Or was it infatuation because he was out of my reach, between my initial marital status and the physical distance; that stretch of water they call the Irish Sea? And the most troubling one of all – was I setting myself up for the biggest fall of my life? We lived in two different worlds, after all.

Thinking too long about it troubled me. Could I have fallen so hard, and so quickly? For the first time in my life, I'd followed my gut instinct. That overwhelming, burning urge in the pit of my stomach that willed me to go with the flow – to see where it took me. Being in love was the most fabulous feeling in the world, I was ecstatic each time I saw his photo flash up on my mobile with an incoming call. He took up so much space in my head.

But alongside that intense ecstatic excitement of being in love also came an undeniable vulnerability. Every day I fell deeper in love with

---

him, meaning he had the weapons to slice me that bit deeper, if he should choose to do so. If he decided the distance was too much, or if he were to see something in me he didn't like, as he had done before with my many predecessors.

With thoughts like these swirling round my head, and troubled by worries about our future together, there was zero chance of falling back to sleep. No matter how much I loved John, I couldn't ever picture myself living there, in that tiny community. It wasn't me. I would suffocate in a place like that. Everybody was entwined in one way or another, compared to the reassuring anonymity of the city. Mind you, I nearly drowned in a sinking marriage before I realised I was the one holding the life jackets. Maybe there was another way.

It was early days, but I toyed with the idea of looking for a job in Dublin. I could rent somewhere in the city, at least we'd be in the same country. It was less than a three-hour drive. And John seemed to be in Dublin himself regularly enough. That was, if he ever wanted to see me again after I spewed up my steak and red wine, redecorating his beautiful, previously untouched countryside.

I crept out of bed to escape the horrors of my own torturous mind, pulled on his grey hoody and my dark jeans, and quietly exited the room on tiptoes, careful not to disturb sleeping beauty. Downstairs, in the kitchen, the gleaming counter tops reflected my shameful hangover back at me.

I pulled on my new pink Hunters and a body warmer I found hanging in the utility room and made my way out the back door into the fresh air. The morning was overcast and breezy, but I felt naturally drawn to the beach, drawn instinctively to the rugged emerald of the unruly land and the familiar smell of abandoned seaweed, just as I was physically drawn to John. I wondered if this path had been mapped out for us by a higher source. What were the chances of meeting the man of your dreams at three o'clock in the morning of a hotel bar while on a hen and a stag? Unlikely, but undeniable.

The cattle grazing nearby took no notice as I glanced approvingly at the solitude of my surroundings and inhaled the fresh morning air deeply, working on my breathing. Anxiety haunted me from the drink, but also from the strangeness of my new-found freedom.

I pulled myself onto a large rock overlooking the rock pools and pulled the body warmer tighter around me. Surprisingly, I relished not being able to see or hear another soul. It was like staring at my very own slice of the world in that moment.

I was a long way from the city, but it came as a relief to me this morning, strangely safe and sheltered from the responsibilities of the real world. A sense of comfort stemmed from the knowledge that I could escape everything and everyone, for a weekend at least. I hadn't realised quite how much I needed a break from my normal, if you could call it a normal, life.

Random mismatched thoughts whirred around my head, swirling like the waves of the ocean that I watched. I contemplated the intensity of my connection with John. He was the ying to my yang, the gin to my tonic, and the strawberry to my champagne. Life was more colourful in his company. It did seem too good to be true. But it wasn't, not when I stripped it right back to basics. His life was here, mine was across the water. My friends, my family (albeit only half of them were talking to me at present), my job.

The thought of starting again, whether it be here, Dublin, Edinburgh or anywhere else for that matter seemed increasingly unappealing. But I had a horrible feeling the magnetic pulling force drawing me to John might outweigh anything else in the end.

I couldn't believe I'd found him. Whatever it took, long distance relationship or not, I had to go with it. He was like no one I'd ever encountered in my life. And I wasn't going to lose him after working so hard to free myself in order to be with him, but none of it was going to be easy.

A sense of calm enveloped me. I somehow persuaded my inner control freak to accept that I didn't have to come up with all the answers today. And *I* didn't have to come up with them at all. We did. I wasn't in it alone. And that knowledge empowered me. I'd finally met my match, my equal.

'So, this is where you're hiding.' John's voice broke the silence, startling me, from behind.

'You frightened the life out of me!' My hand clutched my chest, resting over my speeding heart.

'Not nearly as much as you frightened me when you were gone from my bed when I woke up. I thought you were headed straight for Knock Airport after meeting The Fockers last night.' He sniggered at his own joke, witty despite his hangover.

'Your parents are fantastic. I adore them.'

'I'm fairly sure the feeling is mutual, *Baby Bear*."

'I'm so sorry I was a state last night. I haven't been sick like that with drink in years.'

'Yeah, I tend to have that effect on women, it's a fine line, you need to drink enough to find me attractive and a finer line again to be able to hold it down afterwards.' He climbed onto the rock next to me and put his arms round me protectively. 'You're the only woman in the world that can vomit gracefully.' He kissed the top of my head and wrapped his strong arms around me.

'One of my many talents. And you are gorgeous. You know you are. Stop pulling the ginger card with me. Your father told me about all the pretty women you'd brought to the pub before.' I attempted to be light-hearted, but there was an element of curiosity apparent in my tone that, try as I might, I couldn't disguise.

'Did he happen to tell you they were all bat shit fucking crazy? For a ginger, I've been stalked more times than I can count.'

'I can't help but wonder about your past, seeing as everyone else around here seems to know more than me...' It wasn't that I wanted a detailed description, but I couldn't help question why he was single. He was such a good catch.

For once, he abstained from his usual witty comeback, sensing my need for reassurance.

'I don't know what it is, to be honest. My parents always wanted to see me settled. I dated loads of girls. I've kissed a lot of frogs in my time, there's no denying it. I've done things I'm not proud of. Who hasn't? I've been ready to meet someone for a couple of years now, but it just didn't materialise.'

I sat quietly, willing him to carry on, to let me know him more. To let me in.

'I'd go out with a girl, but within a month or two I'd see something I didn't like. It could be something as stupid as a spot on her face, or the way she laughed or chewed her food. Once I saw that particular trait, I couldn't unsee it. And then in my mind it grew bigger and bigger until it was all I could see. And then I'd have to call it a day. You'd swear I was Jamie Dornan with the pick of the women, the way I was carrying on, but I couldn't help it. I couldn't settle for anything less than perfect.'

'So, should I be sitting here waiting for the bullet?' I said gingerly, excuse the pun.

'Don't be ridiculous.' He squeezed me tighter into his chest. 'I told you before, I'm convinced there must be a film crew hiding around here in the bushes somewhere filming a reality TV show "You've Been Framed" Ginger Special.'

'Now who's being ridiculous?' I leaned into his shoulder.

'But was there nobody serious before? Have you ever been in love?' Would he ever tell me anyway? He had an exceptional talent for using humour to avoid the question.

'No. There was nobody serious. Not before you. Like I said, I kissed a few frogs along the way. Once, I thought it might have gone somewhere with someone, it was the only time somebody called it a day with me. I thought I was hurt at the time, but it was my pride that was injured more than my actual heart. I saw her around a few times afterwards and knew well she wouldn't have been for me, anyway. Plus, my parents didn't take to her.'

'I can't imagine your parents not liking anyone.'

'Well, that just goes to show the nature of the beast, possibly a narrow escape.'

'And are the frogs all local?' I couldn't help but wonder had we crossed any in passing, or would we be likely to?

'Some of them. Some of them are married now with kids, some of them are still stalking poor unsuspecting bastards like me.'

'I can't imagine living like that, with the skeletons of your past walking round in broad daylight, having to acknowledge them, running into them on a daily basis. Is it not a bit awkward?' That was another massive benefit to living in a city, if you didn't want to bump into someone, the chances are you wouldn't.

'I don't give them a second thought, to be honest.' His tone oozed sincerity, reassuring me of his complete and utter lack of genuine interest in anyone before. The frog analogy put everything in perspective.

'You can ask me anything, Lucy. I'll never lie to you. No matter how ugly the truth is. I'd rather spend the rest of my life alone than with the wrong woman.'

'I admire you so much. You're so strong it's unreal. I don't know where you got that old head on your shoulders from, but I'm glad you have it. Look at me, the pure opposite. I married the first wrong one that came along, because I honestly didn't believe there would ever be a right one. It's absurd when you think about it. We're a right pair, aren't we?'

'We are, but I wouldn't change any of it, because all the tiny insignificant details of our lives are exactly what led us to being here. I wouldn't swap for the world. It made us who we are today and brought us together.'

He was right, and I knew it, but I couldn't help feeling the earlier years could have been put to a lot better use and I said so.

'The only thing that could be put to better use right now is this morning.' He pulled me to my feet, lifted me down from the rock and led me by the hand back to his four-poster bed. Sunday mornings didn't get any better.

Chapter Seventeen

FRIDAY 14TH SEPTEMBER

I was at the tapas restaurant in Winchester with the girls.

'Well, fill us in, Lucy. I'm dying to hear all,' said Ruth, eager to hear the gossip from last weekend. Though I rented a room from her, because of both our busy work schedules, we were like ships passing in the night.

'I'm not dying to hear all,' Clara said, between mouthfuls of spicy potatoes. 'In fact, I've heard so much about John fucking Kelly, I'm practically in love with him myself. I could pretty much draw a nude portrait of him, I've had so much visual.'

'Sorry, not sorry,' I said with a shrug.

'Well? Does the rug match the carpet?' Ruth asked boldly, leaning closer for the gossip.

'Absolutely. And what a wonderful carpet it is.'

'She came home walking like John Wayne!' Clara grassed me up without a second thought. 'You should have seen her trying to sit down on her saddle seat. It was priceless. She had to work standing up for the first half of the week. I suppose that's what you get for having sex eleven times in two days.'

'Girls, in fairness, I was making up for lost time. It had been years,' I defended myself with a grin as I remembered.

Another one of our friends, Katie, joined us for dinner. She didn't get out as much as the rest of us as she had two toddlers.

'It's all fun and games until you have to push a tiny human out of your vagina. Make the most of it, I'm telling you, those lazy Sunday shags in bed, the kitchen sex, the shower sex, the lot. It's not nearly as fun when you have two little people biting at your ankles and you can't even sneeze without peeing in your knickers,' she advised us.

She gave off holy hell about those kids, but she absolutely adored them. She often regaled us with mundane stories of motherhood that had us doubled up with laughter, assuring us she would have the last laugh. She claimed by the time we had children, hers would be old enough to wipe their own arses and reach the cereal in the morning.

'Such a week I've had. My period was late,' she said solemnly. 'I nearly fucking died. The fear was real. I couldn't even look at David. His life wouldn't be worth living if he'd got me pregnant again. I can barely cope with what I've got, let alone adding another one to the mix.'

Ruth slapped the table in hysterics. 'You were angry at David? My biology isn't great, but I was sure it took two.'

'Listen to me girls, three times I've booked him into Harley Street for that fucking vasectomy. Three times he cancelled the appointment with a variety of weird and wonderful sudden onset illnesses. Though, he miraculously recovered from them, the second, the appointment was cancelled. I told him straight, I have pushed two humans out of my vagina! I've done enough for this family! The least he can do is endure a minor procedure. It's only a local anaesthetic, it can't be that bad.'

I spluttered my wine, struggling to laugh, swallow and breathe all at the same time.

'He calls it major surgery,' Katie continued. 'He'll need major surgery if he doesn't go through with it the next time. Mark my words.'

The young couple on the table adjacent to us were in stitches, having heard every single bit of our explicit conversation.

'I don't know what you're laughing at,' Katie addressed them pointedly. 'It will be you two next. This is how it starts.' She gestured at the two of them holding hands over the table, downing her wine and pushing the glass out for a refill, determined to make the most of her childfree evening.

It was so liberating to know I didn't have to rush back, or face Rob when I got home. It was hard living out of one room, but in some ways, it made it easier; no mess, no tidying, and it was all mine. I thought about him far less frequently than I thought I would. Sometimes whole days passed where I almost forgot I was ever married to him. It was mad. The guilt crept in occasionally, but I tried to remind myself that it was my life, and I had to live it my own way and do what made me happy.

Sometimes when I was enjoying a particularly happy moment for myself, that little devil appeared on my shoulder to interrogate me. Do you really think you deserve to be this happy? Where do you think poor Rob is now? You haven't even called him to see how he is. I tried to swat him away, like flicking my hair off my shoulder, but at times he was persistent. I downloaded one of those meditation apps on my iPhone to help me banish him for good. I only listened to it twice, it bored the life out of me. I had to try and conquer my demons myself. No one was harder on me than I was on myself. If any one of my friends had been in my position, I wouldn't have batted an eyelid. I certainly wouldn't have talked to them the way I talked to myself. I just didn't expect it to be boring old, sensible me that fell unexpectedly but undeniably in love with a ginger guy from the Wild Atlantic Way as it's referred to. Though girls prefer to call it The Wild Atlantic Willy.

'So, we digressed.' Ruth brought me back in the moment, nudging Katie with a conspiring wink. 'Clara may have heard the details, but we didn't. Do tell.'

I looked down into my glass as I remembered the events of the previous weekend. My lips curled up into a grin that extended to my eyes. 'Seriously girls, it was unreal. The best I've ever had.' I circled my finger round the edge of my wine glass and allowed myself to remember.

'Oh fuck, look at her, she's got it bad,' Katie announced.

'Are you seeing him again?' Ruth asked.

'Seeing him again?' Clara stated incredulously. 'She has nearly every fucking weekend booked up until Christmas with him! God forbid anyone wants their teeth cleaned. I caught her blocking of days in her work diary for 'course days' this week. You know what a compulsive planner and OCD freak she is!'

I took no offence. It's been years since I gave them anything to talk about. I was actually enjoying it.

'And is he coming here at all?' Katie's chocolate eyes danced at the prospect. 'He might be.' I didn't want them interrogating him too early on.

'Ah ha. We need to meet this ginger fella we keep hearing so much about. I'm dying to get a right look at him, see what all this fuss is about. He must be really something special to impress Miss Prissy Pants here,' Katie teased.

'If you think I'm letting you bitches anywhere near him, you can think again! God knows what you're liable to say to him.' I cringed even thinking about it.

'We could tell him about the time of the dental hospital Christmas party, where you were so drunk you went home, let yourself into the house, kicked your stilettoes off and heated up the left-over food in the fridge. Apart from you weren't actually home, were you? You were two doors down from where you should have been,' Katie slapped the table, exhaling a deafening belly laugh.

'That's absolutely hilarious. He needs to know what he's letting himself in for!' Clara nodded in agreement.

'It wasn't that funny girls, it could have happened to anyone,' I protested feebly.

'It was hilarious! Unless you were the family hiding out in their own back garden, dialling 999 because there was a drunk woman in their house, eating them out of house and home.'

'Don't remind me.' I winced thinking about it. 'Thank God the police saw the funny side of it.'

'John would love to hear that story,' Ruth assured me. 'It's actually one of my favourites, I'm only sorry I wasn't around at the time to see it.'

'And you wonder why I'm not letting you anywhere near him?'

'Ah, we are only teasing,' Clara said. 'We wouldn't really tell him. Much.'

The restaurant was emptying. It was getting late, but we had no inclination to move.

'Any word from Rob?' Katie asked.

'Not a dicky bird,' I said.

'No news is good news,' Clara said.

My shoulders tensed at the mention of Rob.

'Did you hear that Take That are doing a reunion tour?' Ruth said, with a shrewd glance in my direction.

'Oh my goodness! We need to get tickets!' Katie latched on to this information immediately and I breathed a sigh of relief at the change in conversation. Ruth was always so good at sensing my moods and rescuing me. Despite this, the devil had returned to his position on my shoulder, tormenting me with the same line. I didn't deserve to be happy. It wouldn't end well. You reap what you sow.

Chapter Eighteen

SATURDAY 22ND SEPTEMBER

In certain places, Dublin reminded me of Edinburgh. The narrow, cobbled streets extending like tiny branches from an old oak tree. The gothic architecture and historic monuments seemed familiar, as did the carefully manicured gardens of St. Stephens Green. They reminded me of Princes Street Gardens.

An all too familiar sight was the many tragic homeless people, camping out in ragged blankets, holding cardboard signs begging for enough change for a hot drink or a bite to eat. The distinct smell of stale cigarette smoke hovered in the air between us. It broke my heart to see them that way. I nearly offered to bring them home with me and cook them a good meal. Instead, I handed over what little change I had and felt as guilty as sin for being as lucky as I was. It rapidly put life into perspective.

The striking contrast between the poor living day to day on the streets, and the wealthy department store shoppers with their Louis Vuitton handbags and fur coats seemed more apparent here than in my smaller hometown of Winchester. Maybe it was just more noticeable as an outsider looking in. I clung to John's arm.

'What are you thinking?' he asked.

'Just how lucky we are.' I tightened my grip on his arm again as we passed the eighth person lying in a rotten tattered sleeping bag with a starved, but loyal, mongrel by his side, huddling for warmth from the damp autumn chill.

The orange leaves littered the cold wet ground and dark thunder clouds hovered threatening from above. The weather matched my mood, even though I was with my favourite person in the whole wide world.

'I know. I often think the same.' He clasped his hand over mine. 'Whatever problems I've had this year are minor in comparison.' 'You've a good heart, girl.' His blue eyes bore into mine.

'I doubt my ex-husband would agree with you there, but that's another story.' I couldn't muster a smile, although I'd intended it to be a joke.

'Well, he should have appreciated you when he had the chance. The man's a fool, thankfully. Or you wouldn't be here now. Now, Miss Morbid Pants, let's go for a drink and try to enjoy the weekend. We won't solve the problems of the world today, let's enjoy each other's company while we can. As wonderful as you look on FaceTime, I prefer you in the flesh.'

'You're right. I'm sorry.' I attempted to pull myself together, even though the lingering guilt of being so happy continued to tarnish my mood.

I'd been questioning my life a lot. The devil's increasingly frequent appearance on my shoulder tormented me until I felt like shit for something or another. If it wasn't Rob, it was my lifestyle, or my shopping habits. Maybe I'd have to give that Calm app another go after all.

I tried to remind myself my dad died at the young age of forty-nine, and although it was important to be grateful and to be aware we should do as much as we could to help other people, we also had a right to enjoy our own lives as well. In fairness, I worked hard for it.

We turned the corner of Grafton Street Green and John led me into a tiny pub with low ceilings and wooden beams. Pictures of Irish GAA sporting legends hung dusty on the walls alongside ceramic pottery ornaments that wouldn't have looked out of place in my eighty-six-year-old granny's house. I was fairly sure the barman didn't stock prosecco. I ordered a Bailey's coffee to warm me and hopefully cheer me up.

It seemed to do the trick. By the time I'd started on my second, I'd forgotten what I was supposed to be feeling bad about. Instead, I let myself fall a little more in love with John Kelly as he gave me a run-down of the Gaelic football memorabilia on the walls. I had no interest in the football, but I could listen to him talk all day.

'This is my kind of pub, girl.' He often called me girl. I liked it. It was said with such affection. If anyone else called me that, it might have sounded patronising, but from his lips, it sounded sensual.

'It reminds me of somewhere my father would have brought me. In the early days, my dad would pick us up on a Saturday and drop us back to my mum's on a Sunday. Shared care they call it now, the joys of the broken family. He used to bring us to pubs often with a beer garden so he could enjoy his pint and let us play in the sunshine. And in the winter, he'd bring us into a traditional pub like this, but there would usually be live music,' I said.

'Every Irish childhood involves eating Tayto in a pub while your parents got tipsy. And we're all fine for it,' John said.

'My dad used to do karaoke. He was actually pretty good. Of course at the time I was mortified listening to it, like all kids tend to be embarrassed of their parents! I only wish I could hear him sing it again,' I said.

'Well, sweetheart, I'm not normally one to shatter people's dreams, but you definitely did not take any of your father's genes in the vocal department,' he assured me.

'What do you mean?' I pretended to be shocked, holding my hand over my heart in mock offence.

'Honey, I heard you singing in the shower last week and it sounded like a cat's mating cry.'

'Hmm. I was thinking of applying for X Factor this year I'll have you know.' My twitching lip gave me away.

'I'll save you the cost of a stamp. You have many talents, but singing is not one of them.'

'Huh. Where are we going tonight?' I changed the subject.

'We're going to a party,' he said, taking a sip of his pint.

'I love parties.' A great excuse to put on a dress.

'One of my best friends got engaged last week. They're having drinks in The Shelbourne tonight,' he said.

'I can't wait to meet your friends,' I said, though I wasn't entirely sure if that was true. I'd had a mixed reaction from John's best friend, Owen, who was still being a little overprotective as I was "the married woman from England". Even though my final divorce papers were hopefully only days away.

'Julia was Jack's lodger for four years. You couldn't make it up,' he began. 'Then suddenly they had a row one night about a fucking plant or something, and he went into her bedroom to apologise, and as far as we know, he never came out since.'

'That's a lovely story. It's funny though, isn't it, how it happens so differently for everyone. Imagine they lived together for four whole years. It's crazy,' I said.

'I keep telling you, honey, I have read the script to our story. You are moving West. It's only a matter of time.' It wasn't the first time he'd said something to this effect. Though I didn't contradict him, I still couldn't see it.

We made our way back to the Hilton Hotel we'd checked into the night before. We'd developed a soft spot for them after that first weekend in Bristol.

I drew the blackout blinds and climbed into the big, crisp-white bedsheets for an afternoon nap before the aforementioned evening events. The Bailey's had relaxed me. A smile crept onto my face as John's hand slid round my waist from behind, inching inside the flimsy band of my carefully chosen underwear.

We made love slowly, tenderly this time, taking our time exploring each other and enjoying the build-up to our inevitable climax. Each time was different. I hadn't thought it possible to top the first week-end, but as we got to know each other's bodies better, we teased one another to the brink until one of us exploded.

Tired from the week at work and the travelling, I fell into a deep dreamless sleep with John's knees tucked into the backs of mine, his arm under my pillow, the other round my waist.

The sound of voices echoing through the hotel corridor eventually woke me from my slumber. I crept out of bed quietly. John seriously loved his sleep. If it was even possible, he looked paler when he was tired, and he'd had a long week at home on the farm. One of the heifers had gotten into trouble delivering her first calf, and the vet had been called. Mother and baby were ok, but it was touch and go all week. It was so far removed from my week on the other side of the water, but it gave us plenty to talk about.

I filled the bathtub and immersed myself in delicious smelling bubbles. A few minutes later, I heard him approach and shuffled forward to make room in the tub.

'Hello, sleepy head.' He slipped into the bath behind me.

'Jeez, you'd tire a man out, girl. You're insatiable.' Yet it was him that was currently fondling my breasts, tenderly running his fingers over my nipples.

'If you're awfully tired, I suggest you stop that immediately,' I warned him, feeling the deep stirring of arousal.

'I suppose I did get a bit of rest there,' he conceded, his hand stroking slowly down over my stomach, teasingly toward another part of me. He played with me, toying with me, running his fingers up and down until I felt like begging him to touch the most intimate parts of me.

'You like that?' he whispered into my ear from behind.

'You know I do.' I could barely think straight, silently pleading with him to give me my release. The man was a mind reader.

He stroked me repeatedly, until heat spread through my groin and down my thighs, my toes curling in anticipation. I was tense, ready to blow any second.

I loved watching his hands rubbing relentlessly over the most sensitive part of me, seeing him so confidently enjoying the power he had over me in that moment. I couldn't hold it any longer, my entire body shuddered to a powerful climax. Though he was behind me, I felt him grin from ear to ear. He loved what he did to me, how he could take me and turn me into a quivering wreck any time he felt like it.

I regained my composure, waiting for my heart to slow to a normal rate before turning round in the soapy water to straddle him. He was more than ready, turned on from turning me on. I placed his hands

THE SEVEN YEAR ITCH

back onto my nipples, dominating him as I began to slide up and down the length of him, slowly at first, then increasing the pace, watching his face as he battled to prolong the experience. It was my turn to smile, knowing without a shadow of a doubt that what we had was better than anything either of us had had before.

Afterwards, I slumped forward onto his chest, grateful for the scrunchie that pulled my unruly curls into a messy bun on top of my head.

'You are something else.' He kissed my neck lightly before I pulled away. As hot as the sex had been, I wasn't exactly comfortable and we both laughed as I navigated my way less than graciously out of the bath and into the comfort of one of the hotel's heavy robes.

I popped open a bottle of Moet from the minibar and poured us both a glass. John drank his in the bath, I sat at the dressing table next to him and applied my make-up for the evening.

'You don't need half that shit you put on your face, Luce,' he said affectionately.

'I like it. It's more for my benefit than yours,' I told him truthfully.

'How many times have I told you, girl, when you have it, you have it. And trust me, you have it.'

I'm not quite sure what 'it' was, but he clearly intended it as a compliment. I slipped into a black bodycon dress, plain in its design, with thick straps and a scoop neck which showed a hint of tanned cleavage. It stopped exactly on my knee and I teamed it with simple black peep toe stilettos and a small black clutch.

John let out a long, low whistle and raised his eyebrows approvingly at my attire. 'Do you have any knickers on under there?' he asked huskily.

'I might let you find out later.'

'Every man in Dublin is going to be looking at my woman tonight,' he said.

'I very much doubt that. Maybe it's you that needs to go to Spec-savers? But if Brad Pitt himself walked through that door right now, I'd tell him to get lost and stop annoying us.' I downed the last of my champagne in one mouthful.

He helped me into my black, knee-length belted over coat and lead me out into the corridor where we took the lift to reception. We got a taxi to the restaurant John had booked; it was called Fire. It was classy, but understated, like himself. We had a private booth dimly lit with candles.

John told me about the week's work on the farm, how Hugh and Sam had been so good to stay all hours. I found myself only half listening. The other half of me wondered what I'd possibly done to deserve to be with this wonderful man. He was everything I hadn't realised I needed; strong, confident, witty, sexy. The only problem was the sea that separated us. I sighed unintentionally.

'Am I keeping you awake? Sorry, I know this farming craic isn't exactly what you're into,' he said.

'Sorry. It's not that at all. I was just wondering how many teeth I'd have to clean before I could buy my very own helicopter so I could come home to you every night.' I attempted to make light of the situation.

'Honey, you are so silly sometimes.' He laughed at me in a childlike manner. 'You won't need a helicopter; the house is only fifteen minutes in the car from town.'

'Hilarious, aren't you?' I sipped my wine quietly, unsure of what else to say on the matter.

'Don't panic. It's all going to fall into place, I promise you.'

'Why? Are you thinking of exporting antiques to the UK?' I asked more sharply than I had intended to.

'There are five dental practices in Ballina,' he said. 'I'm not saying you have to move here, but at least there are options. Let's give it until Christmas and we'll talk about it seriously then. I know we can't go on travelling indefinitely every weekend, and I'm only sorry its mostly you doing the legwork with flights and trains and everything else. I'm just tied with the farm and everything.'

'I don't mind coming here for the weekend, I'd actually travel a lot further if it meant I could be with you...'

'But?' he prompted me quietly.

'But the goodbyes get harder every time I leave you. And in all honesty, I'm not sure I'd ever be able to live here.' There I said it out loud.

'Wait until Christmas before you rule it out. These weekends will give you a chance to get a feel for the place, find your feet before you commit to anything. Look, I know what you've just come out of. I know it was hard, and you probably don't want to get all serious and bogged down again too soon.' He was so understanding, but he was wrong. It wasn't that I didn't want to get serious with him, quite the contrary in fact.

'It's not that at all.' I was desperate to reassure him again I had no interest in "spreading my wings", as he put it. Oh, I had an itch alright. An overwhelming, desperate longing for it to be scratched. And scratched every day, preferably multiple times. But there was only one person that could do that, and he was sitting across the table from me and I told him so.

'I know our friends would all think we were completely crazy if we told them the conversations we're having already, but when you know, you know.' He was as sure as himself as ever. Easy enough for him, he wasn't the one thinking about moving countries.

In fairness, he had a lot more to leave behind than I did. His house, his farm, his business, his family and all he'd ever known. On the flip side, I hadn't lived at home since I left for the Royal College of Surgeons at nineteen years of age, but I'd since worked hard to build a business myself. I was self-employed, and had acquired many loyal patients over the past few years. I'd formed friendships stronger than some of my family bonds. And there was my mum, of course.

No matter how hard I tried, it was impossible not to overthink the situation. I was used to being so sure of my life, so completely in control. I was like a tumbleweed blowing in the wind, wondering which direction the breeze was going to take me.

'I can read you like a book,' he said. 'Don't worry about the details tonight. I adore you; you hopefully adore me. We will make it work.' He reiterated the same line he'd used before. 'It took me thirty years to find you, I'm not going to let you slip through my fingers. Besides, my father would kill me if I let you get away now.'

I hoped his father hadn't ratted me out on the L word. I hadn't said it to him myself, despite knowing that was exactly what it was, from very early on.

I changed the subject quickly to lighten the mood. 'Have you taken that Godawful stag head down from the wall yet?' He laughed, as I'd intended.

After dinner we walked the short distance through the city to The Shelbourne. John led me into the bar and placed my coat on the back of a barstool. I hovered a few feet away as he ordered our drinks, scanning the room to see if I could pick out Jack and Julia.

A short, petite woman with shoulder length highlighted hair made a beeline for John. She strode towards him in a manner that made me think she knew him, and well, by the way in which she put her arm round his waist, reaching on tiptoes to kiss his cheek. She couldn't have been more than five-foot three, a short red dress detailed her tiny waist and child-like frame.

An uneasy feeling crept into my stomach, but I couldn't bring myself to look away. Her behaviour left me in no doubt now that she knew him intimately. It was mirrored in the surprise on his face, surprise that she was here. A flashback of this afternoon, John's hands on my body, gave me a brief flicker of satisfaction and quelled the green-eyed monster. He turned to see if I'd clocked the situation, discomfort apparent in the tightness of his smile. A smile that didn't fully reach his eyes.

I couldn't hear the words they exchanged, but I got the impression from the way he stared at me that he was about to point me out. I deliberately looked the other way.

A man wearing a tweed jacket and dicky bow approached me from out of nowhere.

'You must be Lucy?' He was about five-foot ten and slightly stockier than John. He too had red hair.

'Jack? It's a pleasure to meet you.' He couldn't have come over at a better time.

'Likewise.' He adjusted his dicky bow, pulling at the neck of her shirt.

'Congratulations on your engagement.'

'Thank you. I'll introduce you to my fiancée now.' He nodded at John and raised a hand as a greeting.

John arrived back with a glass of champagne for me and two crystal tumblers filled with some sort of top shelf whisky. He'd eventually managed to extract himself from the blonde. Out of the corner of my eye, I saw her scrutinise me from head to toe and made sure to smile my brightest smile.

That little niggle of jealousy lingered in the pit of my stomach. It was the first time I'd truly experienced it, never previously caring enough in the past. Intuitive as ever, John placed his arm around me protectively. The woman in red shot daggers at us. If looks could kill my head would have been ripped off my neck.

'Yellow Spot,' John said, handing Jack a glass.

'Twelve-year-old?' Jack smelt it as he swilled it around the glass.

'Yes. Congratulations.' John gently tipped glasses with Jack, then me. 'You've met Lucy, I see.'

'I clocked you as soon as you walked in. I see I wasn't the only one.' Jack raised his eyebrows slightly and shrugged his shoulders as if to say what can you do?

'Fucking pain in the arse,' John muttered. She was now only about three feet away from us, subtly moving closer to us to get a better look. As she lingered nearby, I noticed the fine lines crinkling around her heavily pencilled eyes.

Though her figure was child-like, she was nearer to forty than thirty.

'We must introduce Lucy, to Julia,' Jack prompted loudly, and gave us a nudge in the other direction. We scooted rapidly across the bar to the other side of the room.

'One of the infamous frogs?' I asked quietly, only a couple of metres from

Julia.

'Long story. But in short, she's a frog who was determined she was going to turn into a princess for me. It was never going to happen. Ever. I'd been drinking all day at a wedding, and she pounced on me in the residents' bar sixteen pints later. I was absolutely hammered; I barely remember what happened.' He placed both hands on my waist, pupils intensely into mine. 'She's an absolute lunatic, she stalked me for months afterwards. I told you, I'm not proud of my past, sweetheart.'

Relief flowed through my blood to my clenched fists and tight shoulders and I began to relax again. Everyone has a past. Still, it never ceased to amaze me how people could do intimate things with people that they didn't even particularly like. To men, it was purely about the physical release, to women, it often meant so much more. The differences between the male and female brain always fascinated me.

Our conversation halted as we reached our destination by the sash windows. 'Julia, congratulations.' John kissed her cheek.

Julia was five-foot five, with short black hair in a pixie cropped style and widely set aquamarine eyes. Her sallow complexion was flawless.

'This is Lucy,' John said, and Julia kissed me on each cheek, welcoming me warmly.

'I would have known you anywhere,' she said pleasantly. 'John's been showing off your pictures on his phone for weeks now.' She tilted her head back and giggled, pointing at John. I couldn't place her accent, but it wasn't Irish. 'Thanks for that, Julia,' John said, the tips of his ears turning as red as his hair.

'I'll have to start photoshopping if he's going to flash them around the place.' I twisted my hair round one finger, unable to shake the feeling we were being watched.

'It's great to see John has finally met somebody too. We thought he'd never settle down,' she enthused. 'Perhaps now he'll stop bringing my fiancé out drinking whisky into the early hours, when they are supposed to be on a "working dinner",' Her grin showed she didn't mind in the slightest.

'I wouldn't bet on it,' Jack said. 'At least not until she moves over.'

It seemed everyone had my future concluded already. Part of me was flattered they felt John was serious about me. Another part couldn't even contemplate having to start again in a new place. Especially one where frogs lurked around every corner.

Two drinks later, I'd forgotten all about the woman in red, instead enjoying the company of Jack and Julia. It transpired that Julia was Lithuanian. They were planning to get married over there the following year.

At the risk of losing my seat, I excused myself in search of the ladies' room.

'Are you ok?' John checked as I got up from the barstool.

'Perfect.' I reassured him with a kiss.

'If we were dogs, you just did the equivalent of peeing on me,' he said, a small smirk curling his full lips.

'Nothing like marking your territory.' I winked and passed gently by him.

I found the ladies' toilets without a hitch, but was unexpectedly stopped in my tracks on my return by the woman in the red dress, who apparently had not forgotten about me. She examined me distastefully as she blocked my path. 'Hi.' Her voice harboured a hint of boredom, like she knew everything about me already and I was lacking. Or maybe I was projecting.

'Hi.' I acknowledged her as warmly as I could manage, reverting to my professional "I'm At Work and I Have To Be Polite To Patients Because They Are Paying For My Service" kind of smile. I attempted to bypass her, but she sidestepped, blocking me again.

'I know John,' she stated bluntly, like it was supposed to mean something to me.

'That's great,' I said, still smiling, not entirely sure where this was going. Having a distinct height advantage, I glanced over her head, hoping my knight in shining armour was somewhere in the vicinity, because if I ever needed rescuing it was now.

'No, I actually *know* John,' she repeated it like it should mean something. Like I cared about anything that occurred prior to the twenty-ninth of June this year. I shrugged in disinterest, refusing to take the bait. Her steely eyes burned into mine. If she stood there much longer, she was going to get a crick in her neck from gawping upwards. Never was I more grateful for my six-inch stiletto addiction, literally rising above the drama.

I smoothed my hands down over my black dress and waited for whatever line she felt compelled to deliver.

'It won't last,' she warned, 'he's incapable. I've tried.'

'Our relationship is really none of your business.' My smile evaporated. I refused to wilt like a flower. I hadn't been through what I had, to be intimidated by a five-foot, Barbie in need of Botox.

'Don't say I didn't warn you.' She practically spat the words from her pinched mouth.

I crossed the room swiftly back to John and necked the drink he had been holding for me.

'I thought you were taking it easy tonight?' He waved my empty glass under my nose and turned to the bar to fetch me a refill.

'Wait,' I said. 'I'll come with you.' I didn't want to get caught again, and I was determined to maintain a united front, not wanting the frog to think she'd succeeded in driving a wedge between us.

'Is everything ok?' Concern crinkled at the corner of his eyes.

'Your friend wanted to warn me about you.' I couldn't quite meet his eye for fear there was actually more to the story than he'd let on.

'What did that daft bitch want now?' His jaw clenched with temper.

'Just wanted to tell me she knew you, and to warn me that you'd never settle.'

'That's the thing about living in a small town, when you don't know what you're doing, at least everyone else does.' His voice was dangerously low, and a vein pulsed in his neck. I'd never seen him angry before.

'Look, I shouldn't have said anything.' I didn't want this to ruin our night.

'Of course you should say something. How dare she think she knows me, because of a drunken kiss years ago? It's a small town, we all have a past, but don't let anyone allow you to think they know me. Not for a second. It couldn't be further from the truth. In all honesty you're the first person I've ever really let in. For fuck's sake I actually love you...' His eyes blazed and drilled into me, then he blinked and lowered his gaze to the floor. His feet shifted but before he could turn away, I clutched the back of his neck and pulled him towards me. Our lips met, slow and firm. I silently rejoiced in the words that had escaped him. It was everything I wanted to hear; needed to hear; every day. His kiss was loaded with more promises and I moved in deeper, falling a little bit more, but relieved to know we were of one mind.

'You know how I feel about you.' I breathed into his mouth, millimetres from mine.

John whispered into my ear, 'There are girls you spend a night with, and there are girls you spend your life with. There are girls you buy a drink for, and there are girls you buy a diamond ring for. You know which one you are.' He squeezed my waist encouragingly.

I couldn't have put it better myself.

'Time for us to go home,' he said in a low, husky voice. 'I want you to really mark your territory.'

'With pleasure.' We bid our goodbyes and hailed a taxi back to the hotel.

Chapter Nineteen

TUESDAY 25TH SEPTEMBER

As much as I couldn't see myself leaving my beloved city, the days and especially the nights became increasingly hard without John. Was it a sign of weakness that I was so emotionally dependent on him already? Or was that what a normal relationship felt like?

I ached for him so badly I seriously contemplated moving over to the wet wild west just to wake up with him each day. I had it so bad, I barely recognised myself. But it seemed we were growing together. He regularly reminded me that, as new as this was to me, it was also new to him. We were in it together. I took some small comfort in that.

Chapter Twenty

SATURDAY 29TH SEPTEMBER

John had popped into town to pick up some chocolate croissants and a newspaper. I perched on a stool at the island, sipping a black coffee. The sharp bang of the front door made me jump, before a uniformed policewoman strutted straight into the kitchen. My heart lurched violently into my mouth. For a split second I jumped to the worst conclusion, wondering if there had been an accident. My knuckles turned white as I clasped my hands in anticipation.

'You must be Lucy, I'm Jane. I live next door,' the woman introduced herself and I kicked myself for not immediately realising who she was.

Why is it that I'm so quick to jump to the worst scenario? Possibly because I couldn't believe I'd found someone like John. On my darkest nights, I worried not only that he might leave me, but that he might be taken from me another way.

'Jane.' I stood up to greet her, looking apologetically at my leggings and John's T-shirt. I hadn't yet showered, hoping he might join me when he arrived home.

'I was meaning to drop in before, but I kept missing you. Shift work.' She shrugged her shoulders. The Garda uniform was a bit off-putting, but true to form, Jane had a face full of beautiful make-up on.

She was another stunner. High cheekbones, perfectly set dark eyes and full lips. John's neighbours were no joke, I'd seriously have to up my game. The women were like the women from Wysteria Lane.

'It's so lovely to meet you. I've heard so much about you,' I said.

'Well, that can't be good. Mind you, I haven't had to arrest John yet, so it mightn't be too bad. I'm on my break from work and I passed John on the outskirts of town. He said you were here and it might be a good time to say hi.'

'It's perfect, sit down I'll make you a coffee.' I went to the Nespresso machine.

'How do you find the place?' she asked.

I gave her the same answer I gave to everyone. It rolled off the lips these days. 'It's absolutely beautiful, but very different.'

'Aye. I know. I'm from Donegal myself.' That explained her absolutely fabulous accent, different to anyone else I'd been introduced to. It was a soft, distinctive lull that I could listen to all day.

'Blow-ins,' she said.

'Sorry?'

'We're blow-ins. That's what they call us. Those that aren't from around here.'

It was nice to meet someone who didn't grow up with everyone else, or have a story about everyone they met. In that moment, I knew we were going to be great friends. I'd found an ally in this tiny town. We exchanged a grin in an unspoken agreement.

John returned ten minutes later to find myself and Jane sitting in the sunroom with our coffees, me clutching my stomach as she regaled an incident where she'd had to arrest a man for drink driving. When she pulled him over to breathalyse him; he had no trousers on, and no underwear either. His wife had caught him in bed with her sister and thrown him out, literally with his trousers round his ankles.

'I knew you two would get on like a house on fire,' John said over the laughter. The tears streamed down my face as she explained that the man in question was actually wearing a baseball cap, which he then used to hide his man parts as best he could.

'Poor, Michael Maloney.' John knew exactly who she was talking about, small town and all that.

'No, poor Mary Maloney more like! The silly mare took him back after that,' she said in horror. 'Can you even imagine?'

'Well, I suppose I'm not exactly one to be judging anyone else,' I confessed.

'At least you left your husband,' Jane said bluntly. After a split second of uncertainty, the three of us erupted in another bout of belly laughter.

'No secrets in this town.' The more other people talked about us, the less we'd have to tell them ourselves, I concluded.

'We'll get dinner organised the next time you are over,' Jane promised as she pulled her coat on and slipped out the front door back to the police car.

'I'll look forward to it,' I called after her.

'She's so lovely,' I said, as he closed the front door.

'I knew you'd get on. You have too much in common not to. She's a really decent girl. But don't cross her in that uniform by all accounts.'

'Don't think I don't know exactly what you're up to, Mr Kelly,' I chastised him, gently smacking his backside.

'What?' He feigned total innocence, but a mischievous glint in those blue eyes gave him away.

'Making sure I have a solid support network this side of the water in order to entice me to move over. Dangling the carrot in front of the donkey! I know your game.'

'Happy anniversary by the way.' He brushed a stray crumb from my lips and kissed me.

'Of course, how could I forget? The twenty-ninth! Happy anniversary. Can you believe it's only been three months since we met?' Worryingly, I couldn't imagine my life without him in it.

'Should I be expecting the p45?' I joked.

'Nope. You're stuck with me. And now you're officially the longest relationship I've ever had.'

I wasn't sure if I was supposed to be delighted with his last statement, or concerned.

Chapter Twenty-One

THURSDAY 4TH OCTOBER

I sometimes met my mother in Southampton after work. Westquay shopping centre was open until eight and we liked to look around the shops before going to our usual Italian restaurant on the harbour.

'How are you, sweetheart?' She leant over the red and white chequered table mat, squinting in an attempt to analyse me. I'd forgotten I was supposed to be grieving a broken marriage, when in fact it was relief I felt, tinged only by a little guilt over my newfound happiness.

'I'm good, Mum, honestly. Please don't worry about me. I'm fine.' I pushed my lasagne around my plate.

I was nervous in the knowledge it was high time I told her about John. It had gone so far; I didn't know exactly how to broach it. I hadn't wanted to tell her prematurely and give her another thing to worry about. One bombshell at a time was quite enough. She wouldn't thank me if she incurred any additional wrinkles on my behalf.

'I can't help but worry. You'll know yourself one day. I hope.' She always said that to me, but until recently I knew there was no chancing of me understanding what it felt like to worry about your own flesh and blood, but the future seemed full of possibilities again.

I chewed a mouth full of garlic bread and decided to just brave it.

'You never asked me if I met somebody else,' I whispered, conscious of the diners either side of us.

Her head snapped up from her food so quickly I almost laughed. She looked at me silently for a second before the obvious reply. 'Well? Did you?'

I nodded, letting her digest this unexpected piece of information for a moment. She took a sip of her glass of red wine before pleading, 'First, please tell me he doesn't have any children, and second, tell me he lives nearby.'

'One out of two isn't bad?' I brushed an imaginary fleck of dust off my navy blazer to take the attention from my face, feeling the blush creep into my cheeks.

She put her fork down and stared at me, waiting for me to spill the beans.

'He doesn't have any children,' I confirmed. Well, not that I was aware of.

'So, where does he live?' My mum had only just got me back to England, after seven years in Scotland. She was going to be unimpressed with my next statement.

'He lives in Ireland.'

'Ireland?' Widening eyes stared at me like I'd gone mad.

'I met him on Heidi's Hen,' I said.

'Heidi's Hen?' She repeated everything I said, attempting to make sense of it.

'I met him in the residents' bar,' I said sheepishly.

'But if he lives in Ireland...' she trailed off, confused.

'I've been there several times, for the weekend,' I admitted.

'But when?' She seemed hurt, excluded, albeit unintentionally from my life.

'I went when everyone thought I was at Katie's or Clara's the last few weekends. I'm sorry I didn't tell you before, but I had to make sure there was something worth telling.'

'So, presumably you think there's something worth telling now.' She tucked her hair behind her ear, struggling to get her head around the new information.

'You always said someone else would turn my head,' I reminded her.

Numerous times, she had tried to warn me, but I was still in that oblivious mind state of not believing in real love, unlike the love that I had since experienced.

I hated that I had turned into one of those women who threw their normal lives out the window, transforming into an unrecognisable version of themselves, but in all honesty, it was worth it. My feelings for John far outweighed my need to be right. Our relationship was more important to me than anything before, which is why the deeper we got involved, the larger the small problem known as the Irish Sea, became.

I didn't disclose the extent of the situation, she'd probably go grey overnight in shock. Plus, even though I knew I'd turned into one of those crazy, infatuated in love kind of women, I hoped to hide it from my friends and family for a little longer.

'I won't say I told you so, but I knew you would meet someone else.' A small nod of her head demonstrated her delight at having been proven right. 'What does he do? How old is he? Is he married?' she added lastly, as an afterthought.

'No, he's not married! He has a farm.' She raised her eyebrows at this news and pushed her plate away from her. The young waiter returned, took our used dishes and asked if we'd like dessert.

'No thanks,' we replied in unison, waiting for him to leave before we resumed our conversation.

'A farm? It's hardly your scene darling, is it? I expected you to say he was a banker or a lawyer or something.'

'Well, he has an antiques business as well.' I informed her, playing mindlessly with the stem of the wine glass, glad my secret was finally out in the open.

'Hmmm,' she mused.

'Mum, I adore him. Even if it never worked out, and I never saw him again, after that weekend in Bristol, I knew my marriage was over. Once I saw something like that existed, there was no way I could stay.'

'Look darling, it's no surprise to me you split up with Rob, God love him, he was never ever going to be a match for you. You that's so outgoing, bubbly and ambitious. He was so quiet and lacking in ambition. He never would have been able to keep up.'

'I couldn't see it in the beginning. I just wanted someone for myself,' I tried to explain, but she cut in over me.

'Do not feel the need to explain yourself to me. Or anyone else, for that matter. You have one life, my girl, make the most of it. I'm actually kind of glad you met someone else. Although I am surprised by your choice. At least I know there's another person looking out for you,' she reasoned.

Her view was a little old school, she thought that most women needing looking after by a man, even though she had raised me to ensure I was more than capable of supporting myself, financially, emotionally and in every other way. But she was soothed by the knowledge that someone else had my back.

'Let me show you a picture.' I pulled out my phone from my coat pocket. She took out her glasses to get a better look.

I found a picture of John I'd taken that weekend in Dublin. She took the phone out of my hands zooming in on his gorgeous face.

'Is he ginger?' Shock tinged her tone.

'He certainly is,' I said with a giggle. 'And the best-looking man I've ever laid eyes on. Oh Mum, wait until you meet him. He's so funny, and so kind, and so good to me. You are going to adore him.'

'Hmm.' She didn't look convinced, possibly because he lived in another country. 'So does this mystery man have a name?'

'John. John Kelly.' I grinned as his name fell from my lips.

'And where exactly in Ireland does John Kelly live?' She asked.

'The west. County Mayo.'

'Lucy, you do realise why it's called the Emerald Isle?'

'Mum, I'd go to Saudi Arabia to visit this man. It could be a lot worse.'

'It could be a lot better. Could you not just find a nice Englishman?' She rolled her eyes dramatically, but I could tell she was secretly happy for me.

Chapter Twenty-Two

SATURDAY 13TH OCTOBER

'So, what's this big news you have for me?' John asked as he manoeuvred the Audi round the narrow winding roads I had become so accustomed to, from the airport to his house.

I had known for forty-eight hours and it had been killing me not being able to tell him. I so badly wanted to do it in person. The excitement shone from my grinning face.

'Patience, my dear,' I said.

'What are we waiting for? The local newspaper to arrive before you can give the exclusive?'

'You'll find out soon enough.' I'd held it this long; I could wait another few minutes.

Eventually, he pulled into his stone cobbled drive, kissed my cheek, and offered his usual greeting. 'Welcome home.'

Collecting my small, red suitcase, he pulled me into the house and through to the kitchen. As though I was weightless, he lifted me onto the island, wiggled his hips between my legs and kissed me again firmly on the mouth, his tongue teasing mine unfairly.

It still made me weak inside, and he knew it, wielding it over me like a weapon.

He broke away suddenly. 'Now, for the love of God, woman, will you please put me out of my misery?'

I hadn't realised how much it had been annoying him, but it appeared my wonderfully straight talking, joker boyfriend actually hated surprises.

'Can you hand me my luggage up?' I patted the island next to me and he flung the case up quickly. 'Easy, you might break something.'

He rolled his eyes as I took my time slowly unzipping the case, eventually locating a white standard looking office envelope. It gave away nothing on the outside, but the contents were enormously valuable. I handed it to him gleefully and removed the bottle of Moet I'd purchased in the duty free this morning.

Ripping it open, he scanned the typed lines. I watched his face as he processed the words, and then fist punched the air with a triumphant whoop. It was the most enthusiasm I'd ever witnessed from him for anything outside the bedroom.

An embarrassing trickle of tears escaped my eyes as he kissed my forehead then popped the Moet.

'Congratulations sweetheart.' He handed me a glass of bubbling liquid, which could have done with a stint in the fridge. We clinked our crystal flutes together, and he wiped my tears away with a gentle stroke of his thumb.

'I thought it would never arrive. I'd been holding my breath the last few weeks. It had taken longer than expected, and I'd worried Rob wouldn't go through with it. But there it landed, on the doorstep at seven fifty-five on Thursday morning. The relief swept through my veins like a wave.'

'You are the most amazing divorcee I have ever met in my life,' John said, handing back my Decree Absolute.

'Thank you.' I looked to the ground, feeling almost shy.

'Keep it somewhere safe, girl. You never know when you might need it.' He winked at me with a glint in his sparkling eyes.

I was a long way from thinking about marriage again, but at least now I was a free woman. I had the paperwork to prove it.

There had been no word from Rob throughout. It was a relief. I didn't want to have to keep going over things again and again. At last, it appeared I'd crossed the finishing line of a difficult few months. Sometimes I wondered how he was, but I tried not to dwell on it. Our eyes are on the front of our heads for a reason.

We brought the bottle and our two glasses through to the sunroom, and sat together squashed on one end of the enormous sofa. The faint autumn sunlight weakly penetrated the church window. Content with his arm wrapped around my shoulders, I inhaled John's familiar masculine aroma, and enjoyed the feel of my face pressed snugly into his chest. His arms were like home.

I allowed myself a few quiet moments of reflection on how far we had actually come, before slowly pulling open his crisp baby blue shirt and kissing his neck in a manner that was only going to end one way.

Chapter Twenty-Three

FRIDAY 19TH OCTOBER

Two hours in the departure lounge of the Aer Lingus flight bound for Knock Airport had become the norm for me each weekend. I knew most of the air stewardesses, and a couple of other regular commuting passengers.

My friends and family thought I had gone mad. Like, completely lost the plot, stark raving lunatic mad. Yesterday Clara announced she thought the novelty would have worn off by now, reminding me winter was coming and travelling every week in ice and snow would further complicate the situation.

She had no idea. None of them did, but if I had to walk to Ireland, I would do it. I was so deeply in love with John Kelly, I even frightened myself with the lengths I would go to just to be with him. A life without him was unthinkable.

We'd established certain routines, and it was these small familiarities that comforted me in amongst the chaos of the travelling. If I landed on a Friday night, we often picked up a Chinese before going to his parents' pub. If I landed on a Saturday, we usually fell straight back into bed at lunchtime. The weekends meant an early start for both of us. John preferred to milk the cows himself on a Saturday to give Hugh and Sam a break, and to keep his eye on 'the girls'. I had to be in

Gatwick ridiculously early. My alarm was always set for five o'clock. I had to leave Winchester at six. I usually drove to the airport and parked my car in the short stay car park.

My life without Rob had become far more complicated, yet I didn't want it any other way. Well, that wasn't strictly true; if John Kelly said he was moving to England in the morning, it would be the answer to my prayers, but even then, I knew it was never going to happen. The more I thought about it, the more I accepted if we were to have any kind of future together, I would have to move.

Each weekend I spent in Mayo, the thought of living there became less of a shock. The weekends provided the opportunity to test the water, which was probably John's intention all along, and why he said we would talk about the serious stuff over Christmas.

That particular Friday night was different, special. I was about to meet John's sister, Hannah, for the first time. She lived in Ballina with her husband and their two sons. I'd missed her the last few times; she was always working. I hoped she'd like me. John was so fond of her. I always wanted a sister, a sister-in-law I could get on with would be a close second. Not that I was planning on getting married again anytime soon.

On the plane, I pulled out my Kindle and settled into the third book in the Twilight series; I was addicted to Bella and Edwards hopeless love story.

A heavy man of about fifty approached, just as I was getting comfortable.

'Excuse me, I think I'm in there next to you? Twenty-seven A? Is that right?' His accent was a soft Irish lilt.

'You're in the right place.' I shuffled my legs towards the aisle, so he could sneak in past me.

'You're a bit slimmer than me.' He pushed in past me awkwardly before sitting down.

'No problem.' I hoped he wasn't going to be a talker. I'd had a few of them and I wasn't in the form for chitchat.

'Are you travelling for work or pleasure?' he said, and my heart sank. I reluctantly placed down my kindle for a minute.

'My boyfriend lives in Mayo. I go over most weekends,' I explained, as I had done several times over the past two months. I loved the word boyfriend, it made me feel young and full of hope.

'Oh wow. It must be love.' He fought to adjust his seatbelt over his large paunch.

I smiled but said nothing, hoping this would draw a natural end to the conversation.

'So where did you meet him?' He refused to take the hint, ignoring the passenger safety demonstration, as the airplane wheels began to move along the runway at high speed.

'In Bristol.' I didn't elaborate. I had the Kindle in my hand, ready to return to it should there be enough of a pause in the conversation that it wouldn't be considered rude.

'Is that where you're from?' I took a deep breath, before replying as politely as possible.

'No. I'm from the Isle of Wight.' Whether I liked it or not, I realised I was about to spend the next hour and fifteen minutes engaging in small talk. Luckily, I was excited and subsequently more tolerant. If he'd caught me on a Sunday, on the way home, I was usually in a far more sombre mood, knowing it would be a long week until I saw my love again.

'Wow, The Isle of Wight,' he repeated. 'I've never met anyone from The Isle of Wight before.'

If I had a pound for every person that ever uttered those words to me, I would be a millionaire. I used to get it all the time in Scotland.

'What's it like?' Curiosity tainted his tone.

'It's small, pretty, but over-populated. Touristy in the summer, and like a retirement village in winter.' I'd had practice at summarising it quickly over the years. Conversation usually then followed the same route, people tended to ask if it was tax free, like Jersey (it wasn't and neither was Jersey for that matter). Or they asked about house prices.

'And what are the house prices like?' So predictable.

'Slightly cheaper than the rest of southern England, because it's not exactly an ideal commute to London, having to get the ferry every day.' It rolled off the tongue at this stage.

Thankfully, the flight attendant arrived with the beverages. If I couldn't read my Kindle in peace, I was at least going to have a glass of wine.

'Can I get you a drink?' he offered.

'I'll have a glass of wine, but I'll get it myself thank you. I'll get you one if you like?'

'Red or white?' he asked, as she approached with the trolley.

'Red please. Have you any Malbec?' I was more than capable of buying my own drink.

'I'll have the same thank you,' he chipped in over me and handed her a twenty euro note. If I didn't already feel obliged to make small talk for the next hour, I did then.

He seemed like a nice man, but I'd been making small talk with patients all day and I was exhausted with it.

'So, what about you?' I asked, more out of politeness than interest. The hostess moved on to serve the passengers in the seats behind us.

'I'm a dentist,' he said. I nearly choked on my glass of wine.

'You're kidding?' Such a coincidence.

'Do I look like I'm joking?' he said, with a perfectly straight but definitely unwhitened smile.

'Just a massive coincidence. I'm a hygienist,' I told him, and he chuckled.

'Birds of a feather flock together.' He smiled at me with a shared understanding.

'Where did you study?' It was par for the course; it was such a small world we probably shared some of the same colleagues along the way.

'Birmingham. Mind you, that was a good few years ago now. What about you?'

'Edinburgh,' I said.

'And do you enjoy being a hygienist?' He seemed to genuinely wonder.

'I absolutely love it. I get all the benefits of working with the patients, but without the full responsibility of being the dentist. And I'd honestly hate to make dentures and do root canal treatment.' The shudder that ripped through my shoulders appeared to amuse him.

'Do you like being a dentist?'

'I used to. But now there is so much red tape and paperwork. I spend more time writing up notes for patients than actually treating them.' He sighed.

'I can relate.' Every second page in the tabloids held an advert with a 'no win no fee' offer of legal advice for dental negligence.

'It's one of the reasons I'm moving home. Things are still a bit simpler in the west of Ireland. We are about twenty years behind the UK. Hopefully I'll be retired before all the fine print bullshit is introduced. Excuse my language. I probably have another fifteen years of work left in me, part time that is. I'm too fond of the golf to be working full time these days,' he said.

'So, you're moving home?'

'Yes. My wife is delighted. She wanted to return long ago, but the kids were in college and it was never the right time. But now, I have a son who is a teacher in Dubai and another who's an engineer in Canada. If we don't make the move now, we never will. It's a good time to buy in Ireland again now. Not good for them, of course.' He was referring to the crash after The Celtic Tiger era.

'So, do you have a job to go to?' I was curious about him starting again at his age, fair play to him.

'No. I bought over a dental surgery in a town called Ballina. I'm going to renovate it and extend. I'm hoping to have it up and running early in the new year. Have you heard of Ballina?' He asked, before taking a sip of his wine.

You couldn't make it up. It was almost funny.

'My boyfriend is from Killala,' I said. I still hadn't got this stranger's name, or given him mine.

'My wife is actually from Killala. I bet she'd know your boyfriend, or his family at least.'

'I'm Patrick, by the way.' He extended his right hand clumsily over the arm rest. 'Patrick O'Mara.'

'I'm Lucy O'Connor, it's a pleasure to meet you.' I meant it. The conversation had turned out to be far more interesting than I'd anticipated. It had been worth downing the Kindle for.

'So, Lucy, where are you working now? If you're flying out of London, I can only presume you're no longer in Edinburgh?'

'I work in Winchester. I've actually got two lovely places, I'm lucky.' Good jobs were hard to find, regardless of any profession. I was lucky I loved both places. I'd heard horror stories from some of my hygienist friends about unpaid invoices, no nursing support and blunt instruments.

'Well, if you happen to be looking for work this side of The Shannon in the new year, I will certainly be looking for a hygienist.' He put his hand into his suit pocket and handed me a business card with Patrick O'Mara embellished above an Irish mobile number.

I took it gratefully. 'Thank you. You never know.' It seemed a lot less unlikely, than it had two months previously.

'What does your man do?'

'He's a farmer.'

'So, you will be looking for a job down the line.' He winked at me, knowing I didn't have a hope in hell of persuading John to move to the UK.

'It's beginning to look that I way...' I was only fully beginning to appreciate the extent of it myself.

We passed the hour with him hypothetically asking what instruments a hygienist would like in a new surgery. I had it in the bag. Thankfully, I had the foresight to be polite to every human I met, regardless of whether it had been a long day or if I was tired. If my mother was in my position, she'd have called it fate.

I left the flight with a new ally, a potential employer, and a lot more hope than I expected to feel about the uncertainties that lay ahead of me.

John waited for me in his usual spot at the arrival area in Knock, one shoulder leant against the wall, as cool as a cucumber as usual. He wore a close-cut navy jumper that depicted the blue of his eyes. I was so utterly obsessed with him; I was sure that every other woman in the world must want him. Clara and Katie assured me that wasn't the case.

A flicker of excitement crossed his even features as he took my bag from me. 'You look good enough to eat,' he whispered in my ear, and kissed me.

'You look pretty good yourself.' I revelled in the security of his strong arms around me, his chest against mine.

'If only we didn't have to go straight to my mother's house, I'd have those clothes off you before you got up the stairs.' His eyes ran the length of me.

'Promises, promises. I'm looking forward to dinner at your mum's. And I can't wait to meet your sister.'

'She's a headcase. You will love her,' he promised, as he helped me into his car.

It was dusk. The sun had set in the midnight blue sky, and I was acutely aware that Clara had made a valid point. The clocks were due to change, winter was setting in. I didn't relish the thought of our travel plans being interfered with, when the little time we spent together was so precious.

'So, I only got a job offer on the flight.'

'What kind of job?' He glanced at me, his eyebrows knitting together, immediately suspicious.

'The guy in the seat next to me was a dentist.' My voice echoed a level of smugness that I couldn't hide.

'You are unreal. Where is the surgery?'

'He bought a practice in Ballina. He's renovating it, hoping to open in the new year.' I Googled his name while John drove us through the winding country lanes. A picture from his LinkedIn page appeared in the search results, and I flashed it under John's nose.

'You are the jammiest woman I know. Luck just seems to follow you.' From the tone of his voice, I gathered he was excited.

'Well, he didn't actually offer me the job, but he said he'd be looking for a hygienist in the new year. Besides, I'm sure I used all my luck up the night I met you.' I winked at him, refusing to count my chickens.

'You have it in the bag, honey, and you know you do.' He slapped my thigh, openly ecstatic with the evening's developments.

'You can't fight fate.' He quoted me.

'Hmm. We'll see.'

'We should celebrate.'

'Not yet. I don't want to jinx things.' I was adamant. 'And let's keep it between us for now, it mightn't come to anything yet.'

I recognised the landmarks we passed all the way from the airport to Killala. I could drive from the airport to John's house myself at this stage. As we turned a bend in the road, a herd of cattle were being moved from one field to another, completely blocking the road.

'Traffic jam?'

'Welcome to the west, honey. Country life. We could be here all fucking night.' He tapped the steering wheel impatiently and sighed at the hold up.

We crawled along the narrow road, a few feet at a time, before John pulled off the road into a small by-road. He engaged the handbrake and undid my seatbelt.

'If we're delayed, we're delayed. There isn't a lot we can do about it. But I'm damned sure I'm going to make the most of twenty minutes alone with you.' He pulled me over the armrest and onto his lap, as though I weighed nothing. I squealed, struggling to get a leg either side of him to comfortably sit on his lap.

He pushed his hands under my jumper dress, they were freezing cold from the steering wheel.

'Can I help you with something, Mr Kelly?' I whispered into his left ear.

It was only just beginning to get dark, but he didn't seem to care. Neither did I for that matter. I knew what he wanted. As if we hadn't already given the neighbours enough to talk about.

'You certainly can,' he murmured, kissing my neck and rubbing his hands over my bra and pulling it down shamelessly.

As his fingers traced the lace borders of my stockings, I could feel his excitement beneath me. Placing his finger in my mouth, I sucked it lightly, using my other hand to undo his jeans. He pulled up my dress, kissing my breasts, the fact we could get caught only adding to our excitement. He pulled my underwear to the side and straddled him, both of us groaning with pleasure as I slid up and down the length of him. Neither of us lasted long. He pushed his face into my chest to muffle the sound of his climax.

'You are one seriously sexy cat.' His head fell forward onto my chest.

'You bring out the best in me.' I assured him, secretly surprised at my lack of inhibition. He drove us back onto the main road again, the 'traffic' clear, and both of us satisfied, for the short-term at least.

. . .

'Where were ye?' Mama Bear asked, opening the front door wide and kissing both of us on the cheek as a welcome.

'That flute, Freddie thought Friday evening was a great time to move his cattle. We were stuck there for about twenty minutes.' John winked at me over her shoulder.

'Come in. Come in. Welcome home,' she said warmly.

John's parents' house was a beautiful four-bedroomed bungalow which also backed onto the sea but at an outlet slightly further on from John's house. It was warm and cosy; the open fire roared as we were led into the sitting room.

A short auburn-haired girl, who looked no more than fourteen-years-old sprinted across the wide hallway and flung her arms around John's neck happily.

'How's my big brother?' Her tone was a mocking, babyish one, as she squeezed his cheeks between her fingers.

'Have you got your heels on, Hannah?' He delivered a friendly dig on the arm, referring to the fact that short as she was, she'd actually managed to reach his face.

'Lucy?' She opened her arms, offering a warm embrace.

'Jesus, how did he pull you? It must have been the accent that got you, was it?' She joked at her brother's expense, and for all the piss taking, it was clear to everyone in the room the two absolutely adored each other. I wondered for a split second would I ever get used to this culture, where every insult was intended to be more endearing than the last.

'Where's that bull of yours?' John asked, looking around the room for Hannah's husband, Matthew.

'Ah, working unfortunately. I came with The Two.' She nodded towards the direction of the bedrooms, where the boys were apparently already sleeping.

Papa Bear entered the room at that moment, his hair damp from a recent shower.

'Baby Bear.' He came to me first, enveloping me in a warm hug. I smiled from ear to ear.

'He's still doing it for you, I see,' he acknowledged with a hearty rumble.

'You have no idea.' A vision of only ten minutes earlier flitted through my mind, and I blushed thinking about it.

'Dad.' John greeted his father with a fist pump.

'Are ye hungry?' Mama Bear returned to the sitting room with a tray full of smoked salmon, homemade soda bread, and a bottle of champagne under her left arm.

'Open that will you, love?' She handed the bottle to Graham and returned with five champagne flutes.

'I've a roast lamb in the oven, but it won't be ready for another half an hour. I thought Lucy's flight might be delayed. This will keep ye going for a while.'

John and Hannah pretended to jostle elbows to both get the biggest slice of the soda bread. It was obvious they were very fond of each other, despite the jibing.

'How was the flight, Baby Bear?' John's father asked between mouthfuls of delicious salmon.

'It was grand.' I'd unintentionally adopted their terminology in a subconscious effort to fit in.

'Ah, tell them Lucy!' John urged, handing me a glass of champagne.

'There's nothing to tell yet.' I shot him a warning look, which he blatantly ignored.

'She sat next to a dentist on the plane who happens to be opening a dental practice in Ballina,' he blurted.

'Jeez, John, God forbid it was a secret,' I said, rolling my eyes.

'He can't hold his own piss. He never could,' Hannah told me. I was seeing a different side to John in the comfort of his own home house and his immediate family. He dropped the cool as a cucumber persona, seeming completely relaxed, borderline childlike. It was refreshing to see what lay behind the cool, understated mask. In this environment, his childhood home, he was peeled right back to his boyish self.

'His name wasn't O'Mara by any chance, was it?' Mama Bear asked.

'Actually, it was.' There was no denying it, literally everybody knew everything about everyone else in this tiny town.

'His wife, Breege, was in my sister's class at school, they've been in

England for years.' She confirmed what I already knew. I nodded in agreement, devouring my second slice of soda bread.

'I heard he bought Gilroy's old surgery,' Graham said.

'They could do with knocking the place and rebuilding it if that's the case, never mind renovating it.' John seemed to know the exact site.

'It was a great contact to make, even if nothing comes of it.' One of us had to keep it real here.

'Ahh, we'll make a good country woman of you yet,' Hannah promised me. Despite my initial doubts, the thought of it wasn't as ridiculous as it had once seemed.

Dinner was fabulous. John's mother was an extremely talented chef; the gravy was rich and the meat succulent. We drank two bottles of red wine over the table between us.

'Who is working in the pub?' It suddenly occurred to me.

'My cousin, Charlotte,' Hannah answered.

'How lovely.' Would I ever remember all of these extended relations?

Mary brought in a homemade apple and lemon tart with ice cream for dessert. Even though I was fit to burst, I managed to polish off my portion.

John held my hand under the table, stroking my fingers as they chatted about people I had no knowledge of. I was happy to listen, to enjoy their easy company. I couldn't have been made more welcome anywhere else in the world.

A loud cry echoed across the walls from down the corridor, and Hannah jumped to her feet to grab baby James before he could wake his two-year-old brother up as well. She brought him to the dining room and placed him straight into my arms.

'Here's your aunty-to-be.' She nudged John as I took the baby in my arms.

James wore a baby blue sleep suit and a growbag with tiny blue whales printed over the cotton. I smiled in delight as he looked up at me curiously and pulled his tiny fingers through my hair.

'She has the knack for it, John. Look out!' John's father warned him.

'This time next year, I can just see these two here with their twins! One of them to mind each.' Hannah eyed her baby with a loving look in her eye.

John glanced subtly at me for a reaction, but neither of us commented. The funny thing was, I never wanted children, never considered it as even a remote possibility. Yet here, in this very moment, after consuming a fair few glasses of wine, it seemed to be not an entirely unreasonable prospect. An acute, longing pierced my core, and I wasn't the broody type. I didn't even like kids. But I loved the thought of John's children, imagining their beautiful red hair and Irish accents.

I began to stroke James's fine tufts of blonde hair. Slowly but surely, his eyelids began to flutter. John's mother nodded approvingly as the child slowly drifted back to sleep.

'A natural, I told ye,' Hannah said, taking the child and bringing him back to his bedroom.

'I've a suggestion to make, say no if you don't fancy it. I won't be offended.' Papa Bear rose from the table.

'No, Dad, Lucy doesn't want to leave her keys in the fruit bowl.' John, the joker as ever, made himself laugh.

'You've your mother's sense of humour, son.' Graham dismissed John's joke with the wave of a hand. 'I thought we might take some blankets outside and a few hot whiskeys and look out at the stars. It's such a clear night. Cold but clear.'

'That sounds lovely.'

Graham gathered several woollen blankets from the hot press as Mary boiled the kettle. Outside, we sat on folding fishing chairs; the blankets wrapped around our shoulders.

My breath momentarily clouded my vision as I exhaled into the crisp moonlit night. I'd never felt more alive, here in this foreign country, welcomed as one of John's family, and loved by the most amazing man I had ever met. A deep sense of contentment immersed my soul like never before. I looked up into the clear starry sky with my hot whisky, John's hand loosely entwined in mine. He squeezed it and we exchanged a look. He had me, and he knew it.

Chapter Twenty-Four

SATURDAY 20TH OCTOBER

'Tea or coffee?' John asked, as I walked sleepily into the kitchen and ran my fingers through my bed head of matted curls. He'd been up since the crack of dawn to milk "the girls".

'Coffee please.' I knew I'd had a drink the night before. We had such a fabulous evening in John's parents' house, they were wonderful company. I could see why he considered them friends as much as parents they were so entertaining, frank, funny and open.

They brought their life experiences to the table, and they were more than happy to share them with us. It was such a relaxing environment, everything at their own pace, no rushing or racing, no outside noise, no one disturbing the peace.

I was beginning to appreciate the appeal of living in the countryside. If I wanted to sit outside in Winchester at night, with a hot whiskey and gaze at the stars, the neighbours would think I'd gone off my rocker. Plus, there would be no peace between the man in number 77 coming home drunk and shouting at his wife, the kids in number 79 fighting over whose turn it was on the PlayStation, and every cat in the street screeching out a mating call in hope of a little company. There was no comparison really.

I'd always considered city living as the better quality of life, but my eyes slowly opened to another way. It was astonishing really; I was preferring this way of life. The houses in estates and apartments in the city that previously seemed so ideal, convenient and perfectly centrally situated, now seemed overcrowded and claustrophobic. I liked the privacy and the peace of the country.

'You have to do it all over again tonight, honey.' John reminded me, putting his arms around my waist and nuzzling his face into my neck, bringing me back to the present.

We'd arranged to go out for dinner with the neighbours, Jane and Trisha and their husbands, who both happened to be called Michael. I was looking forward to it. I couldn't wait to get to know both women better. Trisha was like an open book, shameless, hilarious and lots of fun. Jane was more private, slightly more reserved, very classy, and she had a sensitive side to her which really appealed to me. Both women were absolutely beautiful in their own ways.

'Do you think I could get my hair blow dried in town this afternoon?' I asked John, sorry I hadn't thought to book something earlier.

'Sure. My friend's girlfriend is a hairdresser. I'll ring her now for you.' He Googled the number on his phone and once he got past the pleasantries, he had an appointment booked for me less than a minute later. Another advantage to living in a small place. If I were looking to get an appointment like that on a Saturday in Winchester, I'd have had to ring around about ten salons, praying one of them had a cancellation.

John dropped me in town half an hour later and told me to ring him when I'd finished. He was going to carry on with a few more jobs while he had the chance. Hopefully that would mean he could lie in with me in the morning.

The salon, Bella Hair & Beauty, was modern and bright and overlooked the fast-flowing river Moy.

'Lucy?' A blond petite girl asked.

'That's me.' Probably the only stranger in the place.

'Come on over.' She motioned to the vacant chair and placed a black waterproof gown around me. 'I can't tell you how nice it is to meet you.'

Was there anyone in this town who hadn't heard about John Kelly's married woman from England? My accent gave me away, in case my face didn't.

'Thank you.' I didn't really know what to say, because I was still none the wiser as to who she really was.

'I'm Natalie. I believe you met my husband-to-be, Luke, already. On the stag,' she reminded me.

'Your husband was the stag?'

'Yep. They certainly came home with a few stories.' She giggled.

'Everyone has a story.'

'So, what are we doing?' She ran her fingers through my long hair.

'A curly blow dry, please.' She led me over to the basin.

'Will you make it home for the wedding?' Natalie asked, lathering soap onto my scalp.

'Oh, I don't know.' I hadn't thought about it, but now she mentioned it, John had said there was a wedding in December he wanted me to accompany him to. It must be the one and the same.

'You should come. It will be a good day,' she said, rinsing the shampoo off.

When she finished, I rang John to collect me. The salon was a ten-minute drive from his house, (a real ten minutes, not an Irish one). I sat in the waiting area and watched the people of the town pass by the window.

No matter what walk of life you came from, whichever way you look at it, people are more or less all the same all over the world. Everyone so consumed in their own life, their problems, their joys, or just getting from one day to the next. I watched a harassed mother battling to get twin boys and a toddler safely over the pedestrian crossing, a shabby looking old man smoking a pipe as he walked aimlessly down the street, and a teenage couple hand in hand laughing at some private joke.

Something inside changed. I don't know if it was my attitude or perspective, or just the events of the year that enabled me to see things differently. I felt more content, beginning to notice the small things in life were actually the big things. Until I'd met John, I always focused on the big things; the holidays, the next night out, the next class I could enrol in. I constantly searched for the next thing to occupy the gaping void in my life and to validate myself.

John pulled up outside double parking on the pavement like he owned the place. He had no problem doing exactly what suited him. Part of me admired him for it, and part wondered if it was a good trait that he was used to doing whatever he pleased with no repercussions. He waved at Natalie through the window and gave her a thumbs up.

'Want to go for a drive?' he said, after complimenting my hair and assuring me they only had the best hairdressers in the west of Ireland. Yet another incentive to entice me to move.

'Sure. Why not.'

'What did you think of Natalie?'

'She's lovely,' I said.

'Will you come to the wedding with me?' He placed his hand in its usual position on my lap, as he drove one-handed through the small town, nodding at most of the passers-by in greeting.

'Is it not a bit odd that I don't know them though?'

'Not at all, honey. There will probably be three or four hundred people there.'

'Wow. I don't think I know three hundred people. Well, apart from my patients. But I wouldn't be inviting them to a wedding.'

'Would you be inviting me to a wedding?' he asked, his full lips curling into a cheeky smirk. I knew exactly what he was implying. It was more of a "Would you invite me to a wedding if we were the ones getting married," rather than bringing him as a guest.

'One day maybe, if you're good.' I glanced sideways at him and he laughed.

The thought of getting married again was oddly enough something I would consider, in the right circumstances. Although I had always assured my friends and mother if I ever got out of the first one, I'd never tie myself to a person in that way again. But the thought of being tied to John literally and figuratively was overwhelmingly appealing.

He was without a doubt my favourite person on the planet. It was exactly the opposite to what Clara had predicted, instead of the excitement wearing off, it seemed to grow. My need to be with him was just as strong if not stronger than it was before. He physically drew me to him. I felt whole with him, like there was nothing else in the world was as important as us being together. Our relationship was still new to both of us, but it was glaringly obvious it was on a higher level to anything either of us had experienced before. I'd only been pretending to play grown-ups before. There was nothing pretend about my feelings for John. They were so real, they were openly raw in places.

The only thing that frightened me, was that if John Kelly were ever to hurt me, I feared I would ever physically recover. I prayed to God that would never happen, because I simply didn't know what I'd do without him.

————

The restaurant was in an old majestic looking castle called Belleek. It had been restored to its original glory, on the edge of the woodlands only five minutes outside of Ballina. The drive to it was slow and steep. It was unfortunately too dark to appreciate much of the scenery.

I wore a black jumpsuit teamed with cream heels and my favourite cream Mulberry clutch bag, aiming for understated, with a hint of sexy, like my boyfriend. He looked so good in a pair of navy slacks and a white shirt that I'd happily have eaten him instead of dinner.

'This place used to be a disco, years ago. Mam and Dad could tell you a few stories about it.' I didn't doubt it for a second.

The ceilings were high, and the stone walls and floor looked cold, but the roaring open fires were welcomingly warm. Jane, Trisha and the two Michaels sat on antique looking armchairs in the bar area, menus on their laps and drinks in their hands.

'Lucy.' Trisha bounded up, giving me a huge bear squeeze again.

'I love your dress,' I said.

'Penny's finest,' she said, dusting off the black long-sleeved fitted pencil dress proudly. When you had a figure like hers, you could wear a bin bag and look fabulous.

'Hi Jane.'

Jane had her own style, sporting a high neck burgundy long-sleeved chiffon top and a tasteful black leather skirt, thick tights and suede ankle boots. Her make-up was a work of art. The boys shook hands in greeting, and we ordered more drinks before heading to the dining room.

The dining room had cold stone flooring, low ceilings with wooden beams and low hanging lanterns. Cream coloured candles were carefully positioned on each table. The worrywart in me screamed fire hazard, though the ambience was relaxing and romantic. Several other couples were already seated; the quiet hum of chat could barely be heard over the tinkling music from a pianist playing in the corner. John sat opposite me on the same side as the two Michaels, and I sat in between Jane and Trisha.

'We've never done this before.' Trisha announced loudly, and we laughed. 'What?' She looked slightly put out. 'I'm only saying John never had anyone to bring before.'

'Thanks, Trisha, keep digging,' John said, as the boys sniggered together.

'It's maybe not that he didn't have anyone to bring, Trisha, more like maybe he didn't have anyone he wanted to bring before.' Jane tried to sensitively correct her friend and neighbour.

'Well, as neighbours, I'm just saying this is the first time we've all been out for dinner together.'

'The way you're going, Trisha, it will probably be the last,' warned her boyfriend with a laugh.

The waiter interrupted to disclose the specials and take our order. I glanced around, taking it all in. It was like being in a time warp, suits of armour hung on the wall and flags with proud family crests were mounted for all to see.

I was happier than I ever thought I could be only a few short months ago, surrounded by these new friends I had only just met, yet I felt so comfortable with them already.

John sat back from the table; his arms folded over his chest subtly observing my interactions with the girls as he made small talk with the men. He was trying hard to line everything up for me, to make moving here a viable option; the support of his family, new female friends, now possibly even a job on the cards, thanks to last night's encounter.

Jane and Trisha described their favourite hotels in Ireland, insisting which ones John had to bring me to, by the sound of it, there was an abundance of them. I mentally tried to remember a few. Their company was effortless, and I had a deep satisfying feeling I was finally fitting in somehow. I was happier than I had been in years. John gazed at me across the table, he knew exactly what I was thinking, a small smile playing on his lips as he leaned across and took my hand.

Chapter Twenty-Five

SUNDAY 21ST OCTOBER

Leaving John had become the hardest part of my week. I hated walking through the departure lounge knowing there was an ocean between us until the next time. I hated that I couldn't just jump in the car and get to him, that I had to rely on flight schedules, trains and boats. Such a lot of variants that could go wrong.

For all my previous ways of longing for, and needing plans, I found myself longing not to have to make a plan; just wake up and be there and do as we felt on that day.

Times were changing. I barely recognised the person I was when I with John, but I liked her. I was stronger, happier, and way more confident.

Regular travelling meant permanently readjusting to the completely different cultures. Despite being only an hour's flight away, the people and the way of life were light years apart. I went from the quiet, remote solitude of John's country house and family, to landing into chaos on the motorway, traffic jams (not ones consisting of cattle), long, drawn-out diversions, toll roads and people everywhere swarming the streets like ants. By Friday I was used to city life again and when I landed in Knock again the serenity and laid-back attitude to life seemed to shock me again. I was all over the shop. It was one extreme to another.

I couldn't go on like this and we both knew it. But was it too soon to take up and leave and start again completely? I didn't know. When I was away from John, a part of me still worried it was too good to be true, and it wouldn't last. Why should our love be different to anyone before us? The ones I'd seen soar high, full of excitement, wonder, and promise, before crashing and burning, hitting the ground at high speed; an accident destined to happen.

When I was with him, I was in absolutely no doubt. It was the other half of the week I struggled with.

Chapter Twenty-Six

SATURDAY 27TH OCTOBER

It was Katie's thirtieth birthday, and I wasn't going to Ireland. The thought of not spending the weekend with John filled me with dread, even borderline panic. I was jittery without his reassuring presence. It was hard enough to do the weekdays without him, let alone the weekend as well. I was convinced in my absence he'd realise he was far too good for me. This side of the Irish Sea, I doubted myself, doubted the logistics, doubted everything.

Did everybody feel so insecure at the start of a new relationship? It wasn't a feeling I was used to, and not one I liked either. It was a roller-coaster, and I hate fairground rides. The high was so extreme, half the week I was ecstatic to be with John, surviving all the long hours travelling on adrenaline, beyond excited. But the other half of the week was often abysmal without him. I kept busy between work and my friends, but the aching for him was unbearable. The distance was a permanent reminder of our separate lives. I felt almost paranoid when I couldn't get hold of him, not because I didn't trust him, but because I didn't trust him fully not to break my heart in some way. Part of me felt that would be karma for leaving Rob for him.

In the darkness, when sleep eluded me, I was my own worst critic. The demons continued to haunt me, questioning whether I deserved to be happy after everything that had happened. Maybe it would be healthy in the long run for me to have a weekend away from my new-found love obsession.

Rhinefield house was on the bucket list. We'd made a list when we left college of all the places we would go to when we started earning proper money and this fabulous hotel caught my eye; a luxurious listed building steeped in history, and almost on my doorstep. As I checked in, I was apprehensive but excited to be reunited with my trusty sidekick, Raquelle. Nobody could feel down in her company. This was the woman who sang Sinead O'Connor at karaoke like her life (and eyelashes) depended on it. Passionate, off key perhaps, but she made up for it one hundred percent in enthusiasm.

Afternoon tea was booked for three o'clock. I had enough time to dump my belongings in the room and touch up my make-up before meeting the gang. The rooms were plush and traditional; heavy burgundy drapes hung as curtains in the room, and complimentary chocolates sat on my perfectly plumped pillow.

I put on a long-sleeved black dress, aiming for simple yet sophisticated, sprayed my signature Chanel Chance and headed down the wide, lantern lit corridors to be reunited with my girls.

The drawing room was an enormous circular space with a triple height dome like ceiling. Mahogany bookcases lined the walls from the floor to almost the roof and held every type of book imaginable. I was in absolute awe. I could have happily sat there alone, leafing through the mountain of wonderous literature.

'There you are,' a voice whispered in my ear, startling me.

'Rach!' I flung my arms around her tightly. The girl was like a sister to me. I had told her my deepest darkest secrets, when I was too ashamed to even say them aloud to myself.

'Have you bitches forgotten it's my birthday? Break up the love affair.' Katie landed on top of the both of us.

'Is it really?' I feigned shock. 'We'd completely forgotten, if I had known I would have brought you a gift.' I smiled and pulled out a Jo Malone bag from behind my back.

'Happy birthday, sweetheart. Hope thirty is your best year yet.' I squeezed her tightly in a warm embrace. It was like old times, back in the college days where we were the only family we had.

'Where's Theresa?' I asked, looking round.

'Ha. Late as usual. Do you even have to ask?'

We took our seats at a table in the window, overlooking the flower beds.

In she walked then, as glamorous as ever. Theresa was our Irish friend from the Hygiene School. Typically Celtic, she had pale skin, brown hair and blue eyes. She was far cooler than any of us, following fashion closely. Some of her outfits were light years ahead of us, yet she carried them with confidence and style. Today was no different; she rocked a pair of slim-fitting high waisted navy slacks and a cream lace high necked body suit, pearl jewellery and a vintage hair slide.

'Better late than never, bitches.' She shrugged, waiting for the slagging she knew was coming her way.

'Ah, you're early really, Theresa. For you anyway. I expected you to turn up at my fortieth, a decade late.' Katie fondly embraced her.

'Well... neighbour?' Theresa turned to me. 'Quite the dark horse here...' She nudged me, prodding for more information. I'd never actually thought about it before, geography wasn't my strong point, but Mayo borders Galway. It was another pro for Ireland, in these searching times.

'I actually completely forgot you're in the next county! I promise you I will come and see you before Christmas.' It would be a great excuse to get John out of Mayo for a day, maybe we could do an overnight.

'Ladies.' A smartly dressed gentleman approached us to take our drinks order.

'Champagne please,' we answered unanimously, giggling in the process; the sound echoed round the huge library.

The waiter returned less than five minutes later with a bottle of Bollinger and four champagne flutes. He proceeded to pop the cork and pour a glass for each of us, assuring us the afternoon tea would arrive shortly.

It was such a treat to be together. Days like these were few and far between. I'd forgotten how therapeutic a drink with this lot could be.

Afternoon tea did not disappoint; the sandwiches were made from fresh homemade breads, the smoked salmon was divine and the warm fruit scones were served with fresh clotted cream and homemade raspberry jam.

'Oh, my goodness. I think I have eaten my own weight in clotted cream,' Rachel said, patting her non-existent stomach.

'Shut up,' Theresa said, rolling her eyes. 'If you turned sideways, we'd wonder where you went.'

We were used to Rachel's obsession with her weight. She had a fabulous figure, but she claimed she was a heavy child, and the fear of her weight escalating again seemed to forever haunt her. Yet another reminder that everyone had their own demons.

'So, I've got some news.' Bright eyes glanced excitedly round the table.

'Go on!' I urged, eager for some good news.

'You're pregnant?' Katie guessed. Since she had two babies, it was her initial thought. She was desperate for the day that we would join her in the unpredictable journey of motherhood, promising it to be the greatest thing in the world, but the hardest work known to man, and woman. We'd had a detailed description of both of her labours and she really didn't sell it.

'Don't be daft, Katie.' Rachel brushed her hand in front of her face. 'Or are you trying to say I have put weight on?'

'Put us out of our misery for God's sake, Rach!' Theresa begged.

'I'm getting a boob job,' she announced proudly while we sat with our mouths open, expecting her to say anything other than that. She'd mentioned many times over the years that she wanted to. If it bothered her, then she was as well to do something about it.

'Well fair play to you, Rachel,' I said raising my glass. 'You always said you would.'

'To Rachel's new boobs,' Theresa said. We clinked glasses in a toast.

'Huh-hmm,' Katie coughed to remind us that it was actually her birthday.

'Happy Birthday, Katie.' We chorused like schoolgirls and I signalled the waiter to bring us another bottle over.

Rachel had her surgery booked for two weeks-time and had paid a hefty deposit to a private clinic on George Street.

'So, no babies...' Katie said, cupping her chin in her hands with a pronounced pout.

'Well... I wasn't going to mention it... but...' Theresa began with an enormous smile.

'Oh my God!' Katie jumped off her seat and threw herself at Theresa.

'Best birthday present ever,' she squealed with delight. 'How far gone are you? There's not a pick on you still.'

'Thirteen weeks.' She placed her hand over her flat stomach in a protective gesture.

'Congratulations.' Rachel and I got up and hugged her, though we knew she secretly hated it. She never had been, nor ever would be a hugger. She awkwardly returned the cuddle, patting us each on the back as we teased her about her loath of PDAs.

'I'm so happy for you both,' Rachel said. Theresa's husband Patrick was a lovely guy from a large family. Family was very important to both of them.

'I can't believe it. This is the best birthday present ever.' Katie repeated, naming all the nursery treasures she had kept for whichever one of us would be next.

'Looks like it's just you and me left doll,' Rachel whispered quietly as Katie grilled Theresa on the details of her pregnancy.

Rachel and I had always previously been on the same page when it came to wanting kids. I thought better of telling her I would actually birth John Kelly's babies in the morning.

Chapter Twenty-Seven

FRIDAY 2ND NOVEMBER

Two weeks was an awful long time to go without seeing John, even with the daily FaceTimes, calls and texts. The weekend apart had reminded me, part of me was missing when we were apart.

He apparently felt the same, pouncing on me as soon as he got me through the front door, taking me there and then on the island in his kitchen. Afterwards we lay together, sprawled out on the couch in the sunroom, arms wrapped around each other tightly, listening to the rhythmic sound of the sea only a few metres away, a bottle of red wine breathing on the coffee table next to us. He sat up slowly and poured a glass for each of us.

'I missed you, girl.' A sincerity exuded from his startling blue eyes, but the worrywart wondered if there was a 'but' coming.

He opened his mouth a couple of times, but seemingly thought better of it, closing it again just as quickly, further igniting my niggling worry.

'I missed you too, so much.' I clasped his hands in mine, holding them tightly. 'Is everything ok?'

'Everything is fine,' he assured me. 'It's just...' There was that unspoken 'but' again. Did he have something to confess? It was hard to shift my suspicious nature; I was naturally insecure, coming from a family where my father had affairs regularly. Could something have happened last weekend when I wasn't here? I felt sick thinking about it.

The devil on my shoulder whispered it would only be what I deserved after leaving Rob. Who did I think I was? It reminded me.

I had to mentally slap myself. For God's sake, the man just told me he missed me, and he certainly showed me how much not ten minutes earlier. I held my breath, silently forcing a small smile, willing him to tell me whatever it was he needed to get off his chest.

'It's just...' he started but stopped again immediately in order to take a sip of his wine, for what seemed like a lifetime. In reality, it was probably only seconds. 'I... I love you.' His words were softly spoken, almost shy.

My lips curled into an almighty grin; sweet relief sailed through my core. It wasn't the first time he'd said it, but it was the first time he intentionally said it. My cocky, confident, self-assured, cool as a cucumber boyfriend was feeling shy about saying that of all things. My heart soared.

'I love you too, John,' I told him fiercely. 'I have done from almost the second I laid eyes on you.'

'Phew. That could have been awkward.' He pretended to wipe the sweat off of his brow with the back of his hand. Crisis averted. Placing his arms round me again, he guided my head to rest on his chest and shuffled backwards onto the couch trying to find a position that was comfortable for both of us. I breathed his masculine scent, my favourite smell in the entire world. I wished I could bottle it.

'The thing is, Lucy, I know we said we'd talk about it at Christmas, but I can't stop thinking about everything. I want you here. All the time.' He glanced down at me as he spoke, gauging my reaction.

'Ah.' I always knew it would come to this. I knew he'd never leave his life here. And why should he? He had everything; his work, his home, his family, the farm. Recently, I'd come to appreciate the attraction of living here; the countryside, more space, the advantages of living in a small community. And, in fairness, I'd already made a couple of friends, thanks to him. There was also the possibility of a new job in the not-too-distant future.

Though the thought of moving over permanently became increasingly appealing, I still couldn't be sure I was ready. It was a massive commitment.

The prospect of being with John daily would win out at some point though, I had known it deep down for a long time. It was inevitable.

'Is that an *ah* yes or an *ah* no?' He looked at me tentatively.

'It's not a no,' I said quickly, desperate for him to know I wanted to be with him.

'But?' It was his turn to wonder.

'I'm mad about you, John Kelly. I have been since the minute I met you. I've said it numerous times. I'd go anywhere in the world to be with you. I love you.' It rolled off the tongue a lot easier the second time.

'You're holding something back from me.' He was as intuitive as ever.

'What if I give up my job, give up my life as I know it, move over here and then all of a sudden you see something in me that you don't like?'

We both knew only too well that was the way things had always been for him before. I did not want to end up on that list. I needed to be one hundred percent sure.

'I can tell you now, you are nothing like anyone I have ever been with before,' he assured me. 'I dread the day you ever get those eyes tested and see what you've landed yourself with.' He attempted to make light of the situation, but I couldn't bring myself to even smile.

Sensing it was a matter that was above his usual humorous diversions, he tried again.

'Lucy, I know it, I've known it for a long time, that you are the woman I've been waiting for. I wish you could just trust what we have and go with it. I promise I will never let you down.'

'You mightn't mean to...' I whispered, overcome with emotion all of a sudden.

'I'm not your father,' he said gently.

He pulled me into his arms again and held me quietly, letting me have a few moments to gather my thoughts.

'You don't need to decide immediately. I'm not going anywhere, but you're as well to know how I feel at this stage. I can't really go anywhere, Luce. I'm not in a position to move countries and in all honesty, you know that I don't want to. I know it's a massive ask on you, but I promise you, I will make it worth it. We could be so happy here together. I want to wake up with you every day.'

'More wine, please.' I held out my glass for a top up, deliberately changing the subject. We both knew this was coming. He'd said what we both knew needed saying if our relationship was going to progress. I was ecstatic he felt that way. I so badly wanted to be different to the ones before me. But it was daunting when I said 'moving countries' out loud.

He topped up my glass and kicked his feet up on to the couch. His arms resumed their position around my shoulders.

'I can't believe I had to say it first. Twice,' he said referring to the earlier 'I love you'.

I laughed, releasing a build-up of nervous energy. Our relationship had progressed to the next stage.

Chapter Twenty-Eight

TUESDAY 13TH NOVEMBER

The white envelope in my scrub top pocket, practically burned a hole through the fabric. I felt the weight of its intention so acutely. I scrolled down the list of today's patients on the computer screen to find I had several of my favourites booked in.

At ten-thirty there was Alison, a sixty-three-year-old grandmother who had sole care of her only granddaughter because her own daughter was unfit to parent her; she was a heroin addict who had repeatedly fallen off the Methadone Weaning Programme, desperately searching for her next hit. Alison's stress levels were usually through the roof, and subsequently her desquamative gum condition flared up regularly and painfully enough for her to attend my appointments at least every ten weeks. We'd built up a great relationship over the last four years and she often confided her problems, grateful to have an ear to listen with the knowledge it was in complete confidence. She'd had a hard life; I didn't envy her.

My eleven o'clock patient was a gentleman who, two years ago, had been diagnosed with prostate cancer. It had thankfully been caught in time and treated. He was now recovering well.

My eleven-thirty patient was a fourteen-year-old school girl, who had almost as many fillings as she did teeth. Her mother had booked her in with me to discuss her oral hygiene habits and sugar consumption.

Twelve o'clock was a new patient I had never met before. Notes stated he was a thirty-four-year-old smoker with no other medical conditions.

And twelve-thirty was one of my favourite patients who I'd treated for periodontal disease from my very first day at Appollo, seeing him every three months without fail ever since.

This was what was hard to leave. If only I could live with John and bring my favourite practice and patients with me. Unfortunately, life didn't work that way and I had to make a choice.

———

'You're leaving?' Maria said, shocked at my news.

As far as bosses go, she was the best I'd ever had, more than fair, generous and loyal. And an overall lovely human being. I couldn't have got through the last few months without her, and my other lovely colleagues who brightened my day just by being there. They had been my constants, never judging, always supportive.

'If I don't go, I'll always wonder. I'm sorry.' I hung my head. She had been so good to me.

'I can't say I'm entirely surprised. I'm just shocked at the timing. It seems very soon, Lucy.' She was disappointed to be losing me, but a maternal concern glinted in her chocolate-coloured eyes.

I could imagine what it looked like from the outside. The rebound. I'd thought of it all, and what other people thought was no longer significant. The only thing that mattered was being with John.

If it didn't work out, I could move home. Okay, she would have found a replacement for me by then, but I could wait in the wings and hope for maternity cover down the line. I prayed it wouldn't come to that. Prayed I was making the right decision.

I agreed on Sunday to try it. The thought of leaving him again for another long week ripped my insides apart. We'd both wish the hours away until the weekend began again. And the weather was turning, flights and trains would become unpredictable and impractical. John was over the moon.

I needed to be with him. It was that simple.

'Are you sure?' She reluctantly took the envelope from my trembling hands.

'I'm not sure of anything. Apart from that, I need to be with him,' I told her honestly.

'I wish you all the best. I hope it works out for you, really, I do. I'll always have a job for you, if you ever decide to come home. I mean it.' She placed a warm hand on my back, as she opened her office door.

Clara sat behind her computer on reception, her face pointed into a downward pinch. She knew exactly what I had done, and I got the distinct impression she wasn't impressed.

'Wednesday Wine Club?' I suggested the usual midweek drink.

'I've got an awful feeling I'm going to need one.' She flicked her black hair back from her shoulders, eyebrows raised. I blew her a kiss as I walked into my surgery, holding back the tears.

Chapter Twenty-Nine

WEDNESDAY 14TH NOVEMBER

I sat in the usual spot in the Italian restaurant, waiting for my mother to arrive, pretty sure she would be even less pleased than Maria and Clara about my news. She arrived, the image of glamour in a slim-fitting pencil dress, attracting stares from the neighbouring tables. She could easily pass for forty instead of fifty. I only hoped I got those genetics.

'Hello, darling.' She pecked my cheek, no doubt leaving her usual trademark cerise lipstick all over me, and slid into the seat opposite, already looking round for the waiter to order our usual glass of wine.

'Mum. You look great. How are you?'

'Good, darling, thanks. I'd be better if I could get a glass of wine, it's been a long day.' My mum worked as an administrative manager in the hospital.

The waiter must have felt eyes penetrating the back of his head as he cleared a nearby table. He came over immediately after he had finished.

'I'll have a glass of red please.' She gestured for him to bring another one for me as well. However much she thought she needed it before, she surely would in a few minutes.

'So, what's up?' She turned her attention to me, lines of concern creasing her forehead.

'Nothing's up.' I took an enormous gulp of my wine.

'Sweetie, I knew you before you even knew yourself. What's eating you?'

May as well crack on with it so. 'I resigned. From Maria's.'

'What? Why would you do that? You love that job.' Surprise formed in her features, and no wonder. I'd repeatedly told her how much I adored working there.

I looked down at the table, trying to find the right words to tell her I was leaving.

'It's him, isn't it?' It suddenly dawned on her.

I nodded my head, lost for words.

'Honey, do you not think it's a bit soon? For God's sake, the ink is barely dry on your divorce papers.' She was worried, but I also sensed a little anger with me for leaving her again. I hated disappointing her, and that was exactly what I was doing.

'I love him, Mum. I've just got this undeniable feeling in my gut that it's the right thing. I really think he is the one.'

'You know I'm all about the gut instinct, Lucy, and I hate to say it, but you thought you were doing the right thing when you married Rob – look how that turned out.' Ouch. Talk about brutally honest. Not many people could get away with it, but if my own mother couldn't tell me straight, then nobody could.

'Everyone makes mistakes, Mum,' I reminded her gently.

'I just want the best for you,' she said. 'And I don't think running off to Ireland is going to solve your problems.'

'I'm not running anywhere. I gave Maria eight-weeks-notice, but the way Christmas is falling with holidays my last day will be Thursday the twentieth of December.'

'That's only six weeks away,' she exclaimed. 'Do you really think this is the right choice? Is it not just an infatuation? The seven year itch maybe?' She tried to reason with me.

'I've never felt an itch like it, if that's what it is.'

'I'm worried about you. And I hate the thought of losing you again,' she confessed.

'It's not far, Mum.' I may as well have been talking to the wall.

'I suppose you're young. If it doesn't work out, you can always come home,' she conceded, taking another sip of her drink.

'Thanks for the vote of confidence.' I raised my eyebrows in disdain.

'Sorry, Lucy, if I'm not overjoyed at the prospect of losing you again. You'll know yourself one day when you have children.' I absolutely hated it when she used that line.

'Look, Mum, it's not like I'm going to Australia. It's an hour flight away. And like you said, if it doesn't work out, I can come home. I need to go, to try. Or else I'll never know. Maybe you're right, maybe the whole thing will blow up in my face, maybe that's exactly what I deserve after leaving Rob. Who knows? But if I don't go, I will wonder for the rest of my life. I can't lose him.'

She seemed to get the message for now as she sat back in her chair, the immediate tension slowly dispersing.

'When am I going to get to meet this mysterious man of yours?' She resigned herself to the fact that it was going to happen, and knowing her, she was already planning on keeping the enemy close. That was exactly what John would be, if he ever hurt me. He was already sailing close to the wind by being Irish.

'This weekend,' I said, mentally hoping I could persuade him to come this way for once. It was important she met him. Hopefully, it would put her mind at ease once she saw how amazing he actually was.

'Wonderful.' Her clipped tone did not match her words.

Chapter Thirty

FRIDAY 16TH NOVEMBER

I couldn't get out of work quick enough, it was becoming a bad habit on a Friday afternoon, but I was beyond excited to have John on my turf. The day had dragged. I checked the clock fifteen thousand times, much to the annoyance of poor Helen, my nurse for the day. She had to put up with my impatient huffing and puffing.

Eventually I finished, fled and parked up my little BMW on one of Winchester's backstreets, where I could abandon it for the entire weekend, if necessary. I left my little red case in the boot for now, having booked us into the hotel round the corner for two nights for a bit of privacy away from my usual lodgings at Ruth's house.

Straightening my black dress, I flung a cream-coloured scarf loosely round my neck, grabbed my handbag, and crossed the street into one our local haunts, a pub called The Bishop on The Bridge. The name spokes for itself; a beautiful spot with a beer garden overlooking the river. Inside, it was spacious and bright; one of the nicer pubs we frequented.

I pushed the door open, spotting John right away. He sat in the corner, with a bottle of Heineken, flicking through the local newspaper. I took a minute to admire him, drinking in that red hair, pale skin, and beautiful blue eyes. He dressed casually in a navy pullover, jeans and Timberland boots. The all too familiar butterflies partied in my stomach, and my heart raced in his presence.

He glanced up, sensing he was being watched and I couldn't prevent the grin that ambushed my face. It was surreal to see him here, in one of my favourite haunts. I'd wanted to show him off for so long.

'How are you, gorgeous?' He stood to greet me and I literally flung myself at him without any shame.

'It's great to have you this side of the water.' I kissed him fully on the mouth with zero concern for my recently applied Mac.

'Easy, girl.' He winked at me and squeezed my butt. 'Let me get you a drink.'

'Sit down, I'll get you one.' It was the least I could do when he'd come all this way.

'Don't be daft.' He ushered me into the seat next to his. 'Prosecco?'

'Thank you.'

He returned swiftly from the bar, with another drink for himself as well.

'What kind of pub is this you sent me to? No Guinness or Heineken on draft. Your man behind the bar tried to flog me some home brewed local shite, but I can't say it sounded particularly appealing.'

'How was your journey?' I snuggled in, enjoying the warmth of him, and the smell of him, fully able to appreciate his accent again this side of the water.

'Don't get me started on that.' A crease formed on his forehead as he remembered. 'I honestly don't know how you do it every week. It was an eyeopener.'

'That bad?' It had become so routine for me. I'd learnt to get on with it. Organisation was key, and I was grateful to be able to do it.

'Three feckin' changes on the train. And each one more wedged than the previous. Sardines in a tin, literally. A total invasion of privacy. There were mums trying to shove buggies in crevices that they really shouldn't have. People pushed against my front, back and side. It was wall to wall; the smell was rancid and the humidity from all of those jostling bodies was disgusting. I thought I might vomit at one point.'

I tried to stifle a giggle.

'How do people live like that?' he asked disdainfully.

'They know no other way,' I said simply. 'If your commute is like that every day, you get used to it; grateful if the train arrives on time, grateful for that tiny space because all you want to do is get where you have to be.'

It was good for him to experience the flipside of the coin. He was spoilt where he lived in a lot of ways.

'Anyway, who are we meeting?' He changed the subject.

The pub was filling up. It was almost six o'clock, and the offices were emptying for the weekend. Young professionals loitered at the bar, ready to let their hair down after a busy week at work.

'Clara, who you met at the hen, of course. Ruth who I live with, and Katie, one of my best friends from college.'

'Great.' A sarcasm echoed in his tone. 'I'm sure they're going to make mincemeat out of me after your resignation last week.'

'They just want to see what all the fuss is about. They couldn't let me swan off with a stranger without giving you a bit of grilling.' I was excited at the prospect of my friends getting to know the man that had completely and utterly stolen my heart, in a manner that none of us ever dreamt possible, least of all me.

'It'll be fun.' I took a mouthful of prosecco before adding, 'wait until my mother gets hold of you tomorrow.'

I thought I saw him swallow hard, but I was distracted by the noisy arrival of the girls.

'Hello,' Clara said, hugging John with a giggle, 'I can honestly say I didn't expect to see you again, but stranger things have happened.'

'Not to me they haven't.' He took the piss out of himself in his usual manner. 'I dread the day she gets those eyes tested.' There was a couple of seconds' delay as the girls processed his accent and translated into something comprehendible, before they dissolved into pealing laughter.

'I'm Katie,' she said, kissing my boyfriend on the cheek.

'Nice to meet you,' he said warmly.

'Watch this one,' I warned him, mocking my college friend. 'Morals of an ally-cat.' I winked at her and we cracked up at our own 'in' joke.

'Those days are long gone,' she assured us, 'I'll have you know I'm the sensible one out of these mad bitches these days. Worse luck.' John laughed along with us. He was swiftly receiving an accurate picture.

'I'm Ruth,' she extended her hand in a formal, accountant-like manner. She was the last one to join our friendship group and subsequently a little bit more reserved. John shook her hand politely, then generously went to the bar to buy the girls a drink, and give us a thirty second window to talk about him.

'Swit swoo,' Katie said, approvingly.

'Best-looking ginger I've ever seen,' said Ruth.

'That accent, love. It's enough on its own,' Clara said.

'Shh girls he's coming back. Behave please. I'm begging you!' I urged.

'Where is Rachel? Is she not coming down for the weekend?' Ruth asked, scanning the pub in dismay.

'Sadly not,' I told her, 'she's recovering from her surgery.'

'Oh my goodness, is she okay?' Ruth hadn't been at Rhinefield House.

'Oh, she's perfectly fine. Delighted with herself, actually. She feels like a new woman. Literally,' I said, pretending to honk Ruth's bust as her eyebrows shot up in realisation. She clamped a hand over her mouth to stifle the shock.

'She did not?' Ruth was flabbergasted.

'She certainly did. We have the pictures to prove it.' Katie pulled out her iPhone and began to scroll past three hundred pictures of her kids to find a photo of Rachel's new boobs.

John put his hands to his head. 'Oh Lord,' he said, rolling his eyes to the sky. 'I clearly didn't think his weekend through.' He was only feigning embarrassment, being in his element surrounded entirely by women. He grabbed my hand under the table and squeezed it tightly as he listened to the girls debating the logistics of Rachel's boob job. Katie was concerned if she would be able to breast feed one day, Clara wondered if she'd ever be able to sleep lying down again. I listened quietly for once, enjoying the banter, delighted to have John here with me.

Three glasses of prosecco later, we decided it would be a great idea to bring John to the tapas restaurant. Thankfully, he had drank as much as us, if not more, and he'd need it to put up with the lot of us.

Katie had given him a detailed account of how she had only marginally avoided a caesarean section, but with hindsight she would have taken it had she realised what the episiotomy involved. She didn't hold back on the details, explaining to him how she shuddered every time she heard the word 'vacuum' ever since, even if it was in a completely different context from the cleaners in her work.

Ruth grilled him about his work and business. She could be a little blunt sometimes, unintentionally of course, but everything in her mathematically logistic mind was either black or white. In her mind, everything was a formula.

She liked to calculate how everything added up in the end.

Clara was quieter than usual. It was still sinking in that I was leaving. She referred to me as her work wife, and as we saw each other most days, she would be more affected day to day, by my absence.

As we piled into the tapas restaurant, even louder than usual thanks to the alcohol on empty tummies, she sat next to me at the table and took my hand loosely.

'I can't actually believe you're really going to go.' A sadness shone in her darkening eyes.

'Neither can I. A couple of months ago I would have never dreamt it a possibility. But it feels right though, you know? For once in my life, I'm just going to go with it.'

She nodded, but I could see she wasn't a hundred per cent with me.

'We'll do the Wednesday Wine Club on FaceTime,' I promised.

'It won't be the same,' she said, glumly. The gin and tonic had made her sombre.

'You're right, love. It won't be the same. But it's all we've got, so we will do it. And you can come to Ireland, you'll absolutely love it, I promise. And I'll come home all the time.'

Instead of reassuring her as I had intended, Clara looked more worried, almost borderline panicked. Her eyes flitted from Katie, to Ruth, to mine at a rapid rate. Something was wrong clearly, but my senses were dull from the prosecco.

I noticed the problem, just as the problem noticed us.

Rob had arrived at the restaurant with a new woman in tow.

I hadn't seen him or even spoken to him in weeks. He looked well, wearing jeans and a white shirt that someone had clearly ironed for him.

His date was pretty. I tried not to look, not because I cared. I honestly felt nothing, not a single thing; I was completely indifferent to the situation, more concerned about Rob seeing me with John. Although there were five of us at our table, he knew Clara's fiancé, Ruth's fiancé and Katie's husband so that just left one anomaly.

Silence descended upon the girls, a silence John couldn't miss.

I raised my glass of wine to Rob and his new woman. 'Cheers,' I mouthed across four tables.

In fairness, he looked as horrified and awkward as I felt. He nodded abruptly, lifted the menu up to half cover his face and began to talk animatedly to his date. He seemed to be holding a conversation with her – more than he'd ever done with me.

'Awkward,' Clara said. I winced, not wishing to draw further attention to the situation in front of John. The last thing I wanted was for him to think was that I cared.

'Seriously girls, I don't care. It's actually a relief. I'm happy for them. It's just a shame they're in our restaurant.' I grabbed John's leg under the table, and he put his hand over mine, taking everything in, but not uttering a word.

I had lived with that man for seven years. I knew how he liked his tea: black with half a sugar. I'd been to America with him seven times, met every single member of his family on numerous occasions. But looking at him across the restaurant, I felt absolutely and utterly zero emotion. Did that make me a coldhearted bitch, or did it simply confirm the decision to part had been the right one? I didn't know.

Rob left with the brunette immediately after eating, clearly as uncomfortable as me. He didn't look our way again and left without acknowledgement. I breathed a sigh of relief, as John whispered in my ear, 'Are you okay, girl?'

'One hundred per cent okay, thanks,' I reassured him. So much for the anonymity of the city. Skeletons lurked in every walk of life, apparently.

'Phew,' Katie said. 'That was awkward.'

'It is what it is.' I was keen to sweep it under the carpet as soon as possible.

'Who do you think the new squeeze is?' Clara said, topping up my glass to the brim.

'Who cares?' I reminded them, and they took the hint. All attention returned to John, much to his despair. After the skinful of drinks, the girls weren't even trying to be subtle in their interrogation anymore.

I cringed as Ruth asked John what his intentions for me were. He brushed her off skilfully, with his usual deflective humour making her laugh, distracting everyone as he had intended.

As we left the restaurant and bid the girls goodnight with multiple hugs, kisses and promises of texts when everyone got home, John took my hand and we walked slowly back to the hotel, via my car in order to collect our weekend bags.

The night was crisp, clear and cold. It was fabulous to be able to appreciate the glittering stars above us. My breath fogged in front of my face as I asked John what he thought of my friends.

'By the way, just in case you wondered, that last question about my intentions...' he began.

'Sorry about that, Ruth's just trying to look out for me.'

He cut me off before I could continue with a raise of his hand. 'They are honourable, just so you know. Whenever you're ready, that is...' He couldn't quite meet my eye, but I fully understood what he was trying to say. I was nowhere near ready to hear it yet, but giddy at the prospect sometime in the future.

As silly as it sounded, I actually liked the concept of being married in a lot of ways. I loved the security of it, the tradition, the thought of our own family unit. I was never one for blowing in the wind, one-night stands or messing around. I could only imagine what heaven it would be, to be married to the *right* man.

Chapter Thirty-One

SATURDAY 17TH NOVEMBER

After a lazy morning in bed, we made our way to Southampton to catch the Red Funnel passenger ferry across to the Isle of Wight. The wind was up and the crossing was choppier than I'd have liked, especially after the alcohol the night before.

John was in great form. The boat didn't bother him, he was looking forward to the day trip. I wondered if he realised what he was letting himself in for, but there was no way I could move to Ireland without introducing him to my mother at least once. She'd never forgive me if I didn't.

The boat docked twenty-five minutes later. My mother waited with a youthful excitement shining in her aqua blue eyes. Nothing made her happier than having her children home, not that we did it often. Home no longer felt like home since she'd let Trevor move in. He stood watching on the side lines with his hands in his pockets, no trace of a smile on his face. He was probably annoyed at the disruption in his weekend of watching sport.

'Hiya, darlings,' she said, pulling me into a massive hug, an excited grin erupted on her face, exposing straight white teeth.

'Mum, this is John.' I introduced the two of them and she gave him a warm welcome, despite her concerns about me running off with him.

'This is Trevor,' she introduced her partner, who reluctantly slunk over, as though he'd rather be anywhere in the world than with us. I'd already given John the heads up, just in case he thought it was only for his benefit, sadly it wasn't. Trevor was always a miserable git.

We hopped into Trevor's jeep, discussing safe topics such as the weather, and the ferry crossing. Mum asked about our night out with the girls. I didn't mention we had seen Rob. I didn't want to bring it up again, and for John to think I cared.

John stared keenly out the window, possibly to take his mind from Trevor's awful driving; far too fast, and hard on the brakes. It was a revelation for him to be able to picture this, the place I grew up.

'Where do you want to go first?' Mum asked, as we left Cowes, the tiny town the boat docked into.

'Shanklin beach,' I suggested. It was one of my favourite spots. I used to spend a lot of time there as a teenager and there were count-less cafes and pubs to sit out at along the seafront.

'Great idea. We'll go for a walk and a coffee,' she said, rubbing her hands together.

'It's meant to rain,' Trevor said, eyeing the sky with his perpetual frown. I averted my focus from the eternal optimist, life was too short for that kind of negativity.

'It will be fine.' Mum would not be deterred that easily.

'So, what do you think of our beautiful Isle?' Mum asked John as he took in the passing scenery.

'It's not what I expected,' he said.

'In what way?'

'It's more built up than I expected.' He eyed the many blocks of newly built apartments, and the town houses lining both sides of the roads. There were cars everywhere. It even seemed claustrophobic to me. I'd been spoilt with space and privacy of late.

'We have a population of about a hundred and thirty thousand people living on an Island that is only twenty-four miles by twelve,' she informed him.

'That is unreal. I live in a much bigger area but the population of Ballina is about ten thousand.'

'Is that why you had to come to England to find yourself a woman?' Mum's tone was breezy, but it harboured an underlying air of suspicion.

A good natured laughed erupted from John's chest. 'I didn't come looking for anything, but I got more than I dreamt of.'

'Just take care of her,' my mother warned him.

'I spent thirty years looking for her. I'm not going to let anything happen to her now,' he promised.

'Hello? I am here, you know,' I reminded them pointedly. 'Can you have this discussion later, if you have to have it at all.'

'Welcome to Shanklin beach.' Trevor parked in one of the bays lining the promenade. We finally had something in common; he was as uncomfortable as I was, with this line of conversation.

We got out the jeep and strolled the length of the promenade, leisurely stopping for coffee and cake at one of the many little seasonal cafes. Outdoor tables and chairs braved the autumn wind. It was fabulous to be outside inhaling the salty sea air. I felt cooped up most of the week in my surgery; to just feel the breeze on my face and savour the fresh air was a pure treat.

Several others strolled the promenade with the same idea. Children played on the sandy beach in front of us with their hats and scarves pulled tightly over their ears. Parents looked on, drinking their tea in peace, undoubtably praying the fresh air would wear the children out before bed time.

I spotted a girl I went to school with and waved at her as she passed by with her four children, the youngest two strapped into a double buggy while the older two ran along in front in a quest for an ice cream.

Mum and John appeared to be getting on well. She seemed to be enjoying his unusual sense of humour. Either that or she was being exceptionally polite as he regaled her with tales of Ireland.

With the familiar sights and scents, a hundred memories flooded through me. Memories I'd made on this very beach over my lifetime. I learnt to swim here, dived through waves at high tide with my friends. Once I lost my bikini top in a particularly strong current, aged fourteen. I was horrified at the time, but I laughed as it sprung to mind again. So many memories I forgot I even had. So many nights I'd sat outside beach front pubs, spent summer holidays with my school friends as teenagers, using fake ID to buy us blue WKDs and Bacardi Breezers.

It was amazing how life had turned out. I'd wanted to become a policewoman, but then ended up as a dental hygienist. I wanted to live in a hot country so I could sunbathe and swim in the sea all year round, now I was moving to one of the wettest climates in Europe. It was unreal, how far removed I'd become from what I thought I wanted.

I hoped to God this time I'd get it right.

————

We had an early table booked at a restaurant called The Boathouse for dinner. It served the best Surf n Turf on the island. The staff seated us at a quiet round table in the bay window, where we watched the sun setting over the opposing Portsmouth Harbour.

The sky was a fabulous shade of coral. As the fluorescent ball descended into the Solent, Mum winked at me in an approving exchange. After spending the day with John, she could fully appreciate the attraction, and was satisfied it seemed to be mutual. We ordered a bottle of Pinot Noir for the table and clinked glasses in a toast.

'Cheers,' my mum said, 'thank you for coming over.'

'It was a pleasure,' John said.

'Take care of my baby,' she said, as I squirmed in embarrassment. I was twenty-seven years old, hardly a baby. I said nothing, unable to sit through the 'you'll know yourself when you have your own children' speech again.

'I will of course,' John reassured her, kissing my hand.

'It's just a shame you live in Ireland,' Mum said, with a heavy exhale.

'It's not that far really. Besides, you never know you might like it so much you could end up retiring there yourself one day,' he said.

'Ha. I doubt it.'

Stranger things had happened.

As Mum and Trevor dropped us back off at the seven o'clock

passenger ferry, her eyes welled with tears, a double-edged sword for her. She seemed happy I'd met someone so lovely, satisfied he cared a lot for me, but it meant I'd be moving further away again. From the lingering way in which her eyes fixated on our departing ferry, it was a thought that she did not relish.

Chapter Thirty-Two

THURSDAY 29TH NOVEMBER

Jackie dabbed the almost black gunge onto my scalp with what looked like a paintbrush. I watched her work in the mirror in front of me, grateful for the barrier cream she'd placed around my hairline.

'So, you're really going to do it?' She stood back checking, examining her handiwork.

'Yep,' I inhaled a lungful of air and slowly exhaled.

Excitement bubbled in my belly for a new chapter, a new start. Sure, I was nervous, but the thought of being with John everyday far outweighed any concerns I could conjure up even on my darkest nights.

I'd been there nearly every week since September. Having Jane and Trish there made it so much easier, and Mama Bear and Papa Bear too. They weren't surprised when John broke the news I was moving and were delighted to see him settling down. His mother told me their home was my home, and I was welcome any time. His father joked about the benefits of upping the weekly mileage, and I'd be lying if I said I hadn't factored that in too. The new year promised a new job. All in all, it seemed like a fairly sound position to be in.

'You'll have to find a new hairdresser.' Disappointment resounded in Jackie's tone.

'Believe it or not I already have the next one lined up.' My mind wondered to Natalie, the girl whose husband's stag had turned out to the best thing that had ever happened to me.

'Have you been cheating on me already and you've not even left the country yet?'

'Only a sneaky blow dry once I promise,' I said.

'Anytime you're home visiting, be sure to call in here for an appointment,' she said.

'Of course. I'll be in touch, anyway. You're not getting rid of me that easily.' Jackie had recently split with her boyfriend of ten years; she too had met somebody else very quickly, and we had been comparing notes along the way.

'I'm dying to meet this Ginger Wonder of yours,' she said.

'Well, when you've washed this muck out of my hair, and made me look a bit more presentable, I'll FaceTime him, and you can see what all the fuss is about.' I took a sip of my black coffee, looking forward to seeing John's familiar features light up my iPhone.

Jackie washed the colour out of my hair and blow dried my unruly mane into a straight sleek style.

After I paid Jackie and she handed me my coat, I tried to ring John. He didn't answer. It was odd, but I assumed he was tied up with the farm.

I bid farewell to Jackie, promising I'd be in touch soon. Outside, it was spitting slightly. The damp air threatened to ruin my freshly blow-dried locks. I half ran, half walked to where my car was parked fifty metres away. Shirley High Street wasn't the nicest area of Southampton to be roaming alone on a pitch dark, winter night.

The doors automatically locked as I sped off in the BMW and drove the twenty minutes back to Ruth's house in Winchester. This was to be my home for less than a month more now. I'd be glad to start laying some roots again, instead of feeling as though I was renting an eight-foot by eight-foot space. John said he wanted me to pick colours for the house, put a feminine stamp on, it as he put it. I'd already told him I'd do no such thing until he took that God-awful stag head down once and for all. Yuck.

I checked my phone again. There was still nothing from John. I squinted at the screen, checking I had reception. Four little bars mocked me. Letting myself in quietly through the front door, I snuck upstairs and straight into my room. I wanted to climb into my pyjamas, and into bed as quickly as possible. It had been a long day and the quicker I fell asleep, the quicker the weekend would begin and I'd be with my man.

My phoned beeped as I got changed, but it was my mum checking up on me. Disappointed rippled through my insides. It was nearly nine o'clock. He never left it this late to call. I hoped he was ok. That niggling feeling hovered in my gut, hinting not all was well. I hated wondering and waiting, needing to hear his reassuring voice.

In the bathroom, I brushed my teeth, removed my make-up, cleansed, toned and moisturised. I was never normally this thorough, but it passed the time while I silently willed the phone to ring. When phone calls were all we had, we tried to keep them regular. That heavy panicky feeling in my chest swelled, pressing down on my sternum. Anxiety invaded my stomach. It was almost eleven o'clock and I'd heard nothing since lunchtime. Something was definitely wrong.

Checking my phone for the hundredth time, I contemplated texting Jane or Trisha, before deciding against it. I didn't want them to think I was one of those crazy, jealous, insecure women, although sadly that's what I felt like. Being in love was mentally and physically exhausting.

I couldn't believe what I'd found in John; I was terrified of losing him. That little devil on my shoulder continued to whisper that I wasn't good enough. Nothing ever lasts; why should this be any different? It took an enormous amount of self-control to ignore him. I had a of habit of replaying every mistake I'd ever made since I was a child, and beating myself up over every bad decision I ever made in my life. It would be a relief when the sun rose in the morning, and I could see things clearly and rationally again in the light of day.

Around midnight the phone vibrated.

John:

So sorry girl, it turned into one of those afternoons. I'm only getting to the phone now. I hope this message doesn't wake you and that you are dreaming of me. I'll ring you in the morning. Love you xxx

Relief washed over me. He was okay, and nothing had changed between us. That fear of him issuing me the p45 hadn't fully left me, despite his constant reassurances.

The other thing that I secretly worried about was that he mightn't leave me as such, but he could be taken from me in a different way. The fear was a product of my father dying young. It had shown me the fragility of life, and how tomorrow was promised to none of us.

I tossed and turned, trying to get comfortable. It took me a long time to drift off. When sleep eventually came, it was broken and fuelled with disturbing dreams. With one leg either side of the Irish Sea, the disconcertment I felt seeped into my subconscious. Change was coming. I was ready to stop worrying about it, and simply get on with it, now the decision had been made.

Chapter Thirty-Three

FRIDAY 30TH NOVEMBER

John didn't elaborate on the events of the day before, and I didn't like to pry. I was late for work, rushing out the door as the phone rang, so I didn't have time to ask too many questions. Besides, I didn't want him to think he had to explain his every move to me. And in the light of day, last night's worries seemed ridiculous.

I hurriedly wished him a good day and hung up, distracted with the knowledge I had to resign at my second job today, Dental Connections. My contract there stated I had to give four-weeks-notice, but with the Christmas holidays coming up they were actually getting six. I'd hung on a couple of weeks longer than I had in my other practice because experience had taught me that people treat you differently when they know you're leaving.

Some patients had been a bit huffy, like I was abandoning them. It didn't occur to some of them I had a life outside of work. I was heartfelt sorry to be leaving them, and I wouldn't be leaving them if there was another way.

I parked up, threw my handbag into my surgery and went looking for Mark. I wanted to thank him for everything he had done for me over the years. I'd enjoyed working at with him, and wouldn't have left otherwise, and I wanted him to know that.

The white envelope in my hand alerted him to the situation before I could even say a word. He shook his head as I stood silently in front of him with the envelope.

'Ireland?' he said.

'I'm afraid so,' I said, and smiled sadly at him.

'I can't believe it. We thought you would go, but it's so soon.'

'I'm sorry.' I seemed to spend a lot of time apologising.

'Ahh. I hope I'm not overstepping the mark, Lucy, but over the years I've come to think of you as a friend as well as a colleague....'

I wasn't sure where he was going with this, but I really shouldn't have been surprised at the following statement at this stage.

'Are you sure it's not just the seven year itch,' he asked, in a tentative voice.

I'd barely heard of the seven year itch before in my entire life, yet if I'd had a pound for every person who said it to me in the previous six months, I'd have been a millionaire.

'I'm sure,' I said, through gritted teeth.

'Well.' He shrugged. 'A person has to do what they have to do. If you change your mind...' he trailed off, but I knew what he was going to say.

'Thank you. I hope it doesn't come to it, but thank you. I've honestly enjoyed working with you all. It's been a pleasure.' I meant it.

Helen strolled into the surgery to inform me my first patient had arrived. The patient was in a wheelchair, so we went to use a surgery downstairs for the morning.

Word spread around the practice like wildfire, people asked me a hundred questions, most of which I didn't even know the answer to myself.

'Where would I work? What was it like in Ireland? Isn't it a bit soon?'

It was a relief to get into the solitude of my car at four o'clock and make the mundane motorway trip to Gatwick. I drove silently, allowing the events of the day to filter through my mind as I tried to process everything.

Things had moved quickly, but it was unavoidable. Eventually I was going to move, so wasn't I as well to get on with it? Excitement bubbled within when I imagined this new life with John, the fun we'd have. Whatever challenges that might arise, we had a solid foundation, having been through so much already. I was certain we could make it work. And so was he.

The phone pierced loudly through the car speakers as I sped along the M25 with only my thoughts for company.

John's name flashed on my digital radio.

'Hello?'

'Hi, honey, how are you?' I beamed from ear to ear at the sound of his voice. That accent had a lot to answer for.

'Traffic is moving along. Fingers crossed I should be at the airport in less than an hour.'

'Great timing for a Friday on those bloody roads.' He could fully appreciate the effort of the commute, having done it himself now.

'Absolutely. In no time at all, I'll be sitting in the bar in the departure lounge with a big glass of red wine. TFI Friday.'

'Brilliant.' He sounded equally as excited as me. Friday nights were our nights. After counting down the sleeps until we could be together again, we tended not to venture too far from the warmth of the open fire. Not to mention the bottle of red that had become another ritual.

'I might be a bit longer getting through Knock; I packed a big case. I thought it would save space in Betsy when I come in the car next month. If I leave a bit more each week, it'll make it easier when I do the big move into yours.'

'You're going to have to stop calling it 'mine' soon enough, Luce. You'll be living here yourself in only a few short weeks, thank God,' he said.

'Hmm. It will take a while to feel like home,' I said.

'Well, funny you should say that.' He laughed nervously. 'I got you a welcome home present.'

'You did not?' Moving in with him, waking up with him every day was the only present I actually wanted.

'I hope you like him,' he said, with a low rumbling chuckle.

'Him? I'm not sure I like the sound of that. It better not be another one of those awful stuffed animal heads that you hang on the wall?' I shuddered thinking about it.

'You're going to love him. Trust me.' I did trust *him*, that was the funny thing. I just didn't trust his sense of humour.

'Okay. I'll text you when I'm on board, so you know the flight's on time.'

'Safe travelling, can't wait to see you, gorgeous.' He hung up.

I briefly wondered what the present could be, before reaching the conclusion it was probably a new bull for the cattle, knowing John.

———

The flight was on time and I managed to get two seats to myself for once. I closed my eyes for most of the journey, touching up my make-up just in time for landing.

John waited for me, grinning as he loitered at the arrival lounge in his normal spot. His long strides enabled him to cross the floor swiftly. That rush of lust when I saw him only got stronger.

I thought I loved him before, but with each passing week it multiplied as he continued to surprise me with his kindness, and his determination in business, both on the farm and in his personal life. He was the strongest man I'd ever met, the most generous and the most insightful. He had a wonderful way of looking at the world. Any time I had a problem over the previous few months, regardless of what it might have been, he was the first person I turned to. His advice, friendship and support had become as valuable to me as his oceanic eyes and the strong comfort of his arms.

As we made the usual drive from the airport he was like an excited child, basking in the thrill of the welcome home 'present'.

We parked outside the front door. As usual, it was lashing rain and absolutely freezing. There was no sign of the neighbours, no lights on around us at all.

'I'm seriously reconsidering my decision to move to this climate,' I warned him as he pushed open the front door and gently shoved us both into the warmth.

'Welcome home,' he said. The shrieking sound of a wailing cat emerged from behind the kitchen door.

My mouth formed a perfect open circle. 'What was that?'

'Go in and see,' he said, his bright eyes glinting.

I pushed open the heavy cream wooden door, apprehensive as about what I would find. An adorable, tan coloured boxer puppy pounced on me. He licked my face with a long, scratchy tongue. I scooped him up into my arms and he took a mouthful of my loose hair and tugged at it with his tiny teeth. Six months ago, I never believed in love at first sight. Now it had happened to me twice in one year. His chocolate eyes gazed into mine, and he wagged his little tail with excitement.

'Oh my God! He is just gorgeous,' I squealed.

'I'm glad you like him. He's yours. Ours. But mostly yours.' John leaned back on the island and took pleasure watching me fuss over our first baby, rubbing his head as he nuzzled affectionately into my neck.

'Was this where you were last night?' I asked, relieved that it made sense.

He shifted awkwardly from left foot to right and bit his nail. 'Not exactly... I picked him up this afternoon.' He ran a hand over the back of his head and opened his mouth to say something, then closed it again. I chose to ignore it. Whatever it was, it didn't matter. Having a puppy together reinforced what I already knew, we were about to start our new life together – a proper couple with no more commuting.

'What's his name?' I asked.

'Whatever you want to name him. He's yours. Another friend for you this side of the water.'

'You're good.' I had to give it to him. He'd thought this one through. He should've written a book. He had so many tricks up his sleeve when it came to wooing women.

He shrugged and laughed.

'He looks like a Harley to me,' I said.

'Harley? That is a shite name. What about Dillon? Or Max or Rueben?' he suggested.

'No,' I said firmly. 'You said I can name him what I like, he's called Harley.' I was adamant.

'Oh look, Harley's left you a present!' John pointed to the floor and put his hands over his eyes in disgust as Harley peed on the previously immaculate kitchen tiles.

'You're as well to be getting used to it. I won't be around during the week for a while.' I headed for the kitchen roll with a little smirk on my face.

'I have Mama Bear lined up for puppysitting during the week, don't worry about that,' he assured me with a wink.

We made him a bed of an old tartan throw, placing it in front of the fire. Harley sprawled out on it like he'd been here with us his whole life. While he snored loudly in front of us, we fell into each other's arms on the couch. I was glad our new baby was asleep; he was way too young to learn about the birds and the bees.

Chapter Thirty-Four

SATURDAY 1ST DECEMBER

The girls had brought me out for the afternoon to a hotel on the outskirts of Ballina called Mount Falcon. It was a beautiful spot, with lovely gardens and a lake.

'Can you believe it's December already?' Trisha was even more excited than usual. Apparently, she loved Christmas, but I was yet to find something that she didn't love. She was like a welcome ray of winter sunshine.

'Don't Trisha, I can't even think about it yet. I have a million things to do first,' I said.

'Ah, well, it's different for you.'

'We'll get there,' I said, taking a scone from the delicate china platter and lathering it with strawberry jam.

'It feels like you've been here forever already though, doesn't it?' Jane said, brushing imaginary crumbs from her heart-shaped face.

'I don't know. I don't feel particularly settled in either place at the moment. I'm constantly in the air. The thought of not having to travel every week is really appealing.'

The end was in sight, I had little patience for hanging round airports. It seemed like precious time wasted, time that could have been spent with John. It would all be worth it soon.

'This place is absolutely fabulous,' I said, marvelling at the tasteful crimson and gold decorations, and the eight-foot Christmas tree occupying the corner of the room. There seemed to be so many lovely places to go in this part of the world.

'Will you be sad to leave England?' Trisha asked, tucking her hair earnestly behind her ear.

'There are lots of people I'll miss; my friends, my family, of course. I'll miss the late-night shopping, my job and my patients. But girls, he's worth it.' I knew it, more than I'd ever known anything in my life. I was certain he was the one.

'And imagine we thought he'd never settle down. Now he's beating them off with a stick.' Trisha said, slapping her leg. Jane shot her a warning look, whatever that was about.

'I just mean he never had anyone serious before you, Lucy,' she corrected herself.

'Luckily for me!' I laughed. 'Frogs, he calls them! As in, "I kissed a lot of frogs before I found my princess".' We erupted with laughter, all three of us.

'Apt,' Jane agreed. 'Unfortunately, we can all relate to that.'

Familiar Christmas music like David Bowie, and Bing Crosby's "Drummer Boy" played softly over the speakers in the drawing room. The year had flown by; the whole thing was a complete frenzied whirlwind. It seemed unreal to be listening to the same songs I'd listened to every festive period, yet this year everything was completely different. Life had changed dramatically in the previous six months. I never imagined I could be that happy. It was almost surreal. I sent up a silent thanks to whoever was up there: a thanks for John, a thanks for these new friends, for this life. I was so grateful for everything.

I was a different woman, for the better in a lot of ways, but also there were a few issues I had discovered within myself that needed a bit more work. It was my New Year's Resolution to confront them head on. John was convinced that when I moved here properly, a lot of those would dispel themselves naturally. I wasn't so sure, but I was sure that one way or another I would get over them. I'd already made colossal progress by simply admitting my truths.

'How's the new baby?' Trisha said. 'I was going to get blue new baby balloons and banners and stick them on the front door, but I thought John would go off the head.'

I giggled; she was probably right.

'He's great. He cried a bit in the night, but they all do that in the first few days.' John was adamant the dog was sleeping in the kitchen, despite my best efforts to persuade him we should let him upstairs. He was having none of it.

'I'll be up to see him tomorrow,' Trisha promised.

'Tell me,' Jane leaned in closer, as if she were about to divulge a secret. 'What are you getting John for Christmas?' she whispered, as if he could hear us from eight miles away.

'Easy. I bought him an Apple gadget his dad recommended. Plus, I booked us two nights away in a fancy hotel in Belfast. That's really for my benefit, girls. I'll need my city fix by then. God forbid my Estee Lauder foundation runs out,' I joked, but I was acutely aware regular city trips would be essential to my survival here, as much as I had come to love the tranquillity.

'I wouldn't be in the slightest bit surprised if he bought you a diamond ring,' Trisha gushed. 'Honestly, we've never seen him like this before. Have we, Jane?' She nudged her roughly with her elbow for confirmation.

'I don't think I'm ready for another ring quite yet, girls,' I reminded them while rubbing the empty space on my finger and ignoring the guilt gnawing at my stomach. The remnants of the band mark had fortunately faded over the past few months but it felt hot to touch occasionally, a permanent reminder of my failing.

'Everyone makes mistakes. You were so young.' Jane tried to alleviate my guilt but it was something I'd have to work on in time.

'I can't afford to make another one... one fuck up is forgivable, I cannot make another. So as completely and utterly head over heels in love I am with that man, I am in no rush,' I confided.

'Don't be so hard on yourself. While you were trying to do your best with a bad situation, others would be busy bed hopping. You were at least trying to stand by your word. Don't beat yourself up about it; I know it's easier said than done,' Jane said in a gentle tone.

I smiled, grateful for her kind words, and for their easy friendship.

Women could be awful creatures, especially to each other. They could smile to your face while taking strips out of you. Thankfully, I had a good radar for those types, and Jane and Trisha were the real deal. The conversations were frank and honest. I had no time for anything less. As different as we all were in many ways, we had so much in common.

'Do you ever hear from him?' Trisha asked, pouring more tea from the china tea pot.

'Who?' I genuinely had to ask.

'Your ex. You don't have to tell us if you don't want to.'

'Not a thing. I'm not sure whether I expected to or not. I saw him a couple of weeks ago, when John was over. He was eating in the same restaurant as us with who – I presume – was his new girlfriend.' I told them.

'No way,' Jane exclaimed, 'what are the chances?'

'I know. I couldn't believe it. Awkward.' I ran my hands through my thick curls as I remembered.

'How did you feel? It must have been so weird?' Trisha asked.

'It was weird, but I was glad to see him moving on. I was more worried about him seeing me with John, but he didn't seem to pay too much attention. Nothing new there.'

'I can't imagine being married to a man and then seeing him with someone else,' Trisha mused.

'It's really no different from seeing any of your exes with someone else, to be honest. There's a lot of emphasis on the word marriage, but it only means something if both people work hard at it. Otherwise, it's only a piece of paper.' Harsh, but true. I'd found out the hard way.

'I guess so.' Trisha was still waiting for her man to pop the question; it was definitely on the cards. Jane was newly married, so she was still in the madly in love phase. I prayed it would always be that way for her.

Later, when we returned to Killala, we sat outside the houses in Trisha's car, with the engine running.

'We'll see you at the wedding next week?' Trisha checked as I opened the car door and wrapped my woollen coat tighter around me.

'Oh yeah. I'd completely forgotten about that.' I smacked my hand to my forehead. I wasn't surprised to hear both Trisha and Jane had been invited too.

'What are you wearing?' I asked her through the wound down window.

'Full length,' Trisha said. 'Go big or go home! Safe travels my dear, see you next week.' She waved as she reversed carefully out the drive and dropped Jane at her front door, in between the two of us. It occurred to me not for the first time today how lucky I was to have these two women as friends as I embarked on the next chapter of my life.

Chapter Thirty-Five

FRIDAY 7TH DECEMBER

It turned out that Irish weddings were massive. The day after the wedding, 'The Afters' as they referred to it, was just a big a deal as the wedding itself nearly. A normal person might die of alcohol poisoning if they were thrown off the deep end into a two-day drink fest with barely a couple of hours' sleep in between. For me, a self-confessed semi-functioning wino, it was like a slice of heaven had fallen out of the sky and straight into my lap.

I floated down the stairs in John's house, feeling a million dollars in a gorgeous navy maxi dress from Coast. It was strapless, with a sweetheart shaped neckline and a split up the right side, giving the occasional flash of painstakingly applied tan.

John let out a long low appreciative whistle as I reached the bottom step and kissed his full lips. 'I feel sorry for the bride,' he said, loyally.

'You don't scrub up too badly yourself.' He wore a beautifully tailored navy three-piece suit, a crisp-white shirt and navy bow tie.

'I didn't have you pegged as the bow tie sort.' I straightened it for him while he looked suggestively down the front of my dress.

'I won't stick it past the church, but its grand for now,' he said.

Mama Bear had taken Harley for the night. I hadn't realised how tying it was having a dog, as adorable as he was, but John's parents were only down the road and more than happy to mind him for us.

John held the passenger door of the Audi open and I slid into the leather seat and tried not to think about the butterflies in my stomach. It was our first big outing as a proper couple, and we'd apparently been the talk of the tiny town for the last few months. I'd normally dispel fears like that immediately with the rationale of 'who in their right mind really had any time to be worrying what other people are doing'. But the fact that Trisha and Jane had heard everything about me before John had even introduced us spoke volumes. Most of the town had heard John Kelly had a new English girlfriend, and a married one at that. We laughed it off, knowing the truth of our own situation was very different, but it didn't prevent a flutter of nervous energy.

It was the first wedding I was attending since my divorce. I wondered how it would make me feel.

'You're quiet,' John observed as we drove to the church. 'Are you ok?' He took a quick sideways glance at me.

'Just thinking.'

'What are you thinking?'

'Everything and nothing.' Too much to explain. He seemed to pick up on my mood, dropping his left hand onto my right thigh for the rest of the journey. For the millionth time, I wondered what I had done to deserve this wonderful man sitting next to me. He just got me. He understood me better than people I'd known for years. When I struggled to find the words I was looking for, he seemed to hear them somehow, anyway.

The church was absolutely ram packed with guests waiting in awe for the big event. The woman in the pew in front of me turned around swiftly to chance a look at the door and nearly took my eye out with her eccentric cerise pink headpiece. The organist began to play, the show was about to start.

Natalie made an absolutely beautiful bride. Blonde, tanned, skinny and stylish with a low cut backless slinky dress and a full-length veil. She virtually glowed. The groom was very handsome in his tuxedo and tie, dark hair and dark eyes. When he knelt at the altar, I saw someone had written HELP on the bottom of his shoes, which gave the congregation a collective giggle.

The church ceremony was the full hour and a half Catholic mass with communion, John held my hand throughout the entire mass, pointing out several of his friends and people he knew. We were in our own little bubble, communicating without uttering a word.

Scanning the faces of curious strangers, I tried to imagine myself as a permanent fixture, struggling to envision it, though it was soon to be my reality. I glanced over at John kneeling in the pew next to me, pretending he was deep in prayer but the lingering look over my cleavage told me his thoughts were far from holy.

Eventually they were pronounced man and wife and we left the church for the hotel. I needed a glass of wine, being in Church freaked me out. I never felt comfortable in them, even more so now. If there were such a thing as hell, I'm sure my recent activity would ensure that's exactly where I'd be sent.

Whatever I needed; my boyfriend needed something else. He had the foot to the accelerator, keen to get checked into our room. The venue was only thirty minutes from John's house but he insisted we book a room, for comfort. My weekend bag was packed with a few essentials: make-up for the following day to mask my pale, tired and undoubtably hung over face − and of course flat pumps in case my feet were in bits from the heels.

The bedrooms were simple but spacious. He pulled me down on to the starchy white sheets and stroked his fingers along the inside of my leg, from my ankle up to my thigh, tracing the split of my dress.

'I like this dress, easy access to my favourites parts.' His voice was low and raspy, and left me in no doubt of his intentions.

'Don't go messing up my outfit now,' I warned him, but he and I both knew he could whatever he wanted to me when he had me like this.

He inched his thumb higher and higher, circling my inner thigh until he reached the edge of my underwear, pulling it to the side, leaving me exposed for him to do as he willed with me. I held my breath as he lowered his face down on to the most intimate parts of me. I finished quickly and he moved to sit on a chair next to the bed.

He patted his lap, motioning me to straddle him. I jumped him willingly; pleasing him, pleased me. Our eyes bore into each other's souls when we were joined together this way. Rocking back and forth, our hearts raced, breath snatched in short fast gasps. I felt complete.

Afterward, we fell lazily back on to the bed.

'You are unreal,' he said, as he had done so many times before.

'So are you.' I snuggled into his shoulder, hoping my foundation wouldn't smudge onto his shirt.

'Don't ever make that trip to Specsavers,' he said, kissing my forehead tenderly.

'I love you,' I said, blissfully content in his arms.

'I love you too.' He closed his eyes peacefully.

I could have happily missed the wedding and spent the afternoon in the hotel room with John, but after a quick twenty-minute power nap we went to the bar to await the arrival of the new bride and groom.

My make-up survived our afternoon rendezvous. I freshened up and reapplied more perfume, before descending down the stairs to my first Irish wedding.

The bar was jammed. It appeared all four hundred guests decided to order a drink at the same time. John swerved through the crowds and managed to get us a couple of gin and tonics. There was no sign of Jane or Trisha, but it was so busy they could be only a few feet away from us and I wouldn't have spotted them. The noise level was that of a school playground. A man sat in the corner of the bar with a guitar, but he could barely be heard over the rumble of chatter and laughter.

Some of the women had gone above and beyond in their outfits, many of them looked as though they had just stepped off the catwalk. Stylish shoes coordinated with colour coded fascinators and hats, and fitted jackets and fur shrugs reflected the seasonal theme. Through the sea of faces, I instinctively zoned in on one. The intensity of her hard stare grabbed my attention, scrutiny smothered her doll like face. She was painted porcelain, pink lipstick, pink blusher and too much eyeliner around her cat like eyes. A tight baby blue dress hugged her tiny petite figure and even though she wore five-inch silver sandals, she still appeared short.

It was the woman from The Shelbourne, the one who had warned me about John. The frog. John followed my gaze, spotting her a moment after me. He pulled me in closer to him and placed his arm protectively around me. Luckily, Jane and her husband, Michael, approached us from the other direction with welcome hugs and kisses.

Jane looked stunning as usual, in a floor length plum purple chiffon halter neck. I was only half listening, as she complemented my outfit, distracted by the dagger piercing my back. I shook off the mild irritation determined, not to let it spoil the fun, and focused on giving Jane my full attention.

'I hope we're on the same table,' Jane said, looking around the room for a table plan.

'You won't be long finding out,' John said as the hotel manager passed through the bar ringing the bell, signalling us to move to the ballroom and take our seats.

Most people seemed in no rush to move, completely ignoring the instruction, but we were keen to see who was at our table. I had an awful sinking feeling we might be put with the frog. I desperately hoped not.

Round tables in the ballroom were each laid for ten guests. Each table had a number displayed on a metal stand, a glass vase full of gorgeous fresh white and red roses and a large church candle with three wicks lit. Fairy lights hung from the ceiling creating a romantic, relaxing atmosphere. It was like something from a fairy tale. A wave of relief swept over me as I realised the frog was not sitting at our table, thank goodness. We were seated with Jane and Michael, Trisha and Michael and two guys I recognised from the stag weekend and their wives, who all seemed lovely. I scanned the room looking for the frog but was pleased to say I couldn't see her anywhere near us so at least I was able to enjoy my dinner without her staring daggers at me.

I exhaled deeply, releasing the tension I'd been unwittingly holding in my shoulders and reminded myself I was the one he was here with; I was the one he told he loved, the only woman he ever had said that to, and the one he had asked to move in with him. I had no reason to feel anything other than wonderful regardless of who else was in the same room as us.

Jack and Julia waved at us from two tables away, they had travelled from Dublin this morning. I was looking forward to catching up with them again, and hearing more about their own wedding plans.

I checked my phone in my handbag to make sure it was still on vibrate. I'd have hated for it to go off in the middle of the speeches. Glancing down at it quickly, conscious of being rude, I noticed I had seventeen WhatsApp messages and two text messages. I scanned through the WhatsApp messages briefly, the girls were debating on different venues for my leaving drinks. Clara wanted to go somewhere fancy, Katie wanted to go somewhere local and Ruth didn't care where we went and reminded everyone to invite Rachel down.

I flicked into the text messages. One was from my mother, wishing us a good day at the wedding and asking for a photo, the other was from a number I didn't recognise.

When I opened it, it was none other than Paddy O'Mara, asking me if I would be interested in a hygienist position in his new practice which was due to open mid-February. Everything was falling into place, the stars seemed to align for us, as though it were fate. As though it were meant to be.

I handed the phone to John under the table so he could read the message. He flashed his perfectly imperfect smile at ticking another box on the checklist.

With Paddy's formal job offer, I was one hundred percent at peace with my decision to move. The weekends were wonderful, but the week days were torture being away from John. I needed a job, an identity of my own, something to be known as, not just John Kelly's woman.

My family and friends thought I'd gone completely mental, turning into one of those lunatic mushy women I used to mock. A part of me still questioned if that kind of love could last. It had only been a few months. The one thing I learnt about being in love, true love – and that's what it was – was, that as wonderful and as amazing and exciting as it is, there were extreme lows as well. One thing about being in love was that it made me vulnerable, I was giving my heart to somebody and trusting him not to damage it; yet handing him everything he needed, all the tools and instructions, to do just that.

I was not used to feeling powerless in that way. I'd never truly cared before. There was no element of risk before because I had nothing to lose. With John, I felt there was a potential for complete and utter indescribable devastation. I'd experienced the real deal and was absolutely terrified of losing it.

I tried to shake off that melancholy feeling and bring myself back to the present. There was some sort of guessing game going on with the guests at each table and I quickly tried to catch up on what I'd missed and join in. John promised me the world, and I didn't doubt he would deliver. I adored him. I couldn't physically get enough of him, I missed him every second I wasn't with him. Thoughts of him consumed me. Every time my phone beeped, I willed it to be him.

'Fifty-four minutes, you heard it here first,' John said.

'No way,' Jane's Michael replied. 'At least I hope not. It will make for a long day!'

'Twenty-six minutes,' Trisha chipped in. 'It will be over quickly.'

What on earth were they guessing while I had been miles away daydreaming?

'I'm going to guess a fast and furious fifteen minutes,' Jane said, sticking ten euro into the glass in the middle.

'What do you think, girl?' John turned to me. I still had no idea what they were guessing.

'Erm... thirty-two minutes?' I picked a random number, and stuck a tenner in the glass, copying Jane.

Waiters and waitresses served every table, offering us the choice of red or white wine with dinner and handing out champagne for the toast. The master of ceremonies rang the bell for the speeches to begin before dinner. At least it would get them over with. If it were me having to stand up in front of four hundred people, I'd rather just get it over with.

The father of the bride stood first, clearing his throat and adjusting his tie apprehensively. He began by saying what a beautiful girl his daughter was, told us a few personal stories from her childhood and one funny, but slightly controversial, account of a teenage incident involving a bottle of brandy, an ambulance and a four-hundred-euro phone bill. The crowd hooted with laughter. Would I ever get the Irish sense of humour?

The groom stood, looking at his new wife in awe. He welcomed everyone and thanked us for coming to their big day. He awkwardly hashed his way through the formalities of addressing the bridesmaids and his new in-laws before getting to the crux of what he wanted to say.

'Even in this day and age it mightn't be the done thing to say at a wedding, but I'm going to say it anyway. Myself and Natalie are expecting our first child in six months. We are delighted to be able to tell you all together.' He put his arm around her shoulders and squeezed her proudly as a loud round of applause erupted from around the room. We stood and clapped our hands vigorously.

'Ah shite, can I change my guess? This has thrown a spanner in the works,' Trisha said, eyeing the glass of tenners, which I then realised were guesses for the length of the speeches.

The mother of the bride dabbed tears away with a finely laundered handkerchief. It put on at least six minutes.

Eventually the best man stood up and gestured for everyone to quieten down. 'I don't know about you lot but I'm absolutely starving so let's get this done with and enjoy the rest of the day.' He spoke confidently into the microphone.

'Hear hear,' the crowd roared, raising their glasses in salute. It was a long day drinking until dinner arrived and I could appreciate how quickly a person could go downhill all too soon on a day like that.

John put his hand on my thigh and squeezed it gently. 'Are you ok, girl?' 'Perfect. Thank you.' I squeezed his hand in response.

'That you are,' he said, planting a quick kiss on my lips, catching the attention of the best man who was still speaking.

'Give it a rest over there, Casanova,' the best man shouted across the room at John caught in a public display of affection. The room erupted in laughter once again as John looked mildly embarrassed for once in his life. He'd warned me about PDAs, yet he was always the first to break the rule.

As the speeches were brought to a conclusion and the glasses raised for the final toast before dinner, Trisha made a show of stopping the stopwatch on her mobile phone.

'Thirty-four minutes and seven seconds,' she proclaimed. 'Lucy is the winner! Drinks on you!'

I couldn't believe it; I'd never won anything. As the waiter passed by with soup and fresh rolls, I handed him the winnings from the glass in the centre and asked him for ten jaeger bombs and a round of drinks. The drinks were well and truly flowing as it was, it probably wasn't the wisest idea to start on the shots. Hung for a sheep as a lamb was one of my favourite mottos. I'd suffer the after effects in the morning.

The craic was mighty, surrounded by my fabulous boyfriend, our neighbours and friends. I felt part of them, a sense of belonging. I kept experiencing these out of body moments where I could almost watch myself from a distance. I appreciated everything and everyone who had helped me get to where I was in that moment, with a bright future ahead of us with my very own Mr Right.

'Not long to go now, Lucy. Are you excited?' Jane leaned in across the dinner table as we ate.

'I can't honestly wait.'

'Shall we go and have a digestive at the bar?' John whispered into my ear.

'Absolutely.' I grabbed my bag and pushed my chair back.

'Where are you two love birds sneaking off to?' Trisha asked, anything but discreetly.

'Mind your own business,' John told her, sticking his tongue out. They had known each other since school, and it was obvious at moments like that. If I had initially had any insecurities about the beautiful women living beside John, they were quashed immediately with the apparent love/hate almost sibling rivalry that only arose from knowing people your entire life. I had recently learnt that John's mother had been in the labour ward with Trisha's mother. There was only three days between them.

As we walked hand in hand, John greeted many people along the way, shaking hands, introducing me as his better half. I met so many new people every weekend I was out with John, I struggled to remember any of them. Faces I could manage, but names were a massive no no, especially if they were Irish names. I could barely pronounce a lot of them; I'd have hated to try and spell them.

He ordered us both a brandy and he pulled out a bar stool for me to perch on, but I shook my head politely. I'd been sitting for the last two-and-a-half hours, I didn't want to sit again already. He sat on it instead and pulled me in between his legs in an intimate stance. Positioning his hands on my hips, he pulled me in close enough to talk over the noise. The band was setting up, as the waiting staff transformed the dining room into a dance floor, dragging tables and chairs discreetly to the side of the room.

'Are you having a good night, girl?'

'I'm having a great time, thank you for bringing me.'

As I leaned into him, I caught sight of the blond over his shoulder. Her burning stare depicted disbelief, so much so that I felt compelled to look away and pretend I hadn't noticed her. I squeezed John's arm to alert him just before she tapped him on the shoulder roughly.

'I don't know who the hell you think you are,' she spat at him.

He turned around, and annoyance flashed over his features at the disruption. 'Jennifer,' he acknowledged her curtly.

'You think you can treat people like shit and get away with it,' she snapped.

'If you want to talk about treating people like shit, I'm not the one here shouting and causing a scene,' he said quietly, calm in contrast to her angry demeanour.

'You will learn the hard way, my dear.' Her tone dripped with sarcasm as she pointed her spindly finger in my face. 'You're no better than any of the rest of us,' she said, rage moving through her shaking hands.

'Excuse me.' John stood up from the bar stool and towered above her, positioning himself in front of me protectively. 'Don't you dare talk to my girlfriend like that. You know nothing about us,' he hissed.

People were beginning to stare; heads turned and conversations nearby halted. The couple next to us nudged each other and John eyed them pointedly until they looked away.

'She'll find out what you're like, John Kelly. The hard way. And maybe that's exactly what she deserves.' She stormed off as thunderously as she had arrived.

John shook his head in disgust at her. 'Some people have no class,' he said calmly, though a few tell-tale beads of sweat lingered on his forehead. 'Where were we?' he said, placing his hands on my waist again.

'What is her problem?' I asked him.

'She a complete nutter. A stalker.'

'Why is she still bothering you?' I asked, confused.

'I have no idea. She's a little obsessed, although I have no idea why.'

'Is it always going to be this way?' I whispered trying not to let my emotions get the better of me. Not easy, especially considering how much I'd had to drink already.

'What way?' he asked.

'Me wondering if every woman in the room is a frog? If every woman has a story to tell about my boyfriend?' Tears threatened the corner of my eyes. 'Lucy.' He took me in his arms. 'How many times do I have to tell you there was no one that meant anything to me before you? Especially not her. I swear on Harley's life.' He attempted to make light of the situation while simultaneously reminding me of the commitment of the dog. He was good, I'd give him that.

The band began to play their version of The Lumineers "Ho Hey" and he led me to the dance floor and put his arms around me. I felt better. It was the newness that threw me. I wasn't used to the whole town knowing our business and people like her forming an opinion on us.

'Let's get another drink,' I suggested as I clocked Jane and Trisha at the bar.

I felt tired, although the party was really only beginning to get started. The months of travelling and worrying were catching up with me. I was physically and mentally drained. I'd have loved nothing more than to crawl under the covers with John, but he was preoccupied with the two Michaels, discussing the potential benefits of getting the three houses re-insulated at the same time, with a foam job in between the walls.

'I'm going to the ladies' room,' I told Jane, turning away.

'I'll come with you,' she said, having witnessed the heated exchange only an hour earlier.

We walked together through the throng of gyrating merry guests on the dancefloor. The toilets were packed, the queue extended out the door. We got in line with the others. The band began to play a few Christmas songs, which could be clearly heard from the toilets.

'Are you ok?' Jane asked tentatively.

'Just tired. I feel like the weeks are catching up on me,' I confided.

'Is it any wonder? But you will have a lovely Christmas. Once you get your things over, you can unpack and settle properly. And we'll get a good few nights organised over Christmas so you won't get the chance to get homesick,' she promised.

'You are so good. I'm so glad you're here,' I told her.

'Ditto. Great to have another blow-in for an ally,' she reminded me of our common ground.

The line moved along slowly, until eventually the disabled cubicle became free. We both went in. I heard a toilet flush next to us and the clipping of heels approach the sinks as I sat on the loo myself. Two women began to talk as they washed their hands. 'You should just tell her,' one voice said.

'What's the point?' said the second voice, which I recognised from less than an hour earlier.

'She should know what he's like. Right now, she thinks the sun shines out of his arse. It will do no harm to bring both of them down a peg or two.'

'They deserve each other,' the voice I recognised as the frog from earlier replied.

'I heard she left her husband for him,' the first voice said.

Jane stood blocking door as I stood up from the loo. She shook her head at me in a silent plea not to go out and confront them, knowing that it wouldn't do any of us any good and they would probably thrive on the drama of the situation. 'She did. The daft bitch,' the frog confirmed in a superior tone.

'You should tell her you spent the night with him last Thursday,' the first said as the blood drained rapidly from my face. I looked at Jane for her to dismiss the accusation, hoping she would brush it off with her hand as nonsense. Instead, she looked at the floor, refusing to meet my eye.

'Why would I bother? Let her find out the hard way.' And with that, the two of them clip clopped off out the door back into the party.

My knees were suddenly weak and unable to support me. I fell back down to a sitting position on the toilet seat, quivering hands covered my mouth in horror. If I'd been there by myself, I might have dismissed it as bitterness or lies, but Jane's reaction confirmed my worst fears.

She knelt in front of me, holding my hand as I sobbed ugly tears of distress, mascara smudged my fingers as I hastily wiped them away.

How could I have been so stupid? Deep down, I knew he was too good to be true. I knew it wouldn't last. I had *always* known love like this never lasts. I'd gotten so caught up in the moment, wishing it to be true, willing it to be different for me, for us, the real deal.

'Jane?' I asked her when I could compose myself enough to utter her name. She refused to meet my eye still.

'Please? What is it? Tell me. Please?' I begged her, make-up running down my face. I couldn't give a shit about appearances now. My insides were crushed, smashed, irreparably broken. Nausea rose to my chest, suffocating me. My breath came hard and fast as my shattered heart pumped furious blood through my veins.

'Maybe it was nothing' Her hesitation spoke volumes.

'Please, tell me, whatever you know. I need to know,' I pleaded. She obviously knew something.

'Her car was outside his house last Thursday night.' Her gentle lull was apologetically. 'Look, it could have been nothing. I thought it was odd at the time. She has a personalised number plate; you'd know it anywhere. I know they have history. It could still be nothing,' she attempted to reassure me.

'Whether or not it was nothing, and let's face it, it doesn't look promising, the worst thing is that I had to hear it from her. If it was innocent, why wouldn't he have told me?' I wiped my face with the back of my hand, fresh tears immediately replaced the ones I'd removed.

'I don't know,' she said, sympathetically. 'You need to ask him.'

'What time did the car leave?' I was desperate for all the facts, even though it made me sick picturing it, picturing her in the house which I was soon to be calling my home. The house we made love in. The house we had cooked in, planned our future together in and shared our hopes and dreams in.

'That's the thing Lucy...' Jane looked really awkward, wring her hands together.

'Oh God, what is it?' I stuttered, pre-empting what she was going to say, although every single cell in me willed her not to.

'It was there all night.' She confirmed what I already knew. I had known something wasn't right that last Thursday from the second I texted him from the hairdressers. He was never as unreachable as he had been that night. I heaved over the toilet, bringing up my dinner.

'I'm so so sorry,' Jane said to me gently rubbing my back. 'I would never have told you if she hadn't said it. It's none of my business. And you never know, it could be something perfectly innocent,' she said, but her natural suspicion leaked through in an undercurrent reflected in her tone. She'd made her feelings on cheating crystal clear when she told me about Michael Maloney. We'd laughed at the time, but we were both equally horrified his wife took him back. If it were Jane's husband, she'd have his head on a spike. I was under no illusion.

We emerged from the cubicle to the quietness of the empty toilets. I caught sight of myself in the mirror above the hand basin. I was a mess, make-up everywhere. I'd aged about ten years in five minutes and my hair looked like it had been dragged through a bush backwards. I didn't give a flying fuck about any of it.

My heart was shattered into a million pieces as I my mind continued to torture me with images of her in John's house; her hands on him, the two of them laughing at me. It struck me hard in the gut – karma. It was only what I deserved.

'You've got to help me,' I begged Jane.

'What do you want me to do?' she asked.

'Go get the key card off John. Tell him I want to freshen up, that the wine's hit me a bit, but I'll be back when I've fixed myself. Tell him you're going to touch up my make-up for me. Just get the key card. I need to get into that room.'

'Ok.' She left me in the toilet alone and I hid in the cubicle, heart-broken, humiliated and ashamed. This was worse than I'd ever felt in my entire life. The devil reappeared on my shoulder, murmuring, 'I told you so.' I pinned my hands to my ears. I couldn't bear to hear it. This was karma in full force. How dare I think I could leave Rob and expect to find happiness myself? How had I allowed myself to fall so utterly and hopelessly in love with John Kelly?

My main priority that second was to get far away from there as fast as possible. I would lick my wounds in private later. I just needed to escape. There was no way I could face him, or her, or anyone else out there. I couldn't for a second pretend to feel like my entire world hadn't just been obliterated in front of me.

Jane returned swiftly with the key card. 'It won't be long before he comes looking for you,' she warned me.

'I know,' I said. I'd immediately assumed he was always that way because he wanted to protect me, but perhaps he couldn't take the chance someone else would talk to me first. I felt sick. I felt stupid. And I needed to leave immediately.

'What are you going to do?' Jane asked.

'I need to get my passport. I'm getting the first plane out of here.' I was on autopilot, desperate to get as far away as physically possible before I splintered into a trillion pieces.

'Would you not just sleep on it?' Jane tried to reason with me. 'I know it looks bad, but what if it's not what she said?'

'If it's not what she said, then why did she say it? And why could I not get hold of him at all on Thursday night? You're the policewoman, the evidence doesn't look good, does it?'

I flew out the toilets and up the stairs two at a time. Jane wanted to come with me but I begged her to go buy me some time and stall John. I didn't want him seeing me like this. I didn't want to let myself down by causing a scene. I just needed to get out of the country as quickly as possible.

Thankfully, I always left my passport in my weekend bag. I glanced around the room that we'd been so happy in only a few hours earlier, the unmade bed taunted me now. How could he do that to me? I tried not to think about it as I balled my dress and threw it into the bag. I pulled on jeans, a vest and a jacket, and the flat pumps I'd packed for the morning. I splashed some water on my face, trying to rid myself of the tell-tale streaks of mascara. It was pointless, the tears refused to stop despite my best efforts.

I fled the room, bolting down the stairs, past reception and into the crisp December air. There were four taxi's outside the front door. The first two were booked already for guests heading home from the long day of celebrations. The third taxi driver took pity on me as I leaned into the passenger window.

'Where do you need to go?' he asked, starting the engine. 'Dublin,' I said.

'Dublin?' Shock lined his face. 'That's a two-and-a-half-hour drive,' he said. I was well aware of that, but there was no flight from Knock until the next day and I couldn't take the chance John would turn up at the airport with some bullshit story I'd be tempted to believe, purely because it was what I wanted to hear. That man had me fully fooled. I genuinely thought he was in love with me. I'd trusted him like no one before.

'I know. Please take me there. I'll pay you double. I just have to get home now,' I begged.

He misinterpreted my tears from my broken heart as some sort of family emergency, or bereavement because he nodded then chewing hard on a piece of gum.

'Thank you.' Relief washed over me as we pulled away from the hotel. I prayed to God I would never set eyes on that place again and allowed my head to fall back against the rest as tears flowed freely down my face.

Chapter Thirty-Six

SATURDAY 8TH DECEMBER

I boarded the Aer Lingus flight from Dublin to Gatwick at six in the morning. My tears eventually dried up after crying the entire car journey. I was told there was space on the first flight out, but I had a three-hour wait in the airport. I sat in the twenty-four-hour McDonald's with the shittiest tasteless cup of coffee, staring into space in shock. I switched my phone off after receiving fifty-nine missed calls from John and countless text messages pleading with me to tell him where I was. He was worried about me, apparently. It would have been laughable, if it wasn't so tragic.

Jane must have caved and told him what had happened because the frantic texts became apologetic all of a sudden. It was at that point I switched the phone off, unable to deal with any more bullshit. I was exhausted, yet I knew sleep would never come.

A devastation like never before consumed me. Never had I allowed a man to get inside my skin like John had. I'd deliberately kept people away so they couldn't hurt me. I'd seen first-hand what 'true love' had done to others. I'd been determined not to let that happen to me.

And yet there I was, my life in a fucking mess. And all my own doing. I pushed my head into my hand, willing the tears not to start again. The shame and the stupidity hurt badly enough but nowhere near as much as the gaping open wound John Kelly had left. It was this bad after only a few hours. How the hell could I go on without him?

For months he had consumed my every thought, my every waking minute and most of my dreams too. I had loved him like I never thought possible to love anyone. I thought he felt the same. I was so complete in his company, so safe, so loved, and at home. His arms had been my home for the last five months, despite being so far from the places I was used to.

When I eventually boarded the plane, I sank into my window seat. I decided if anyone made small talk, I'd give them the whole sordid story, just to get them to shut up. My foul mood must have radiated from me. The woman who took the aisle seat next to me nodded and immediately looked the other way.

Betsy was waiting for me at Gatwick, on the third floor of the short-stay car park. I fell into her and cried yet again, massive hopeless wailing sobs of despair. Each time I thought I had nothing left, I was proved wrong. At least I didn't look out of place crying in an airport car park. I could have been sending off my fiancé to Afghanistan, or waving my sister off, back to Australia.

When I could manage it, I turned the ignition and drove the familiar route out of Gatwick and back down the M25. There was no need for satnav, I'd made this trip countless times in the previous few months. I drove in silence, flashbacks of the day before haunted me. I replayed that moment in the cubicle over and over again. If only I hadn't heard, I would still be there lying in his arms in blissful ignorance. I'm not sure what was worse, living a lie or living without him.

There was absolutely no way I could go back to Ruth's. I couldn't face telling anyone anything, admitting another failure. Technically, nobody was expecting me home until the following day. I pulled off the motorway into a large service station with a travel lodge and decided to camp out here until I could decide what to do with myself.

'Is there a pharmacy here?' I asked the receptionist and she pointed across the car park at a twenty-four-hour Boots. It wasn't even nine in the morning yet but already it felt like the longest day of my life.

I bought a packet of antihistamines, the ones that warned of drowsiness and I took two of them back in the room. I'd been awake for thirty hours. I needed a break from the God-awful situation I was in. I sank under the covers, praying for a few hours of oblivion

It did the trick. I passed out into a deep dreamless sleep for six hours straight. Ignorance really was bliss. I had a brief reprieve from that gut wrenching, devastating heartache. I had no idea how to survive it.

Chapter Thirty-Seven

SUNDAY 9TH DECEMBER

I woke in a crumpled mess of sheets. It had been a long night, but I wasn't ready to face the music yet. Going home would mean telling everyone the horrific truth of the situation, and I was nowhere near ready. I decided there was only one place I could go; the Isle of Wight, to my mum. She was the best friend I had, and although she would want to throttle John Kelly when she heard about this, she might be the only person who could remotely make me feel better, as unimaginable as it seemed.

The car ferry ran on the hour, every hour. I didn't bother booking, merely rocked up and waited. Time meant nothing to me. I was so utterly miserable and sick to my stomach with the awfulness of everything.

I hadn't warned my mother I was coming. I didn't want to worry her, which she undoubtably would do once she realised what a state I was in. I also didn't want to switch my phone on and see any more messages from John Kelly. My heart couldn't take it. No excuses, no bullshit. It was what it was.

When the boat docked, we were ushered off in lines. Driving the short distance to my mum's house, I was reminded of the last time I was on the island – with John. Everywhere I turned, everything seemed to be mocking me. There was no escape. By the time I pulled up on to the empty driveway I was sobbing again, furious aching salty tears of sorrow, and a painful longing for what had been.

No one was home. I sat with my head on the steering wheel for a full half hour before Mum's elderly next-door neighbour, Vera, gently tapped on the window.

'Are you ok, Lucy?' she asked, concern crinkled at the corner of her kind eyes.

'I'm ok, just waiting for Mum,' I managed to utter between the sobs.

'Do you want to come into my house and wait for her?' she asked, offering me tea and warmth.

'No thank you, Vera. You're good to offer, but I'm no company right now.' I wanted my mother, and nobody else.

'If you change your mind, the door is open,' she said with a sympathetic sigh.

Hours passed, but they meant nothing to me. All I could do was imagine the worst. I tried my best to draw a line under the whole horrific thing, but that pesky demon kept flashing images of that bitch Jennifer all over my boyfriend, sorry *ex*-boyfriend, in our bed, in his house. I hadn't eaten since the wedding, but I couldn't have stomached a thing. My nerves were shot, I was completely and utterly drained. I fished out my phone from my bag on the passenger seat and then after looking at it blankly for a few seconds, threw it back into the bag without switching it on.

Behind me, my mother pulled into the drive in her little blue VW. At the sight of my car, she rushed over with an enormous smile and outstretched arms.

'Oh my gosh darling, what a surprise. How are you?' She pushed her sunglasses on top of her head and took a proper look at me, immediately concerned.

'What happened?' Her eyes pleaded as she scanned over me.

'Tell me. What is it?' I guessed from her expression her imagination was running riot.

'I'm ok,' I reassured her through the sobs. 'It's John.' I couldn't control the earth shattering gasps, as she helped me out of my car and ushered me in through the front door. It smelt like home. Like fairy washing powder and clean sheets. The familiarity of it made me cry harder. She held me until I was all cried out again.

'I can't believe I let myself fall in love with him like that,' I told her as she poured us both a large glass of red wine. She handed me mine silently and we sat together on the sofa as she waited for me to elaborate in my own time.

'He let me down,' I said.

'What happened? He was absolutely besotted with you when he was here a few weeks ago. Even I could see that.' In her effort to make me feel better, I actually felt worse. It would have been far easier if she had agreed with me that he was a rotten bastard through and through and I just couldn't see it for looking.

'I don't know. I honestly thought he felt the same...' I hated to even say the words out loud, but I knew at some stage I would have to divulge.

'You know, the thought of my only daughter moving to Ireland wasn't exactly one of the best pieces of news I'd ever received,' she began.

I didn't interrupt her, but she still didn't know what he had done. She took my hand and continued earnestly. 'When I met John Kelly, I wanted to dislike him, I really did. He just waltzed in and swept my only daughter off her feet, like none of us would ever have thought possible. I would have bet money on you never ever having let anyone in the way you let him in, and partially I blamed myself for that, because in all honesty, I have the worst taste in men and probably didn't set the best example along the way. But that was to do with me and my insecurity. Nothing to do with you. You, Lucy, are beautiful, smart and talented. You are way stronger than I was at your age.' I listened, feeling a fraud. Whatever strength she had seen in me had long left at this stage.

'Don't cry. I wanted to dislike that man of yours for taking my baby away from me again.' She took a sip of her wine, and I sat silently waiting for her to continue.

'Lucy, anyone can see John Kelly adores you. And from what I saw of him the last day, he was an absolute gentleman. Much as I hate to admit it, I think you may have met your match.'

I glanced around the sitting room, taking in pictures of myself a few years earlier in a graduation cap and gown, smiling from ear to ear with my newly acquired hygiene diploma, the whole world ahead of me. Little did I know at this stage how much of a fuck up I'd become. A twenty-seven-year-old divorcee, and a delusional one at that.

'What happened, Lucy?' Mum interrupted my thoughts, bringing me back to the present.

'There was another woman.' The words scorched my tongue like poison.

'I don't believe it,' she practically scoffed. 'Who could compete with my daughter?' She seemed to take it as a personal insult to herself. If it wasn't so tragic, I would have laughed at her reaction.

'It's true, Mum. I over-heard her talking about being with John one night when I couldn't get hold of him, and worst of all Jane was with me and she saw her car outside his house. She definitely spent the night with him. I feel like such a fool, Mum. I feel sick to my stomach, but I feel like it's exactly what I deserve after Rob and everything. Talk about karma.'

The tears came again then, like the burst banks of a river. They were relentless.

'Oh, honey.' She put her arms around me in only a way that a mother can. 'I can't believe it. Are you sure? He definitely had me fooled. Are you sure it's what you think? I would have laid money on him being the one for you after I met him. Do you know when you went to the toilet in The Boathouse, he promised me he would look after you. He told me her adored you, and he would make sure he gave you the best of life, even though he knew I'd rather you were here.'

I cried harder again because I had honestly believed it too. But Jane saw Jennifer's car outside his house. And it was there all night. It's not like she parked it there and swanned off somewhere else. There was nowhere else to go. And the fact he knew it was wrong because he didn't answer any of my calls. So, he lied to me as well. If I ever got over this, there would be no more men ever.

'It hurts like nothing ever before.' I flopped back into her deep couch and sighed.

'I know, honey. I know. What did he say when you confronted him?' she asked in a gentle tone.

'Confronted him? I couldn't even look at him. I hopped in a taxi and got the first plane out of there. I couldn't bear to look at him while he lied to me. I didn't want to cause a scene. And I just couldn't even think about saying a last goodbye.'

I'd never known pain like it in my life. It was over-powering, over-whelming, all-consuming. I didn't think I'd ever recover. I was an absolute riot. Greasy hair, blotchy skin and in desperate need of a shower I had no enthusiasm for.

We sat silently, holding hands and drinking wine. There was nothing more I could say, and if there was something else she wanted to say, she held it back. The clocked ticked ominously in the back ground as a thousand childhood memories flashed through my brain of this house, temporarily distracting me from my immediate heartache.

'Where is Trevor?' It occurred to me it was almost eight o'clock and he was nowhere to be seen, thankfully.

'He's in York until Friday for a golf thing.' Thank fuck, we silently exchanged through a glance and both managed to muster a small smile.

'Can I sleep in with you?' I asked her, almost child-like again. I didn't want to be on my own. There was no one else in the world I could share this heartbreak with. I know she felt my pain from the way she looked at me.

'Are you meant to be working tomorrow?' she asked, before we headed up the stairs.

'No, thankfully. Not until Tuesday. Are you?'

'I am, but I'll ring in the morning and tell them I'll work from home,' she said.

'Thank you.' I nearly cried again at her kindness, although that's exactly what I'd gone there for.

'No more tears, missy. You're too beautiful to be crying.' Ha, only a mother would believe that.

'Mum, I don't know if I'll ever get over this one,' I confided quietly in the darkness of her double bed.

'You will, my darling. Of course you will. You are stronger than you will ever know. And you are my daughter, never forget that.'

She held my hand under the covers while I silently cried. Eventually a light and very unsettled sleep came to both of us. No one had my back like my mother.

Chapter Thirty-Eight

MONDAY 10TH DECEMBER

I woke at five in the morning and wondered briefly where I was, before the reality hit me like a freight train. I began to sob again. Beside me, my mother stirred and switched the lamp on.

'You're okay honey,' she said, hugging me tightly. 'You're going to be okay.'

The possibility of further sleep evaporated, so we headed downstairs together, me in her dressing gown and her in Trevor's. She made a pot of tea and we watched the sunrise over the familiar estate. School children sauntered past the window to catch their buses. I glimpsed commuters walking toward the train or ferry. Life moved on, even though my world had stopped. It was once me sauntering down the very same road in my uniform, wondering what the day ahead at school would hold.

'So, what is your plan?' My mum brought me back into my present misery.

'I'm not sure to be honest.' I looked down into my tea for inspiration. 'The only thing I'm damned sure of is that I can't stay here.' I couldn't hack staying in the life I'd already committed to leaving.

My bosses would both take back my resignations in the morning. My friends might feel my pain, and they'd be delighted if I stayed.

Though that would make them happy, I needed to do something to make me happy, if that was even possible.

I'd committed to leaving, to starting a brand-new chapter. And that was what I needed to do. I couldn't stay here wallowing in what might have been.

I was considering taking some time off to go to New Zealand. I had a friend there, she used to be my dental nurse in Edinburgh and she was forever inviting me over. If I liked it, I could work as a hygienist in New Zealand. They accepted the British hygiene qualification; I wouldn't have to sit any exams. The fact that it was on the other side of the world, away from everything and everyone that reminded me of John Kelly, was especially appealing. I didn't need a constant reminder of what I'd nearly had.

I chose not to elaborate on my plans. Instead, I shrugged and drank the scalding hot liquid.

Three cups later, my mum gestured to the phone in my hand and asked, 'Are you ever going to switch that thing on?' I'd been flipping it over from one hand to the other as I contemplated my options.

'I'm not sure to be honest. I considered throwing the damn thing out to sea and starting from scratch again.' I actually managed a tight-lipped smile at the thought. The first in three days.

We walked the length of Ryde Beach, all the way to Seaview and back again, stopping outside a small beach front café for coffee. Christmas music taunted me again. If I had to hear one more word about George Michael's broken heart I was going to scream. He wasn't the only one who'd been hurt. Tinsel and fresh holly wreaths mocked me. I couldn't bear to even look at them, opting to sit outside with our coats on. The morning was blustery but bright. The great outdoors was the only thing soothing my soul, and my mother knew it. I guessed she was trying to heal me discreetly. The great outdoors promised endless opportunity; the wide-open sky, grey or blue, the crashing waves, the oceans that extended into each other washing up anything in its path. It signified freedom, and the minute possibility of hope.

For a few short seconds before that overwhelming sinking sensation of loss attempted to drown me again, I felt maybe one day, there could be life again after John. It was a brief, but it was there, far far away on a horizon I didn't recognise and didn't like the look of.

I still couldn't face the thought of telling the girls, but I'd have to bite the bullet and send out a group message. I couldn't be doing with going over it again and again. I'd say it once and that would be it. I contemplated going sick from work until Christmas, at least that way my notice would be up and I wouldn't have to face anyone, colleagues or patients. It was cowardly, and not how I wanted to leave, but I couldn't go in jolly and pretend my world hadn't been turned upside down.

That afternoon, I was brave enough to switch the phone on. I was immediately bombarded with eighty-two text messages, two hundred and forty-three WhatsApp messages and endless amounts of Facebook notifications. I wouldn't have bothered, only I was supposed to be in work the next day. It was never going to happen. The only company I could stick right now was my mother's, and I was under no illusion anyone other than her could stick me right now.

John's messages relentlessly flew through.

Phone me girl. I can explain. Please ring me Lucy.

I love you.

I can't believe you won't even hear my side of the story.

That one particularly irritated me, as I didn't realise there was any story to tell in the first place, because he didn't willingly volunteer it. I'd have far more respect for him if he did. I thought we had been honest with each other from day one, but I'd been wrong.

I had about fifteen messages from the desperate housewives, Jane and Trisha as they had been irrevocably nicknamed.

Jane:

Are you okay?

Trisha:

Call me. Please just let me know you're safe.

At that second the phone rang in my palm, the shrill tone sent me flying a foot into the air with fright. John's name flashed in front of me alongside a picture of his perfect face. I hit the red decline button, which alerted him to the fact that he knew I was actually looking at the phone. It would have been safer to turn it off again, but I had one person to call first.

I waited for a split second between incoming bombarding calls and rang Clara. She answered on the second ring.

'Lucy? Are you okay?' I shouldn't have been on the missing list yet, but Clara's tone was heavy with concern.

'I'm okay,' I mumbled, forcing a cough. 'Just wrecked and run down after everything. I won't make it into work tomorrow, I'm afraid.' I coughed again, for effect.

'Lucy, please come in tomorrow. I know what happened,' she added sympathetically.

'You know nothing, Clara,' I assured her. 'And I don't want to talk about it. My resignation stands. I'm going to New Zealand for a few months.' My mother looked on with raised eyebrows. I had neglected to mention my plan to her.

'New Zealand?' she shrieked, and a familiar male voice spoke in the background.

'New Zealand?' his voice was cracked, tinged with despair. 'For God's sake, do not let her go to New Zealand.' I'd place that accent anywhere. It used to sound like home. Now it made the hair on my arms stand on end, and not in a good way.

'What is he doing there with you, Clara?' I thought I was let down before, but this seemed more of a betrayal.

'He turned up at work this morning and refused to leave. I told him you weren't due in until tomorrow and he said he'd wait. I didn't think he meant it literally, but he's been sat in the waiting room for the entire day. As I locked the practice up, he was planning on waiting outside for you until the morning. He'd freeze Lucy. What was I supposed to do? He actually booked himself in as a new patient for four cancellation appointments tomorrow.'

'Did he tell you what he did?' I asked her icily. A roaring rage had begun to grow inside me, anger replacing the hurt. How dare he inflict himself on my friends and assume the role of the wronged?

'No, Lucy. I didn't get the full story. I didn't ask, it's none of my business. He said there was a massive misunderstanding, that you jumped the country, Luce. You didn't even give him the chance to explain.'

'There aren't enough explanations to excuse the bare truth. Tell John Kelly he can wait there day and night, I won't be coming. And please tell Maria I'm truly sorry. I'll have a sick note faxed to her in the morning. I have no intention of returning before Christmas, after which my resignation will be in full force. At least if he took four appointments, there will be less patients to call and cancel in the morning.'

'Wait,' Clara and John said simultaneously as I hung up the phone and switched it off.

'He's here?' Mum gathered from my half of the conversation.

'He is.' I exhaled a weighty sigh, but it didn't ease the building pressure on my chest.

'Lucy, it's a long way to come if you know you're in the wrong,' she said. 'The proof is in the pudding,' I said. 'Jane didn't lie.'

The initial shock wore off, and I felt the stirrings of the strongest woman I knew inside. It was about time, because my God did I need her.

'What's this talk of New Zealand?'

'Just an idea, Mum. Maybe a couple of months off work and a change of scenery might be just what I need to get over this. I've had someone else to think about for as long as I can remember. Maybe I should just take a break while I have the chance,' I reasoned.

'Running away won't solve your problems,' she said.

'No, but I'd prefer to lick my wounds far away, somewhere private.'

I picked up her iPad, intending to look up flights to pass the evening, dreaming of lands far away from here. Sunny ones, where I didn't see John Kelly's face in every corner. Even thinking of his name winded me. That sinking feeling rose to the surface, slowly drowning me again.

I didn't want to start again on my own. I wanted to be with him, like we had planned. Why did he have to go and throw it all away? After everything we'd been through, he knew me well enough to know I couldn't tolerate any form of deceit. Why did he have to test the theory?

I closed the iPad and wandered around aimlessly for a while before deciding to run a bath. I filled it with scented oils, bubbles and Epsom salts. I piled my unruly mane of curls into a crab clip on top of my head and sank under the hot water, trying to wash off my troubles. Even taking a bath reminded me of him, sliding in behind me as he had so often done. Closing my eyes, I washed my face and put on a face-mask I found lying around in an attempt to make me feel better.

The weight was falling off me, I could see it as I looked down into the bubbles. For once, I wished I could have been fatter and happier. Knowing John was here was alarming. The draw to him pulled so strongly still, magnetic was our connection. The thought of his arms around me, pulling me into his familiar embrace tormented me in a way I wished I could have forgotten. A stray tear slipped out again despite my best efforts, just when I thought I was improving. If only it had never happened. If only none of us had ever laid eyes on that daft cow, Jennifer. If only he had been here that night instead of at his house. If only I had been there too. It was pointless. I couldn't keep going over it. I got out and decided I needed some fresh air again. Walking was the only time I could think straight.

I pulled on a pair of my mother's skinny jeans, her timberland boots and a fleece I'd left here years ago. It had seen better days, but so had I. As I descended the stairs, she looked up from her phone, surprised.

'Where are you going?' She stood to come with me.

The evening was drawing in, but sleep was the last thing on my mind. The house felt claustrophobic. I appreciated everything she had done for me, even just being here with me, but I needed to get out. To be alone.

'I'm going to the beach for a walk.' I took my car keys off the mantlepiece.

'It's dark. You can't go out there.' She tutted maternally.

'The promenade will be lit. I need the fresh air.'

'Take your phone with you at least.' She knew by my stance; she wouldn't change my mind. 'Be careful.' She reluctantly let me pass her.

It was almost nine at night. There was not another soul to be seen at the seafront, not even a lone dog walker. It was kind of eerie, but I craved the solitude. The icy wind nipped my fingertips. I blew on them and shoved them deep into my pockets, walking the length of the pier with no purpose other than escapism. The night was clear, the stars apparent to the naked eye, my breath visible in front of my face, the moon three quarters full.

I found myself sighing heavily again, picturing his face. Wishing this was all a bad dream. I held my phone in my hand inside my fleece pocket, fingering it, almost caving at the thought of ringing him. I imagined hearing the soothing tone of his voice, the reassurance it used to provide. Oh, what I'd have done to go back in time.

The intensity of my longing frightened me. As a knee jerk reaction, I flung the phone as high and as hard as I could physically manage off the pier and into the Solent. I didn't hear the splash, but it gave me a small rush of satisfaction as I pictured it sinking into the waves, deep onto the floor of the ocean, never to be seen again.

All contact with John and everyone else I had met in Ireland through him gone with it. There was no way I could stay in touch with my new friends now, it would be too hard. I needed a clean break. There was no half measure.

I sat on the memorial bench halfway up the pier and watched as the passenger ferry disembarked and three lonely stragglers got off the boat into awaiting vehicles. I heard a car engine ignite and briefly wondered who they were going home to. A loving wife? A family? Or a microwave meal for one. Who knew? I was again reminded that everyone was just living their own life, trying to get by in whichever way they could. I would get by; it would just take time. Lots of time.

Car lights swept the ground in front of me. The purr of the engine disappeared into the distance, leaving me in silence again, bar the gentle shushing of the current below the wooden panel of the pier. The ferry pulled back out into the sea to return to the mainland for one final trip before the working day was complete.

I stood again and continued my walk towards the end of the pier. The wooden beams beneath my feet were slippery from the splashes of the stronger tide. Speed bumps were positioned every few metres apart on the pier, but you'd have to have a death wish to be speeding on here anyhow.

I thought I was completely alone out here, but in the distance, I glimpsed a figure walking towards me. The silhouette of a man hunched low from the wind. He was tall and of pale complexion, his skin practically luminous under the moonlight. I stopped dead in my tracks, caught like a rabbit in the headlights. My sudden halt drew attention to myself, he glanced up from his own world of thought and stopped too, only a couple of metres in front of me.

'Lucy? Is that you?' His voice pierced the quiet like a knife through my heart, and my eyes squinted to adjust. I couldn't be certain they weren't playing tricks on me.

'John? What are you doing out here?' I knew he was close by; I just didn't realise how close. I knew this man inside out, at least I thought I did. I shouldn't have been surprised at his determination to speak to me when he had come this far.

'I needed to see you. Nobody knew where you were. The general consensus was the only place left you could be was here. Your mother wouldn't take my phone calls either.' He looked sheepish for a moment before taking a step towards me.

'Don't come any closer. Do not touch me.' Tears threatened to break again, pooling in my glassy eyes. I didn't want to go over what happened. I couldn't bear to hear the details, to have them confirmed. What was done was done. I'd far rather have left it the way it was; I didn't want an apology or an explanation. I just wanted to draw a line under it and move on with my life.

'Please, girl,' he said. 'It's not what you think.'

'It's only what I deserve. I'm not exactly Mother Theresa myself,' I consigned.

'I knew you would be doing this to yourself, beating yourself up over something that didn't happen, because you feel like you brought it on yourself. That you somehow deserved this. It's crap, Lucy. And if you'd just listen to me for a few minutes you'd know that,' he said, braving three quick steps towards me.

'So, you're telling me Jennifer didn't spend the night with you, Thursday two weeks ago? The one night of our entire relationship that coincidently I couldn't get hold of you?'

He had the grace to look at the floor.

'It wasn't like that. I have zero interest in her. She landed on the doorstep drunk. What was I meant to do? Put her back into her car?' he said, running a hand over his stubble.

'I couldn't care less what you did with her, unless you let her into your house, our home. How could you do that to me? After everything we've been through.' My voice broke, cracked and pained. I shoved my hands into my pockets again, for fear I might reach out to him. The physical draw was still overwhelming, despite what had happened.

'She wanted to talk. She's got issues. I wanted to let her get them off her chest once and for all. Stupidly, I thought at least that way she might leave us alone if she knew she had said everything she wanted to and still got nowhere. I wish to God I'd shut the door in her face, I really do. The only reason I didn't was because she said she'd jump into the river if I didn't hear her out. She was in such a state and she's pretty fucking crazy as it is, I didn't want that on my conscience. With hindsight, I would have taken my chances. I'm so sorry.'

I had no words as I gazed up at his gorgeous face in the moonlight. He looked like a broken man, tired, dishevelled, even paler than usual. He looked how I felt. But it didn't change a thing. He shouldn't have let her in. Literally and figuratively.

'Nothing happened. She threw herself at me, told me there was something wrong with me if I couldn't just take it for what it was.' His hands wandered to the back of his head as he shook it with regret.

'Stop it, John. I can't bear it.' I winced at the details and raised my hands up to halt him.

'I'm telling you Lucy, nothing happened. She refused to go home, she was crying and shouting. She was furious with me that she couldn't have her way. Then, when she calmed down, she asked me if could she crash on the couch. I felt like I couldn't throw her out into the night in that state.'

'Well, that's exactly what you should have done, John. Because right now you're as well to have done the worst, because it makes no difference now. You put her first that night. You lied to me. You didn't tell me about this, that's lying even if it's by omission. I need complete honesty. You of all people know that.' Frustration bubbled inside, churning in my empty stomach. I wanted to believe him nothing happened, but there would always be that element of doubt in my mind. I couldn't fully trust any man. Especially after what my father had done to my mother.

'I know. Believe me I know, Lucy, but look at me.' He gestured to his blatant state of despair, which mirrored my own sorry self.

'You know how I feel about you. Can't we get past this? I swear to God it will never happen again. She used me; this was her exact plan all along. She knew her car would be seen outside my house all night. I find it hard to believe the lengths she went to, to upset you, to come between us. Please, Lucy, I'm begging you don't let her get between us. Please.'

'It was you that let her get between us. Not me. I wouldn't have let her in the front door.' I was annoyed now, annoyed at her cunning, annoyed at his stupidity, if that's what it was. Anyone could see she was trouble. You don't let that in the door. I felt myself wavering. I wanted to believe him, but how could we get past this? It wasn't just that he had let her in. He hadn't told me. It would have been awful. I'm sure I would have completely blown my lid, but he could have avoided all of this heartache if he'd have been brave enough to talk to me.

It seemed we both had trust issues. Mine were obvious, I wore them on my sleeve. His were more subtle. John didn't trust me not to completely lose my shit over an awkward conversation. I could see his point for a split second, undoubtably I would have jumped to the worst conclusion.

I motioned to the memorial bench, I needed to sit down. He took my hand.

'I'm so sorry, sweetheart. I know how it looked. I promised you I'd never ever hurt you but, unintentionally, I did. I will never, ever let you down. I have never looked at another woman since I met you. You are the only one I want. I've said it before and I'll say it again, it took me thirty years to find you. I'm not going to lose you now.' He pulled me into his arms and my resolve wilted completely.

He felt so good, so strong, so familiar. He felt like home. His mouth found mine, delivering a crushing kiss that swept from my mouth to my heart and back again. The relief was acute, both of us so grateful to be at one again.

'I know you're not ready, but I'm telling you now, girl, one day I am going to marry you. Mark my words. I'm not letting you go. I love you. You are mine, and I am yours.' Determination inched into his chiselled features. 'I'm going to build us a ten-foot wall around the house, with a fourteen-foot motorised gate that only you and I have fobs to.'

'I'm sorry, I immediately jumped to the worse conclusion. I should have come to you instead of fleeing the country. I should have trusted what we had. You know it's not you, I just I find it hard to believe that I'm enough, that you wouldn't want someone else more than me. I'm going to work on it.'

As I stared at John, I realised I should have gone to him. I should have asked him, instead of running. I had been so sure it was karma for my past. I needed to work on that, so it didn't destroy the future.

'We are some pair.' He bowed his head down to mine and kissed me deeply again. The familiar longing spread like wildfire through my core, heating me from the inside out.

I was reminded of a line he said to me that night at The Shelbourne. 'There are women you spend the night with and women you spend the rest of your life with.' He'd already told me which one I was. He'd said it enough; it was about time I believed it. I needed to learn how to trust him instead of assuming the worst at the first hint of a problem. I could have saved us both a lot of heartache the last few days.

'Are you feeling brave?' I asked. He looked alarmed for a split second before the penny dropped.

'Your mother?' he guessed.

'Oh yeah,' I confirmed, leading him back to the seafront to where I'd parked up only a half an hour earlier, a different woman.

EPILOGUE

Seven Years Later...

Saturday 2nd March 2019

Harley barked from downstairs as the rain hammered off the enormous panes of glass. He had become exceptionally overprotective since the little people had arrived. There would be no blondes, or anyone else sneaking in these days.

The weak, wintery morning rays filtered through the cracks of the blackout blinds, naturally rising me from a deep, drowsy slumber. It was almost unheard of in those days to wake naturally. I stretched my arms lazily over my head, hearing my shoulders click before stashing my hands back under the comfort of the warm covers, not yet ready to fully open my eyes and face the day ahead.

The sheets were freshly laundered, the familiar comforting scent of fabric softener emitting from the soft linen brushing against my naked skin.

Life had been unbelievably kind to us. I never imagined feeling so complete. I was more at home here than I've ever been, anywhere else in the world. And that was because of him. His arms were home, and I would never leave.

Seven years on, I still felt it; that powerful stirring itch tormenting me, indescribable in its nature, so distinct. It began in the lower part of my tummy, creeping slowly through me, awakening every single sleepy cell with desire.

I was sure it would have faded at that stage, providing me with long term relief, but no, he was as magnetic as before, pulling me in, daring me to scratch it, despite the situation, despite the time constraints, despite my new role.

I patted the mattress next to me until I found him, oblivious and unconscious, a full night's sleep a rarity these days. His skin felt smooth under my fingers as I traced the hairline of his belly button, stroking him softly, snuggling my knees into that familiar position behind him, nuzzling his neck until he began to stir. He was as responsive as ever.

'What time is it?' Squinted eyes peered at me as he turned to kiss my lips. 'Almost eight,' I said.

'And are they still alive?' he murmured, rubbing his eyes.

'Both snoring still, thank God.' I checked the monitor again, just in case.

I took my husband in my arms, he felt every bit as delicious as he always had. I kissed him slowly, enjoying the feel of him, the scent of his skin and the taste of his mouth on mine.

These moments had been less frequent of late, since we'd had the two babies, but the attraction was just as strong as ever. Time was the issue. We often joked we had more time together when we lived in separate countries, at least the time we had was our own. But we were so lucky, so grateful and so privileged to have a healthy boy and a beautiful baby girl across the hall from us. Grateful and tired!

I twisted my chunky diamond wedding band round the fourth finger on my left hand, the memory of our wedding three years earlier flashing through my mind. It had been a beautiful September day, an intimate civil ceremony with only John's parents, my mum and her new partner, Steve, as witnesses. Our close friends and neighbours had joined us in our after celebration.

They said it would never last. It was impossible. It was improbable. It was unlikely. Yet there we were, seven years later, that powerful attraction still drawing me in, that gorgeous, determined Irishman still surprising me with the love he had not only for me, but for our beautiful children too.

He was still the strongest man I'd ever met, my absolute rock from the very beginning. His strength gave me strength and that was only one of the many reasons why I had so much respect for him, why I loved him so much. I was his from the first night I met him and I would always be his. It mightn't have been the smoothest or the easiest path to true love. But for us, that was what it was.

FOR GERRY

*You are my love story, and I write you into everything I do, everything I see,
everything I touch and everything I dream, you are the words that fill my pages.*

a.r asher

ACKNOWLEDGMENTS

Some elements of this story were very personal to me. I'd like to say a massive thank you to my husband, Gerry, who has supported me continuously and always believed in my dreams. He is my happy ever after, and the best man I know. Some itches were meant to be scratched!

Thank you to my mother, who raised me to be independent, strong and equipped me with the confidence to strive for my dreams, regardless of the obstacles along the way. Thank you to my in-laws, who not only raised the best man I know, but also accepted me as one of their own. They just happen to be great craic as well!

Thank you to my crazy, hilarious, loyal friends who equip me with enough stories to fill hundreds of books over! I love you KK, Rachel, Theresa, Ann, Wenna and Carole, even if we don't get to see each other as much as we did in the days before babies, jobs and husbands took over.

To my new Irish buddies, Jude, Trina, Niamh and my mammy-friends. I say new, but I've been here eight years already (we passed our own friendship itch!). I'd like to thank you for making my transition so much easier, for embracing me into your circles, and for all the friendship, laughter and support along the way.

Thanks to the fabulous Vikkie Wakeham aka Little Miss Booklover for all her encouragement and support and to Aoife for being the best beta reader ever. Thank you to all my author friends who have helped me along the way, especially Margaret Amatt, Emma Farrell, Lucy Keeling, and Adrian Wills. I am grateful for each and every one of you.

And the biggest thank you of all to those of you that took the time to read this book. I hope you enjoyed it. If you did, please consider leaving a review on Amazon or Goodreads.

OTHER TITLES BY LYNDSEY GALLAGHER

ABOUT THE AUTHOR

Lyndsey Gallagher is a romance author based in the west of Ireland. Wife, mammy and dental hygienist by day, she enjoys long walks, deep talks, and the occasional G & T.

Follow her progress on Instagram @lyndseygallagherauthor or subscribe to her website www.lyndseygallagherauthor.com

Printed in Great Britain
by Amazon

10457032R00142